NADINE
DORRIES

SNOW
ANGELS

HEAD
of ZEUS

First published in the UK in 2019 by Head of Zeus Ltd

Copyright © Nadine Dorries, 2019

The moral right of Nadine Dorries to be identified as the author
of this work has been asserted in accordance with the
Copyright, Designs and Patents Act of 1988.

9 7 5 3 1 2 4 6 8

A catalogue record for this book is available from
the British Library.

ISBN (HB): 9781789544817
ISBN (ANZTPB): 9781789544824
ISBN (PB): 9781789544831
ISBN (E): 9781789544800

Typeset by Adrian McLaughlin

Printed and bound in Great Britain by
CPI Group (UK) Ltd, Croydon CR0 4YY

Head of Zeus Ltd
5–8 Hardwick Street
London EC1R 4RG

WWW.HEADOFZEUS.COM

For Paul

Chapter 1

Liverpool, Winter

Malcolm Coffey was not expecting anyone to knock on his door this late at night. He had only just slipped the first forkful of creamy mashed potato into his mouth and settled down to listen to the six o'clock news on the radio. It was his favourite supper, steak and heel pie made by Melly, the daily who came in six days a week and helped him to run his boarding house for seamen that lay close to the docks.

'You're a creature of habit you are. I swear to God, if I left you a pan of scouse on a Thursday instead of the pie, I'd come back in here on a Friday morning and find you'd dropped dead by that oven door,' Melly would laugh, the well-rounded raucous laugh that he heard most nights, slipping back in through the walls from the bar of the Silvestrian next door, long after Melly, in bodily form, had left. Melly made him the same meal every Thursday and, as a man accustomed to regimental order, that suited him just fine.

'I like to wake up in the morning and know exactly what the day will bring, and that includes my dinner – I hate surprises,' Malcolm would reply. He disapproved of Melly drinking in the Silvestrian, known locally as the Silly but it appeared that no matter how much Melly drank – and it appeared to be a huge amount – she still turned up for work on time every morning, completed her duties to his satisfaction and appeared none the worse for it, giving him no grounds for complaint. 'That's a woman who is used to her drink, that is,' his late mother's friend Biddy would say, 'and there's nothing you can do, Malcolm; if she wants to drink what she earns, that's her choice. Don't interfere. I'd clock anyone who stood between me and my vices. If Emily tried to deprive me of my buttered potato cakes or the bingo I'd find another job.' Malcolm took all Biddy's advice with the same degree of adherence he would that of the priest, or his mother if she were alive and, so far, Melly had never missed a day's work. As he settled down to his supper, he was jolted by the sound of Melly's piercing laugh penetrating through his wall; and once again he wished that she would find another public house to drink in.

The fire burnt well in the grate and he had lit the long brass standard lamp with the burgundy fringed shade, frayed and tattered, still soot-stained from the Blitz.

It was the lamp his mother had sat under to read every night of his childhood and he was loath to change it, regardless of how many times Melly complained. 'There'll be nothing left if I try and clean that again.' He would not let it go because with it, he feared, the ghostly image of his mother that he often conjured for comfort, would disappear too. The lamp stood to the rear of the tanned leather armchair with arms wide enough to support an ashtray with his pipe on one side and his opened copy of the evening edition of the *Echo* on the other. It now sat neatly folded, waiting, tempting and the ashtray winked at him in the firelight.

Malcolm lit the fire at six o'clock and not a moment before, regardless of the temperature or the weather outside and the pulling of the cord on the lamp to light the room was a luxury he left until the point where the room was so filled with dusk that the landmarks of domesticity faded into the gloom until he could barely see at all. The polished oak furniture that had once belonged to his parents stood neatly around him and it shone under the years of being rubbed by Melly with daily helpings of wax and elbow grease, the room smelling of lavender polish during the day and pipe smoke at night. The table at which he sat, scrubbed with Vim, was now depositing a thin film of white powder on the sleeves of his jacket, and a faint aroma of bleach competed with steak and heel, tickling his nostrils.

It was at moments like this that he pondered on the

fact that he had almost sold the house, the life, the routine that made him as happy as a man who had lost his family could expect to be. He had to constantly chase up Melly to clean behind the toilet doors and to cease flirting with the coalman, but he couldn't fault her delicious pies. He had pierced the pastry with his fork to allow the steam to rise and was just about to dive in when a loud knock on the door burst his bubble of anticipation. More often than not, according to their sailing rota and the tide table, which was as accurate as it could be, the sea and stevedores allowing, his paying guests rebooked their next stay as they checked out. He grunted with irritation, reluctant to leave the buttery shortcrust pastry, hot and melting, and the wafting smell of rich gravy under his nose.

'Who the hell is it?' he called.

His paying guests each had a key so this must be someone looking for a room. No one knocked on his door for any other reason, unless it was the postman, the milkman or Biddy Kennedy, on her way home from work, and it was too late for any of them. The wind rattled at the windowpanes with such ferocity it felt as though the room itself shook. This was not the weather or the night to be disturbing the routine of Malcolm Coffey, a stickler for everything being done by the book. The only thing he looked forward to, or dreamt about during the day, was his supper – and he often wondered, as he ate, what kind of pie his late wife would have turned out. He had served throughout the war, only to return home to find that he had lost his wife with his newly delivered son in her arms as a result of the bomb that had landed on the maternity hospital during the May Blitz nine months after his leave. He also found himself an orphan too, both his parents having lost their lives by a bomb that hit close to the dockers' steps only two days later. The regimental major had withheld the second news from the dispatches to his posting for over a week, to give him time to absorb the shock of the first.

Malcolm had been serving in North Africa at the time and all leave was denied. Only his parents had been afforded a funeral due to their bodies being identifiable – a funeral he had not been able to attend, but Biddy Kennedy had. His wife and son lay in a concrete grave on what was once the delivery suite of the maternity hospital, both beyond identification and removal. Today, the hospital rebuilt, life came forth over death.

'Biddy? Is that you?' Malcolm called not expecting a reply, reluctant to rise and leave his pie.

'Malcolm, I promised your mam, I would keep an eye on you,' Biddy would say when she called in for a cup of tea. Biddy worked as a housekeeper at the St Angelus hospital, a plum job in the school of nursing, working for Sister Emily Horton; and one of the pleasures in Malcolm's life was to hear all about the antics of the probationer nurses and how they ran Biddy around in circles. Over two thousand bombs had been dropped the week his family died; nearly seven thousand homes had been completely destroyed. Fire had ripped through the dock's side streets. 'Think of me as your mam, if you ever need one, I'm here. You aren't alone, Malcolm,' Biddy would say.

Malcolm had been at school with her own children and not one of them had remained in Liverpool or even in contact with Biddy. He enjoyed her visits. She had transferred from being his mother's friend to his – and more than that, much more. Melly had her own opinions about Biddy. 'That woman mourns her kids,' she would say. 'Not one of the buggers bothers to write to her. Still working her socks off and all those kids, not one of them tips up a penny, a crying shame it is. You want to watch out – she might have her eye on this place, if anything happens to you.'

Malcolm would snort with derision. 'Biddy is looking for an easier life, not to take on more work,' he would reply, irritated by Melly's suspicions of Biddy and left with the depressing thought that there *was* no one to take over, should anything happen to him. No kith or kin of his own to rely on, no legacy to leave... and in his heart, he sometimes wondered what the point was of everything he worked for. A question that had been quickly answered upon his return from the war. The seven-bedroomed Victorian family town house, next to the Silvestrian Public House on one side and the St Angelus hospital at the top of the road, had survived the war intact and it was very soon obvious, given the rapid increase in trade and activity down on the docks, where his new career path should lie. The parlour had been converted into a reception room which doubled up as his sitting and dining room. A hatch had been made in the wall and, from where he sat at his kitchen table-cum-desk, he could clearly see who came in and out.

Outside, the sky had now darkened and the rain fell like twines of ice as it blew up the hill off the Mersey and pelted against the door of the 'Seaman's Stop' bed and breakfast. The door knocker banged again, more force-fully, leaving him in no doubt that it was neither the wind nor Biddy – who would have tapped on the window by now, given that he had put the lamp on – and he would have to leave his pie. Malcolm sighed, laid down his knife and fork and, begrudgingly, rose from his seat.

'I'm coming, give me a minute,' he shouted as he tugged at the napkin that was neatly tucked inside his collar. He picked up the wire spectacles he had removed to avoid them steaming up as a part of his pre-pie ritual, and threaded each arm over his ears. His thick hair was dark and glistening with Brylcreem, worn in a short back and sides, and the only feature to make him stand out in the crowd was one missing tooth to the side of his mouth, his only war wound, courtesy of a nasty fall from a horse. As he made his way to the door, he pondered who it might be from his regular paying guests. There were two ships berthed overnight at the dock and another two due at the bar in the early hours, to be brought down by the tugs in the morning. He had eight seamen checked in who were all out on the town. He knew the tide table like the back of his own hand. The door knocked again, this time with more urgency.

'Jesus wept, I'm coming!' he said again as his footsteps, heavy and hard, marched along the lino-covered hallway. He flung open the door, expecting to see the familiar face of a seaman in need of a bath, wearing a peaked cap with a kitbag slung over his shoulder; instead he was met by a diminutive woman who looked as though she was soaked to the skin.

'I-I'm looking for a room,' she stammered.

Malcolm was taken back and, unusually, lost for words. 'Excuse me,' he blurted back as he craned his neck out of the door and looked up and down the street to see if anyone was watching. In those few seconds his glasses were pebble-dashed with rain, making it difficult for him to see. A female visitor to his door was a rare occurrence and she could not have been more than five feet two, frail and childlike, her dripping dark hair adhered to her face as rivulets of rainwater ran into her eyes. Her cheekbones were sharp and thin, her eyes almost black, her skin a ghastly shade of tallow as she stood almost directly under the globe sulphur light above the front door. 'We don't usually have ladies as guests,' he said.

She was clutching the handles of a blanket holdall, equally sodden, tight to her body and he could see that the shoulders of her coat were dark and soaked through.

'Everywhere else is full,' she almost whispered back to him and he had to bend his head to hear her.

'Can't be,' he blurted. 'There's plenty of rooms about. You just need to knock and ask. Enquire at Mrs Bennett's on Lovely Lane. Here, I'll write the address down. I can tell you're not Irish by your accent – she won't take the Irish.'

'No.' The response was swift. 'I want to be close to the hospital. I *have* to be here.'

'But Lovely Lane is close to the hospital; the nurses' home is opposite the park gates.'

'Please, I want to stay here, it's closer to the hospital.'

He shook his head. 'I've been asked before, but this is a seaman's rest. I sleep two to a room and if I take you in, I lose half a room rate.' He felt uncomfortable. He *did* have a spare room, but a female guest was the last thing he wanted or needed. His guests spoke freely and swore loudly; they wouldn't like it if they came down and found a woman at breakfast and had to watch their Ps and Qs – and God alone knew what Melly, not shy of expressing an opinion, would have to say if she came in and found a woman at the breakfast table. 'There's no fancy frills here that would suit a woman's taste; it's all geared up for sailors. Besides, you wouldn't want to be sharing a bathroom with men.'

He saw the flicker in her eye at that, but, 'I really don't mind, I just need a room. I'm desperate, please.'

At that moment he knew that he had lost, for he could

no more turn away a woman so obviously in need in such foul weather than fly to the moon. She was soaked and the rain was so bitterly cold it hurt his cheeks. If he had opened his door to an animal knocking, he would have let it in. He hated himself for being weak as he sighed and said, 'It's seven and six a week,' his voice making it quite clear he didn't think she could afford it. The woman didn't speak, but rummaged around in the purse she had taken out of her bag and gave Malcolm five green one-pound notes which became an even darker green and went limp in her hands as the rain hit them. He scratched his head. 'Bleedin' 'ell, you staying for Christmas or what?'

She kept her gaze steady and her voice, matter-of-fact. 'Does that mean I can have a room?'

He could detect a slight accent, but couldn't make it out. He felt a hint of shame; she was so cold and wet, how could he refuse her? The weather was foul and his pie was getting cold. 'Come on, bring your bag up. I'm quieter now that Christmas is coming and there is one smaller room I only let out when I have to. It has bunks. You can have the bottom one and the room to yourself.' He stood back and held open the door as she stepped inside and stood under the central ceiling lamp which made her look worse than she had outdoors as it cast dark shadows down over her face. He bent down and took the holdall from her. 'Here, let me. I'll lead the way,' he said as he slammed the door shut. Silence fell as he locked out the sound of the rain and wind. Taking a better look at her, he felt his heart sink. He had seen enough people stay in his lodgings, served with enough men during the war years, to know that this was a woman in trouble. He took a deep breath and bit his tongue. Her money was as good as anyone's and besides, every man, and woman was entitled to his or her secrets. It was none of his business. Christmas was just around the corner, business would be light, the ships from Rotterdam headed back home. He had learnt that when it came to paying guests, their personal lives were none of his business. All he had to concern himself with was swift payment and abiding by the house rules. Malcolm was as stickler for the rules.

'Come on then, follow me,' he said as he walked on ahead. He chatted as he went, only once glancing, regretfully, through the hatch at his cooling supper. 'It's a fry-up in the morning, cooked by Melly; she comes in every day at seven and does all the cooking. I do the porridge because Melly always burns the pan. She helps me to run the place. This is the breakfast room,' he opened a door opposite the parlour and she saw a large trestle table laid out with cutlery and dishes, ready for the morning. 'We serve from seven o'clock until ten and the rooms are cleaned between ten and twelve so we like the place to be empty from ten and guests are allowed back in at three. Melly puts a pot of tea and a plate of Garibaldi on the table, just in case anyone's peckish. They're Melly's favourites.'

He gave her a hard, long look, aware that he was talking more than normal for someone who had earnt himself the reputation, justifiably so, as a grumpy man. He was also aware she wasn't really listening. She looked as though the wet and the cold had penetrated into her bones as her shiver became a violent tremble. He could also see that it took every ounce of her willpower to try and stop it as she clenched her teeth together. He could smell his supper, a vision of his cooling pie, tantalising him.

'I allow no visitors into the rooms because it's the best way to keep on top of the bedbugs. Only one person to blame if only one person has slept in the bed – and anyone who does bring them in is out through the door as fast as the mattress. I will give you your own key. I don't mind what time anyone gets back in at night, mind, I'm not a total tyrant, as long as the door is properly locked. The key is on a wooden paddle, so you don't lose it; if you do, it's the same cost as a night's stay to replace it. There's a paraffin heater in each room and the paraffin is topped up by Melly when she cleans the rooms. Have you got all that?' He turned into the parlour doorway and took a key hanging on a large flat block of wood with the number 2 painted in the middle from a brass hook. Is that acceptable?' He turned to look at her. The colour had left her face altogether and she was frighteningly white. 'Jesus, I've met ghosts with a better pallor than yours,' he said.

She chose to ignore him. 'Anything would be acceptable,' she said. 'I just need a room.'

He picked up a pen on a side table next to the visitors' book and flicked the top off. 'Here, can you sign here?' She was hesitant and looked at the pen as though it might bite her. 'One of the rules,' he said as he noted her reluctance. He knew this moment well. It was one he endured often with seamen. Most liked to remain untraceable, under the radar, just in case one of the dockside girls with an unexpected bun in the oven came looking for him. She reached out her hand and scrawled her details and it looked as though a spider had walked across the page, her hand shook so much. He picked up the book, squinted, removed his glasses, squinted again. 'What's that address, it's not in Liverpool, is it?' He could make out the name, but only just – Eva. It was certainly not a common name around the dock streets. Was that a German name? 'Is it German? Makes no difference to me, queen. The war is long over and I take in people from everywhere. Melly and I, we like to think of ourselves as being very cosmopolitan.'

The woman was staring as if in a trance at the letter rack on the table next to the guest book, at a wad of letters held together with a frayed elastic band, faded, yellowing around the edges from the heat of the lamp, leaning up against the wooden box with 'A Present from Rhyl' carved into the front and which was stuffed full of airmail letters. He caught her eye.

'Oh, yes, I do take in mail, it's part of the service for paying guests and he's a popular sailor, that one. I thought he had a girl in every port until Melly pointed out that they were all from the same person; she could tell by the handwriting. Someone pushed them through the door to begin with and then they started coming from America. One of my regulars, he was. He's not been here for over a year, but some of these tramp ships will pick up a cargo and take it anywhere in the world, then do the same when they reach "anywhere". They can be gone for two, three years or more at a time before they come back into Liverpool. Last I heard, that fella's ship was in the West Indies. Fancy that, eh? The West Indies. I've been to a few places myself with the army, but never anywhere that exotic.'

Malcolm's head was buried in the visitors' book, trying to make out her handwriting, when he heard the thud. His mysterious visitor had collapsed in a heap on the floor behind him. Well, she had signed the book and her money was in his pocket so she was his responsibility. 'Would you credit it,' he muttered as he squatted down on his haunches before her. He lifted her head and she opened her eyes. 'You don't feel well at all, do you love?' he stated the obvious. She nodded her head. 'Come on, let me help you up. There's a very nice pie and mash waiting for you in my parlour and a hot fire – I must have known you were coming. Let's get this coat dry. I'm not letting you get to your bed until you've had a hot meal and a pot of tea inside you and you've dried out a bit. I'll put an extra army blanket on your bed, too, and light the paraffin heater in a minute, to warm up your room.'

She began to shake her head and tried to push herself up. 'I can't be any trouble,' she gasped. 'I can't eat your food.' He hauled her to her feet and put his arms around her to steady her. He could feel the tremble vibrating through her body. 'It's no trouble, honest to God. I get fed up eating Melly's pies – sick of them, I am. I just wish she would cook me something different every now and then.' He was lying and she could tell, but as he spoke, his hand cupped her elbow and guided her to the parlour. 'Look, it's there, on the table, all ready for you. There's a nice bit of cheese in the fridge and bread in the kitchen that'll do me, I won't go hungry. I had a big lunch and look at this…' He patted his ample, well-fed belly. 'Do I look like a starved man? I need to trim this down, not feed it up.'

He was talking too much, almost gabbling. The pain that often settled on his diaphragm and felt like a deep ache had suddenly lifted, the pain Biddy had told him was a combination of grief and loneliness – and Biddy knew all about that. He suddenly felt lighter. Someone needed him, and despite the interruption to his well-established routine, he didn't mind, not one little bit. 'Come on, miss, to the fire with you. Eat – and then you can tell me why it is that out of all the doorsteps in Liverpool, you've turned up on mine.'

As they walked towards the parlour, she turned to take one last glance at the unopened envelopes. She could smell the pie and, despite her desire to be alone in a room and safe, she could not resist. Malcolm turned the dial on the radio and following a hiss and a crackle, the sound of a choir singing 'Once in Royal David's City' washed over her like a wave and filled her with emotion. She turned to the fire, tears stinging her eyes and she wanted to pinch herself. The pains of hunger in her belly had almost dragged her down along the lino-covered hall-way to the food and there before her lay a hot meal. She allowed the man with the warm, cupped hand to guide her by her arm.

Jacob... The name on the front of the envelope had burnt her eyes, the words in the first letter, engraved on her mind. Jacob, he had never been back, never returned. Jacob wasn't here.

Chapter 2

Madge Jones balanced a tray of glasses as she teetered on her heels into the kitchenette at the back of Matron's apartment to find Elsie O'Brien, Matron's housekeeper, at the sink, up to her elbow in soapsuds and Biddy Kennedy, from the nurses' home, lifting a tray of devils on horseback out of the oven. She pushed the green baize door open with her backside and pirouetted in, carried on a wave of excited chatter and clinking glasses which stopped dead as the door swished closed behind her.

'Has anyone gone home yet?' asked Elsie, wearily turning her head as Madge placed the tray next to her on the wet wooden draining board which had only just been cleared of the last load of glasses and dishes. Even though Elsie and Biddy were manning the kitchen and supervising the refreshments and had practically spent their entire evening in the kitchen, Madge had remained front of house, as was in keeping with her role of hospital switchboard operator. There was an unspoken ordering of rank at St Angelus, loosely based on dress and appearance. Setting aside the white-coated doctors who had their own hierarchy, it began at the top with Matron, in her smart navy dress, and moved down through the uniformed nursing staff to the probationary nurses in their pink dresses and starched aprons. Among the non-medical staff, those in the porters' lodge and the operating theatres wore brown coats and there was a distinct and elite group who wore their own clothes to work, like Madge on the switchboard, the secretaries and clerks and it ended at the bottom, with the kitchen, housekeeping and cleaning staff who wore wrap-around aprons. Everyone knew their place in the St Angelus hierarchy and those who could afford it the least were responsible for wearing their own, freshly laundered apron, every day. Despite being confined to the kitchen by Madge, Elsie had still dressed up for the occasion. This had involved removing her curlers, jigging up the black-dyed, tightly permed curls with the end of a tail comb and applying half a tin of highly perfumed Get Set hairspray, which defied a single hair to move out of place. A stark line of steel-grey roots shone out bravely, courtesy of the bare overhead light encased in a bottle-green glass lampshade, as she bent over the sink. Her thin lips were defined and adorned with ruby-red lipstick and her eyes were framed with charcoal. The cumulative effect made her look much older than her years. Under her customary wrap-around apron dress, she had abandoned her usual hand-knitted wool twinset for a dress she had purchased from a stall on St John's market and kept for special occasions. Its last outing had been at her grandson's christening, his father, her son-in-law, Jake Berry the under-porter, was on the other side of the green door in Matron's sitting room and office, playing the role of a sommelier with a bottle of Spanish sherry, the infamous Golden Knight, or golden shite as it was commonly known amongst the St Angelus' domestic mafia. Biddy, who had not dressed for the occasion and had walked across from the school of nursing, had made one sartorial concession for the occasion: she had changed her shoes for a pair of slippers.

Biddy pushed the baize door slightly open and peeped out into the room and the noise of chatter filled the kitchen once more. 'No, not one bugger is showing any signs of leaving yet and why would they with your son-in-law refilling those glasses every two minutes. Look at him, wearing that jacket and dickie bow! He's going to burst into song in a minute. He thinks he's Charles Aznavour, he does. They're all having too good a time to think about moving. Well, until the golden shite gets them, because it always does. Hits you like a brick just as you get to the fourth glass – and you would know, Elsie.' The day Elsie had been found asleep on Matron's sofa, with a yellow duster in one hand and an empty glass in the other, was an issue of such sensitivity it was only ever discussed on the rare occasion she was ill, on a day off, or on holiday, when it was mentioned, always in hushed tones. Elsie controlled the record of the event and Biddy was the only person amongst the St Angelus' staff who would dare to speak of it in her presence. Elsie sniffed in indignation, but would not take the bait and passed straight over Biddy's comment as though she hadn't even spoken.

'Have you got a glass yourself in here tonight, Elsie?' asked Madge peering around and failing to notice the half-empty glass behind a plate of sausage rolls. Elsie turned the tap on, rinsed a plate, and totally ignored them both. 'They'll all need to be carried out at this rate, we don't want you joining them.' The plate clattered into the drying rack so loudly no one would have been in the least surprised if it had broken. Biddy kicked the wooden doorstop out from under it and let the kitchen door swing behind her as she retrieved her packet of cigarettes from the front of her apron pocket. 'Between your Jake's attendance and Mavis's cakes, they'll all be there until Boxing Day at this rate,' said Madge, who slipped off a shoe and rubbed her toes.

'Bleedin' hell. I hope not. God forbid they stay a minute after ten,' said Elsie. 'I'm half dead on me feet. I've been here since half seven this morning and I've barely sat down. My veins are killing me and I can't even feel my feet now. I daren't take my shoes off because I won't get them back on again.' Despite her obvious tiredness, Elsie was as concerned for Matron, the only other woman she knew who worked as hard as she did. 'Is Matron having a nice time out there? I can't believe I was the one who said this was a good idea when she said she wanted to have all the doctors and their wives over for Christmas drinks. That was ten years ago and I should have known it would be a load of hard work. But it sounded such a good idea at the time. Trust me and my big gob. Soft girl, I am.'

Madge reached over to the tray of food cooling on the side and popped a steaming devil on horseback into her mouth, taking a sharp breath and wafting her hand in front of her mouth. Madge was the 'glamorous lady of a certain age' at the hospital. In terms of status, her area of responsibility, the switchboard, was as good as having her own office and she had made it so: a small carpet offcut on the floor, to stop her stool on wheels from wandering back; a spider plant on the top of the switching unit, where it caught the light from the arch window above the office door; the kettle and tea caddy, with four matching Queen Anne Ivy-leaf cups and saucers on a side table in the corner. Not the usual national hospital issue for Madge, because Madge was not your usual hospital employee. She was not one of the army of domestics, nor of the medical secretaries or departmental clerks who enjoyed their own rank and status. Madge was alone, both in life and in work, but her switchboard was, in effect, the nerve centre of the hospital and thus afforded her a special status, given that she was first with all the news.

Madge, as the purveyor of important information, was also queen of the high heels, new hairstyles and fashion. She was the unofficial nod to glamour amongst her peers. Helping Elsie host Matron's drinks party was no reason to reduce her standards of footwear as she slipped her red high heels back on and clattered across the kitchen floor to pick up a tea towel and begin drying glasses as Elsie rinsed them in hot water under the tap. Biddy moved over to the sink and began to tip the contents of the glasses into a bucket on the floor. And so, side by side the three graces of St Angelus stood, one with her arms in the sink, one with a fag in her mouth, the last with a tea towel in her hands. All three lifted their heads to the window before them, one bleached blonde, one dyed black and the other a proud and untouched steel grey, a red tip glowing in her lips. Their reflections mirrored back at them and Madge leant forward to take a better look and rubbed an imaginary smudge of blue eye shadow from the side of her eye.

'I've got that much make-up on, there'd be an avalanche on my face if I cried,' she said as, leaning back, she picked up another glass.

Elsie nodded in agreement. 'You go too heavy on the tutty you do, Madge, all that to catch a fella. I don't know why you bother, it's a bit late now.'

'I do,' said Biddy. 'She's never really had one to speak of who was worth having. None of them are, Madge.

When will you learn? A good man is like the holy fecking grail. You'll be searching forever.'

Madge pursed her lips and looked indignant. 'Who says it's to catch a fella? I'm very happy as I am, thank you,' and then, as if to contradict herself, 'Where am I gonna find one worth having anyway? I know everyone around here, don't I? Half of the good ones never came back from the war, the other half were already married. National shortage there is – I read it in the *Revellie*.'

Elsie made no response as her heart suddenly tightened in her chest and, catching her breath, she plunged the knitted dishcloth into a dirty pan. Madge was right, but like so many others she would pass no comment. There were too many widows – and she was one. Too many sad stories. Too many fatherless children, broken hearts and absolutely no words to be said because one mention of the war years, one unwitting remark, took all conversation down a path of intense sadness. Best not to comment. So little was said, sometimes, it was as if the war had never happened.

'Is that the last glass, Biddy?' said Elsie as the hot water stung her hands.

'Aye, it is; and bloody hell, me fag's soaked,' exclaimed Biddy as she removed the cigarette from her mouth with wet fingers.

Elsie handed Madge the pan to dry and pulled the plug out of the sink. As the grey water drained and gurgled away, all three peered out of the window, momentarily lost in their own thoughts, remembering a loss: Elsie, her husband; Madge the boy she'd met at the Cabbage Hall dance, who had promised to return to her on his following leave, but never did, Madge always choosing to believe he had fallen in action, and Biddy, never the husband who had run off with her Belleek tea service and her purse, but always the children she had reared and never heard from. They looked beyond their own faces into the cold dark night, the wind so strong, it hurled the fat drops of ice-cold rain against the glass with the force of pebbles. The Mersey, visible from the window by day, was fathomless and indistinguishable through the sheets of white gusting rain. A tug blew its horn and Elsie blessed herself.

'There can't be anyone out there on a night like this, surely to God.' She grabbed the crucifix from around her neck and held it to her lips as she chanted, 'Holy Father and all the saints in heaven, protect all the merchant sailors from Liverpool out in that dreadful weather, God love them and save them and bring them all back home for Christmas.'

'Amen to that,' said Biddy as Elsie tucked the cross back into her dress.

Madge picked up another plate to dry and stack and felt a need to change the mood from gloom to glamour. 'Tell you what, Biddy is right, your Jake missed his vocation – he's doing a grand job in there with the bottle of sherry and a tea towel over his arm! Playing to the gallery, he is, and the doctors' wives, with all their diamonds sparkling, they love him, they do.' Madge laughed out loud at the antics of Jake who, as she had left, had been extracting a cork from another bottle as he blew a surreptitious kiss to Mrs Mabbutt, the wife of the orthopaedic surgeon, who was already on her fifth glass and was more than a little tipsy. 'I just heard him telling Mrs Mabbutt it would be easier if she stood next to the sofa to balance herself if she was going to have another top-up. Wobbling all over the place, she was. I said, "What are you doing, Jake?" and he said, "Look Madge, if she sits on the arm of the sofa and she passes out, at least she'll have a soft landing."'

Elsie, leaning back slightly, placed the palm of her hands in the small of her back and winced from the effort of straightening as she laughed at the same time. 'He doesn't want to be the one to pick her up. Have you seen the size of her? She'd kill him with the effort. He's a good lad and, honest to God, I don't know what I'd do without him. Brings my coal in every night for me and he's such a good dad to that lad of theirs.'

Madge opened the door and peeped out into the party. 'Ah, God love her. Sister Horton looks so tired. In the short time they've had that baby, she's aged ten years.'

'Tell me what new mother doesn't?' snapped Biddy. Biddy's life was devoted to Sister Horton and the school of nursing and, more lately, to the addition to Sister Horton and Dessie's family, baby Louis.

'Who'd have thought it, eh?' said Elsie. 'Nurse Davenport not long married with a bun in the oven and Sister Horton and Dessie with their own adopted baby boy.'

'I'll tell you what, though: there's no way that bun wasn't already in the oven before they were married,' said Madge. 'What did Mrs Duffy say, Biddy? Does she think that? If anyone knows, she will. She looks after them all. If the nurses were talking at the home, she would have heard it, surely to God.'

Biddy looked enraged. 'Are you kidding me? I don't know and I won't ask Mrs Duffy – you know what she's like about her precious nurses. You ask her on the bus tomorrow, Elsie. And if it was or it wasn't, it makes no difference; it changes nothing, does it? Whose business is it anyway but theirs? It'll be here soon enough and nothing anyone has to say will change that.'

Madge held up a glass to inspect it for smears. 'Oh aye, I'm not going to argue with that, and she won't have been the first or the last – and I'll tell you something else: you can tell it's a little lad she's carrying. I saw them all in the café at George Henry Lee's a few weeks ago, buying baby clothes. It was just after Nurse Brogan got back from Ireland and very excited they all were, although Nurse Brogan wasn't herself at all. Due at the New Year Nurse Davenport is, but she was that big she'll be lucky to get to Christmas without delivering him.'

Elsie turned the dripping tap off and Biddy said,

'Talking about little lads, I'll just go and check on Louis. He's in the pram in Matron's bedroom, flat out he was when Emily and Dessie brought him in.' Biddy undid her apron ties as she spoke and hung it over the rail of the cooker to dry.

'Let me take those sausage rolls out there, Elsie,' said Madge. 'You go with Biddy and both of you put your feet up for five minutes while you check on Louis; me and Jake can manage for the next half an hour. You can't go until he does anyway, ladies, because you aren't walking home on your own.' Madge disappeared through the door and Elsie picked up the glass of sherry and handed a half-full one that had come back into the kitchen to Biddy with a wink. 'Come on,' she said. 'Let's go and check on him and put our feet up like she said.'

Madge blinked at the sight before her as she walked into Matron's sitting room; just as Jake had anticipated, Mrs Mabbutt had fallen backwards, straight onto the sofa, but she didn't seem to mind as, bright-eyed and flushed, she allowed half the men in the room to reposition her into a sitting pose and asked Jake to top up her glass as she straightened first her skirt and then her pearls. She saw Dr William, deep in conversation with Emily Horton, heads together, whispering. Madge knew from patching his calls through to the school of nursing that Emily had asked him to visit the hospital to give a talk to the probationer nurses about the role of a GP and how district nurses assisted in the community. He also ran the dermatology clinic at St Angelus on a Thursday afternoon. Everyone loved Dr William, and none more than his wife who stood adoringly at his side. Madge moved towards Matron with the tray, but as she passed she heard Emily Horton say, 'Well, of course, but the best person to do that is Mavis Tanner. Leave it with me, I'll have a word with her.' Madge's ears pricked up, her gossip antenna had not been dulled by the late hour and as she placed the tray on the sofa table she pretended to be rearranging a pile of small serviettes. If they were discussing Mavis, it was obviously her duty to eavesdrop. Mavis Tanner was a key member of the St Angelus Mafia and a close friend. No one had noticed Madge, not even Mrs Mabbutt, who was now beginning to doze with her glass, tipped threateningly towards her generous bosom, held precariously in her hand. Madge leant over the boucle sofa, removed it from Mrs Mabbutt's fingers, and placed it on the side table next to her as she strained her ears over the chatter.

'It's important this is kept very confidential,' Dr William was saying. 'The reasons why, I mean. If you could invent something plausible, I would be very grateful. Obviously, Dr Gaskell has no idea and it's not my place, or that of anyone else to tell him – and certainly, Mrs Tanner must not know.' Emily nodded her head and looked thoughtful. 'Obviously, under normal circumstances, I couldn't agree to withhold information, but this is different; and besides, I'm just asking someone to help out. This is not a medical intervention, it's more a social one – and helpful for Mrs Gaskell.'

Mrs Gaskell? Madge was confused. They were talking about Mrs Gaskell and Mavis Tanner in the same sentence. No one knew Mrs Gaskell. She was as unknown as her husband was a legend on the dock streets. Mmm, Madge thought, spotting Mrs Gaskell in the corner of the room, standing next to her husband who was deep in conversation with Matron, maybe it was time she got to know Mrs Gaskell. She picked up the tray and headed over to the corner window herself.

'Mrs Gaskell, would you like a sausage roll? Biddy made them herself.'

Matron, who was perched on the windowsill, leant forward to inspect the offering and made an exaggerated show of sniffing the plate. 'Well, well, they smell delicious,' she said; and, Madge noticed, it was as though Mrs Gaskell was invisible. Madge had spoken to Mrs Gaskell and Matron had not even cared to wait for her reply.

Dr Gaskell took one of the sausage rolls. 'Golly, they do,' he said, without offering one to his wife first. He rarely, if ever, brought his wife to any social functions and was usually the man by Matron's side.

Madge had willingly volunteered to help out at Matron's party, it being a special place to gather information and gossip and it looked as though it was about to pay off. 'It's lovely to see you here,' said Madge to Mrs Gaskell. 'We don't usually see you, do we, Dr Gaskell?'

Mrs Gaskell flushed and Dr Gaskell placed part of his sausage roll into his napkin and, ignoring Madge, helped himself to another. His wife looked to him for reassurance, received none, and flushing, turned back to Madge. 'Ah no, well, I thought now that Oliver was living in the doctor's residence, it was time for me to get out a bit more.'

Madge could see she was uncomfortable answering her question. Everyone knew she was oblivious to the antics of her son Oliver, the wild boy doctor of the hospital who, so far, had only specialised in breaking the hearts of probationer nurses.

'Mrs Gaskell, go on, you try one before your husband demolishes the lot,' she said proffering the tray again. 'Matron, would you...'

'Oh, I will, Madge, thank you,' said Matron, lifting one of the sausage rolls. 'Is Elsie coping in the kitchen? And more importantly, is the little prince, Louis, behaving himself?'

'He's been flat out the entire evening, loving your bedroom, I would say. Not a peep out of him,' Madge replied.

Dr Gaskell snorted with laughter. 'Who would have thought when that little lad was admitted into casualty that he would be sleeping in your bedroom in his pram at your Christmas party, eh?'

Matron shook her head in disbelief. 'I would have had you certified if you'd told me that; he was in such a bad way, almost starved to death.'

Madge looked from one to the other, neither were addressing Mrs Gaskell. 'Did you hear about the case, Mrs Gaskell?' Madge knew she was stepping over the line between staff and guest. Matron turned to Dr Gaskell's wife, as though realising for the first time that she was there and then she glanced at Madge with an expression of mild curiosity.

'Er, yes I did hear,' Mrs Gaskell said. 'It was on the news. An awful, dreadful case of abandonment and neglect. He was found in a garage in a house, wasn't he?' Dr Gaskell looked at his wife as though she had grown an extra head. He had given up long ago trying to encourage her to speak at social occasions. 'I have nothing to say,' had been her rejoinder for years. 'It is your world, not mine. No one is interested in what I have to say, they are all so clever.'.

'Yes, quite. He was almost dead by the time he got to us,' said Matron. 'The police still have no idea who the parents were. This time last year it was and not a sign of his mother. The neighbours in the street said that the couple who lived in the house were extremely secretive, kept themselves to themselves and, apparently, had fled in the night.'

'Yes, I saw the plea for his mother to come forward on the news. They said they thought she might need medical help because there was no record of the birth anywhere.'

'Quite. There were traces of blood on the bathroom

floor, apparently. It looks as though she had him at home in unusual circumstances. I mean, lots of babies are born at home, but their births are registered. Not this one, though.'

There was a moment's silence while they all visualised a lonely woman, secretly giving birth and then hiding her baby in a pram in a garage. Mrs Gaskell broke the silence.

'My husband did tell me he is being adopted by Sister Horton and her husband, Dessie, isn't that right, darling?' She turned to Dr Gaskell and Madge thought that she was sounding more confident, now that she had warmed up. It was obvious to Madge, a perceptive woman, that Mrs Gaskell wanted her husband to continue the conversation, to relieve her of the burden of commenting or passing an opinion alone, to back her up, endorse her words. Her eyes held his face, gently pleading. Madge was taken by her manner and her voice and found herself staring at her. It was timorous, faltering, as though it had been an effort to speak. Madge wondered why she didn't do something with her hair which was white and straight, her face, touched only by a powder that made her complexion look pale and dry.

'Yes,' he said. 'Well remembered. The very lucky young man is in the process of being adopted and he's always about, isn't he, Matron? And Sister Horton is still working here.' Dr Gaskell bit into the puff pastry of his sausage roll and covered himself in an explosion of buttery golden flakes. He had passed the conversation on to Matron as though it were a baton.

'He is indeed always about. Sister Horton is very lucky. The head of children's services has allowed her to continue working here during the adoption process – and why not, I say. In this case, with his medical needs, there was no better solution. The whole thing was such a dreadful affair – the house where he had been found was rented in a false name and there was no paperwork, the neighbours knew nothing, and there was no trace of anyone. The neighbours said that the couple who had left the house were foreign and too old to have children so it wasn't theirs. There was a live-in help, but the neighbour said she left the house six months earlier, so it couldn't have been hers either. So someone looked for an empty house and dumped little Louis in the garage. It was a complete mystery – just thank goodness he was heard and Emily and Dessie fell in love with him.'

'Goodness me, Matron. You are becoming a thoroughly modern detective in your old age and a modern matron too.' Dr Gaskell laughed as he spoke.

'Nonsense,' said Matron, having the grace to look embarrassed. 'Wasn't I the one who pushed for married nurses to be able to work? Don't get me wrong, if children's services had said that Sister Horton had to give up work to adopt, she would have had to make the choice – adopt Louis, or keep her job. Thankfully, it never came to that.'

Madge didn't want to overstay her welcome; taking her leave she made her way into the kitchen to fetch a fresh plate and circled the room, offering out the devils on horseback, bites of prunes wrapped in bacon, pierced with a cocktail stick and drizzled with golden syrup, to the sound of oohs and ahhs. She had heard the recipe on the radio the previous week. Lyle's syrup had not long returned to the shelves in the shops in some abundance and was flying through the tills. It was three weeks to Christmas and she could smell it in the air. The happiness and anticipation, the sherry and the sugar, the cloves and cinnamon. She sighed as she spotted Dr William and his wife sitting on a hard-backed chair talking to one of the other GPs and his wife. Matron had placed Dr William next to the gramophone and he was laughing as he bent to carefully place the stylus on the beginning of a spinning record.

'This takes more skill than removing an appendix,' he laughed as there was a slight scratch before the strains of Bing Crosby singing 'White Christmas' filled the room. Matron's Christmas tree, always the first to be erected and decorated, twinkled in the window. It shone down over the car park and the main entrance to the hospital and out onto the Dock Road. 'I want the hospital to be a welcoming place at Christmas, not the terrifying place it is for the rest of the year,' she was known to say when she was asked why hers was always the first tree to be lit. 'Half of Liverpool still think this place is a workhouse.'

In the reflected light, the crystal glasses filled with the golden sherry shone. Chatter, laughter and pre-Christmas excitement filled the room. Madge patted her hair. No, not a single man in the room.

'Right, back to the kitchen for me, then,' she said, and with a sigh she turned away from the life she wanted to live to the life she had. No sooner had she run a fresh sink of hot water to soak the sticky plates she had carried in, than Emily and Dessie caught up with her.

'Time for us to go,' said Emily. 'We'll just fetch Louis from Matron's bedroom. Has he been good?'

'He has, not a peep; but then, when was that little lad any trouble? Who would have thought it, eh?' Emily tied her headscarf tight under her chin. 'Have you seen that rain?' said Madge, inclining her head towards the window. 'I wouldn't be surprised if he wakes up once you get him out there, so keep him covered.'

'Bet you he doesn't,' said Dessie. 'A bomb could go off and that lad wouldn't wake.'

'Aye, well, let's hope that one is never put to the test, shall we?'

The door opened again and Jake appeared. 'Come on then, Dessie, I'll help you carry the pram down the stairs before Mrs Mabbutt passes out altogether and I have to help her husband with a fireman's lift.'

Dessie frowned. 'Tell you what, I'll get Emily and Louis home and then I'll come back to help, shall I?'

'No, you won't,' said Jake taking his coat down off the

back of the door. 'Dr William and I have got it covered, he's going to help me, should help be required. You never know, she may surprise us all and make it out of the door all by herself. She's been known to see off a bottle's worth of port and lemon at the doctors' wives lunch, so I've been told and she wobbles out of the door all by herself then.'

Dessie looked relieved. 'Well, as long as Dr William is there to help. What an asset he is to the hospital.'

'Oh, he is that,' said Madge. 'I'm registered at his GP practice and he's a lovely doctor too,' she said. 'I thought my heart would break when Dr Marcus died because I didn't think they would ever find another to replace him. But Dr William does the skin clinic here on Thursdays now and Doreen told me that the patients and the nurses just love him in outpatients too.'

'Right, let's go,' said Dessie. 'Thanks for everything, Madge. Where's Biddy and Elsie?'

'They're with Louis,' said Madge, and they pushed open the bedroom door to find Elsie on one chair, her shoes kicked off, fast asleep and Biddy sprawled out opposite in the other in the same state of repose. 'I don't know about Mrs Mabbutt, it's your mother-in-law and Biddy you'll be carrying home,' said Madge to Jake.

'Poor things, they're wiped out,' said Emily. 'Thank goodness Louis was no problem.' She took the handle of the pram and carefully swivelled it around as Dessie secured the elastic over the hooks at the side of the hood to make sure no rain could get inside the pram once they were outside, then with Dessie at the front and Jake on the handle, they expertly carried the pram down the stone steps to the outside of the hospital and gently laid it back down onto the cobbled pathway. All three of them peeped over the canopy cover to check on the little boy.

'God love him, and God speed home, you two. See you in the morning at eight, Dessie,' said Jake, one hand held up in a salute of farewell as he jumped the steps two at a time to go back into the light and warmth as Emily and Dessie set off on the ten-minute walk to their terraced house. The wheels of the large Silver Cross pram glided seamlessly over the cobbles as they strode with their heads bent down, their gaze never leaving the face of their baby boy. Neither noticed the passing bus or the face of Ida Botherthwaite, a night cleaner at the hospital, pressed against the glass, watching them as the bus passed. They were proud parents, two people with a history of loss and despair who had found love together and total happiness in their joint love for their adoptive son.

Only one of them knew that they were living a lie.

Chapter 3

Mrs Duffy, housekeeper at the Lovely Lane nurses' home, age unknown and advancing, had been discussed at the highest levels following a recent decision made by Matron to recruit more nurses from Ireland. New wards were being built to meet the post-war demands of a burgeoning NHS. Along with the new wards, the decision had been taken to expand the nurses' home and build out into the large garden.

'I wonder if it's time for us to politely suggest to Mrs Duffy that it's time to retire,' one of the board members had said at a recent meeting.

Matron sat up in her chair and tumbled her pencil around in her hand in mild agitation. 'It's up to Mrs Duffy to decide when she wants to retire,' she said. 'I certainly shan't be suggesting it. What would be far more useful would be for us to take on a maid to help ease her burden, someone to learn under her. No one, young or old, should be expected to run the place alone when the new rooms are occupied. We will value her knowledge and experience more than ever then. She's a stickler for order and routine – and that's no bad thing today. We know that whoever trains under Mrs Duffy will be well taught.'

The chairman of the board had not agreed so readily. 'That is an extra budgetary expense, Matron. Why would we take on an extra member of staff? Surely the thing to do is to tell Mrs Duffy to retire and take someone half her age on. I mean, you don't run an old nag in a race if you want to win it, do you? Mrs Duffy has been exemplary in her service to the hospital and the nurses, I have no doubt; however, isn't it time to rest the racehorse? Put her out to grass? Bring in a new filly who can do twice the work in half the time.'

Matron had laid down her pencil and taken a sharp intake of breath. Dr Gaskell, knowing the signs well, intervened. 'Captain Rodgers, you are absolutely right.' He spoke slowly, his thoughts forming. He was a man to frame his argument with diplomacy and care. 'As you will have noticed, much of our workforce comes from the surrounding streets and, although it was difficult during the war, now we have no end of young talent and professional people just like your good self, looking for work.'

Captain Rodgers blushed. As the new chairman of the hospital board, he enjoyed both his status and the power it gave him. Like many men who had returned from a long spell serving as officers during the war, finding positions to equal their war status had not been easy. Captain Rodgers was enamoured with his new role and had taken to flexing his opinion far too often for Matron's liking.

'The thing is, Mrs Duffy is what you would call in certain social circles – circles you yourself are familiar with, I am very certain – she is, well...' He looked up to see if he had the captain's full attention; satisfied, he continued, 'An old and very much-loved family retainer and therefore you will understand, more than most, why it is that our natural desire is to keep her on and help her as much as we can, until that inevitable day comes when she makes the decision herself to retire.'

As he spoke, he wondered if he was the only one thinking about the day Matron's retirement loomed. Would she recognise when that day had come? Would he have to fight for her as he was about to for Mrs Duffy? They had carried St Angelus through the war years, through the formation of the NHS and now, into this new era of ward building. They were all getting on. Would anyone fight for him?

Captain Rodgers preened, he lived in a small three-bedroomed detached house, albeit a smart one, in the equally smart Menlove Avenue. The postal address mattered to him far more than the size of the house and he had no more idea of what an old family retainer was than anyone else around the table. What mattered to Captain Rodgers was status and perception – and Dr Gaskell had played his hand well.

'Of course, when you put it like that, I see exactly what you mean. However, may I ask, is that why the new self-contained accommodation at the nurses' home was approved by Matron, for Mrs Duffy to retire to? If so, it means she's never going to leave, doesn't it?' Captain Rodgers said as he placed an exaggerated tick against Matron's suggestion on the agenda before him. The air across the board table crackled, Dr Gaskell aware, as he reflected on the conversation he and Matron had had just before they entered the boardroom for the meeting, that he would have to answer this question very carefully indeed. Matron had known this meeting would become difficult and, in her own way, she had prepared him.

'What happens if and when she does retire?' Matron had asked him when they went through the new plans for Lovely Lane on her desk. 'She will miss the company, will need looking after herself. We can't just abandon her to a life of solitude and no sense or purpose to her day. We are her life, all of us. There is barely a nurse working in this hospital who hasn't been woken up with a cup of tea by Mrs Duffy. No one who has returned after a long and hard night shift to a cold bed because a hot water bottle is always waiting. We owe it to her to ensure she is looked after in her old age.'

His heart broke as he watched her fold the plans and place them back inside the foolscap folder. *Who will look after you, Matron? We all owe you.* 'I do understand,' he had said, gently, 'but how do we get this past the board?'

Matron had obviously thought this through. 'Well, it's not that difficult. You just have to exert your authority over that new and very self-important Chairman, Captain Rodgers.'

Dr Gaskell frowned. 'Matron, Captain Rodgers is a war hero,' and Matron looked only slightly shamefaced.

'Yes, he is and the nation is grateful, none more so than I; however, our board meetings are being turned into a battleground. And if there is one thing Churchill has taught us, Dr Gaskell, it is that brains can outwit brawn – and you have brains. You will say that the lack of housing in Liverpool following the war means that if we are to attract a live-in housekeeper, we need to have accommodation to offer as part of the package. That will reflect in the pay, obviously. This isn't a problem unique to Liverpool; the board shouldn't need to be convinced of the fact that we are in the midst of a national housing shortage crisis.'

'Yes, but your idea is to move Mrs Duffy in, while she is still working as the Lovely Lane housekeeper and to leave her there, even after she retires, which means there will be no accommodation for a replacement live-in housekeeper.'

Matron looked down at her clasped hands and took a breath before she replied. 'I am, of course, very aware of that and I have to ask you to trust me. Only you and I must know that we will look after Mrs Duffy when the day comes.'

Dr Gaskell knew there was no point in arguing with her – Matron always got her own way – and now, at the board meeting, she was silent, knowing she stood a very strong chance of losing her temper with Captain Rodgers, so he was the one left to answer. Brains over brawn, indeed.

He looked up and faced Captain Rodgers square on. Notwithstanding that the man might have left the war decorated, he was now beginning to find him increasingly tedious. 'Yes, Captain Rodgers. I am afraid that following the war, needs must. We have struggled on for as long as we have been able to and our staff put in a heroic effort, but since the formation of the NHS, the demands on the hospital grow daily. It is entirely necessary, if this hospital is to produce the results required by the regional board, recruitment, expansion and investment, both in people and resources.'

'Very well, if you say so, Dr Gaskell. As I am new to this, on this occasion I shall bow to your greater understanding. The decision to extend the Lovely Lane home was made before my time and I'm not sure that if the plans were being presented today, I would necessarily approve them. Change is not always a good thing, you know. I've been looking at the costs and it all appears to be very extravagant to me. Central heating? Whoever heard of such a thing? Certainly not the farm girls from Ireland you are about to inflict on us all.' He snorted with laughter and looked around the table for approval, but there was none as the members of the board shuffled their papers uncomfortably. Matron smiled at Dr Gaskell. They had won this battle, today, but for how long? 'Now, next on the agenda, Matron, a request for the purchase of four new metal drip stands. What on earth for? Can the patients not hold their own drip bottles? We didn't have those in the war – you were lucky to have a drip in the first place.'

Following the meeting, Matron and Dr Gaskell always retired to her sitting room for a post-mortem. 'I don't think I will ever have the patience to sit there and explain to that idiot why it is I need four new drip stands,' said Matron as Elsie poured their tea. 'I mean, what does he want me to do, get nurses to hold the drip bottles? He has no idea. I swear, one day this new NHS will be taken over by men like him, telling us how to do our jobs, and not one of them will have a shred of medical training to speak of. When I listen to him speak, I can see the day when patients no longer come first.' She took the cup and saucer from Elsie. 'I don't know why you are grinning at me, your turn will come. You think it's funny now, but that smile will be wiped off your face when he starts telling you which patients you can afford to operate on and which you can't. Now, all I need to do is recruit someone to help Mrs Duffy. I don't suppose you know of anyone, do you, Elsie?'

Elsie pulled the knitted tea cosy back down over the pot as she thought. 'Well now, I do – Ida Botherthwaite's granddaughter, Gracie – I happen to know she's looking to be taken on. Ida's son is a lazy good-for-nothing and his wife has him and a houseful of kids to look after. She's only fourteen but she's been taking laundry in since she had the strength to lift a flat iron. I met her in the fishmonger's and she asked me did I know of anything going. She has a lovely disposition, nothing like her grandmother. Very bright too, they say.'

'Well, beggars can't be choosers. I want to have someone down at the nurses' home and working before Christmas, just in case Captain Rodgers changes his mind because the next board meeting is the first week in January. So, Elsie, would you recommend her?'

Elsie shuffled the dishes around on her trolley as she thought. 'Matron, if you want me to be honest, I think she's such a grand lass and she would be wasted in Lovely Lane. She has as much about her as half of the girls who come into Lovely Lane as probationers. It's a mystery to me why her grandparents haven't asked you before now to take her on.'

Matron smiled. 'Would Ida think beyond herself?' she asked. 'She's a good enough cleaner, but it isn't lost on me that she's not the most popular in our workforce. Elsie, you have made my mind up for me. I have no time to procrastinate or even interview. If you could offer her the job on my behalf and bring her to Lovely Lane tomorrow, I shall meet her there myself and you can introduce me to her and Mrs Duffy at the same time. I also need to have a word with Dessie. We need to push those works along. He has to go down there and lean on Mr Botherthwaite. A point of no return is where I want us to be, not just a hole in the ground – and that was where we were last time I looked. Do you think Gracie will take the job, Elsie?'

'I think she'll bite your hand off, Matron.'

'Good, that's settled then. I'll see you both there at eight in the morning.' Matron glanced at Dr Gaskell. 'You have been very quiet. What do you think?' she said to him. 'Ida Botherthwaite's granddaughter? Elsie recommends her and that's good enough for me.'

Dr Gaskell picked up his cup and saucer. 'Well, as her grandfather is the works foreman at the nurses' home, I say let's keep it in the family.'

Matron grinned; she loathed a problem, loved a solution.

'Just a thought, Matron, but has anyone spoken to Mrs Duffy about this?'

Matron and Elsie looked at each other. 'Well, not yet, obviously.'

'Ah, well,' he sipped his tea, 'far be it for me to speculate, but if you were looking for a fly in the unguent, I think that may be it.'

★

Elsie had waited outside when Matron took Gracie in to meet Mrs Duffy and start her first day at work. Dr Gaskell's words had kept her awake the previous evening because he had a habit of being right. Mrs Duffy was proud and independent and Elsie had a premonition that although Matron wanted an assistant at the nurses' home, Mrs Duffy might not be quite as keen. As predicted, Gracie had jumped at the chance of the job.

'Thank you, Mrs O'Brien!' She had almost hugged Elsie when she'd called round the previous evening after work.

'Oh, don't be thanking me. It was your pluckiness, asking me did I know of anything going the other day. Serendipity I call it, Gracie. Meet me at the bus stop in the morning, we'll catch the seven twenty. Go and boil some water now, have a bath and wash your hair, get yourself ready.'

Gracie's mother had been even more grateful, if that were possible. 'I've been asking Ida for months to see if she could get Gracie taken on, but she kept saying there was nothing going.'

Elsie sniffed and pulled her headscarf down over her curlers. 'Yes, well, there usually is a job somewhere for family and your dad-in-law, Bertie, does all the heavy maintenance so either of them could have asked at any time.'

Gracie's mother slipped her arm around her daughter's shoulders. 'It's me, Mrs O'Brien, they don't like me, but they shouldn't take it out on Gracie. I have the mother-in-law from hell, I'm afraid.'

Elsie felt sorry for her and wanted to add, 'Your husband is just as bad, love, the apple never falls far from the tree,' but Elsie was wise enough to not pass opinion. 'Never mind, queen, all's well that ends well. She only left school in the summer and she's being taken on now, so you'll get a wage packet before Christmas, Gracie. You just work hard and don't let me down. Mrs Duffy is very protective of her nurses. You keep your head down, make her life easier and it will all keep fine for you.' But despite the fact that Gracie was perfect for the job, Elsie felt a niggling doubt in the pit of her stomach.

'What do you mean, help? I don't need help and I don't want it, either.' Mrs Duffy dried her hands on her tea towel as she walked towards them and looked Gracie up and down with as much curiosity as she would an alien who'd landed in her kitchen, unannounced.

Matron was taken aback, having expected Mrs Duffy to exude a warm welcome. Gracie blinked, rapidly, already feeling very much unwanted. 'Mrs Duffy, I insist – and so does Dr Gaskell. You aren't getting any younger; none of us are.'

Mrs Duffy folded her arms. 'Have you taken on an assistant matron, then?'

Matron, unused to being challenged, blustered, 'Well,

no, not yet,' and then, with greater confidence, 'but I shall soon. You will be having more nurses and I more beds and patients. We both need help.'

Mrs Duffy carefully folded the tea towel and laid it across the bar of the range. 'Well, Matron, when the nurses arrive, we can talk about it then. In the meantime, thank you very much for coming, young lady, but we won't be needing you at all.'

Matron wrinkled her nose. 'Mrs Duffy, what's that smell?'

Mrs Duffy looked around. 'What smell, Matron? I can't smell anything.'

Matron walked past Mrs Duffy towards the range. 'Is there anything in here, other than these eggs on the top?'

'No, nothing,' Mrs Duffy replied.

Matron, shaking her head, whipped the tea towel off the bar and opened the oven door to rescue a tray of black bacon. Mrs Duffy looked sheepish. 'Well, if you hadn't disturbed my routine, I wouldn't have forgotten them!'

'I'm sure. However, this has been discussed and decided at the board meeting yesterday. We need more help, so Gracie stays.'

Chapter 4

Dr Gaskell fixed his tie in the hallstand mirror as his wife stood waiting patiently, felt hat in one hand, his leather gloves in the other. The weak December light that filtered through the oval stained glass of the front door cast a pinkish hue over his reflection. Doris Lillian May Gaskell had never liked the stained-glass window. 'A brace of pheasants,' he had said when as newly-weds they had chosen an image from the glazier's catalogue all those years ago and every morning since it had been put in, the glassy eyes of a dead bird had looked down and witnessed their morning ritual. At the time she hadn't thought to mention that she didn't actually like the design – as long as he was happy, she didn't want to be difficult.

She resisted the urge to shuffle from foot to foot as the chill wind that blew under the doorway presented a challenge to her pale blue candlewick dressing gown, the hem lifting and her ankles freezing.

'What plans have you for today?' he asked as, satisfied with his Brompton knot, he turned to face her with a smile and relieve her of the grey felt hat. It did not pass her by, as she leant forward and caught her own reflection, that the filtered light of the stained glass smoothed the wrinkles of time, passed a light brush over the shadows under her eyes and protected her from the cruel morning light. Her thick chestnut brown hair was now white, thin and fluffy. She no longer bothered with the curlers she had slept in for years and it was now as straight and as stiff as a board. Despite this, she had retained a flash of her youthful beauty: her slim figure and wide blue sparkling eyes had not deserted her yet. He had asked her the same question every working morning for the past thirty-seven years, four months and two days. She lifted her face and beamed up at him.

'Oh, it's the usual Wednesday for me,' she said. 'It's half-day at the shops so I need to get to the butcher's and then, well, not so usual, I suppose... Mrs Tanner from the hospital called around yesterday and I promised I would meet her later today at the Lovely Lane home, to make cakes in the kitchen with Mrs Duffy. Some of the nurses might pop in to help, too. The more the merrier she said.'

Dr Gaskell looked surprised. 'She never said a word to me, and you didn't mention this last night...' he said and looked put out. 'That's not like you. I don't mean the baking, but...'

He didn't have to finish his sentence, she knew exactly what he meant. She had heard him describe her on a number of occasions as 'a bit of a home bird' and he was right; her entire life had been spent looking after her oh-so-important husband, tending his every need.

'Well, I was in bed fast asleep by the time you arrived home last night.'

Her words held no accusation, she was well used to being alone. He had telephoned her, as he always did, because he was thoughtful – but thoughtfulness did not compensate for a cold bed. She had half anticipated his call – it had been his operating list day and she knew there were a number of serious cases who were on the table for lung removal; he had told her this over a plate of shepherd's pie the evening before.

'Hello, darling,' he'd said, 'I'm going to stay, just until my patient is out of the woods.'

Her reply, always the same, had been, 'Of course, darling, but make sure you are home by midnight. Your other patients won't appreciate a tired and grumpy doctor tomorrow.'

Unfair, she knew. He was never grumpy. He looked down at her outstretched hand now and took the black leather gloves from her, began to ease them, a finger at a time, over his hands.

'I know, I'm sorry. It's just such a surprise, Mrs Tanner calling around here. I wonder did Matron know?'

She felt embarrassed, didn't know what to say to the man she had been married to for all the years she had been on autopilot, the perfect doctor's wife. 'Well, I didn't ask and she's hard to say no to, Mrs Tanner – you try it,' she said and finished her words with a nervous laugh.

'Will you be all right?' His expression was concerned, his eyes asking a question she did not know how to answer. 'I know only too well how difficult Mrs Tanner is to refuse. You don't have to go, though, not if you don't want to.' He studied her face, looking for a clue.

She set her jaw and looked him in the face. 'No, I do. I mean, I will. I'm going to go. I want to.' She sounded as though she meant it and, as she spoke, she realised that, actually, she did, in one way. In another, she was terrified and he knew it.

'That's nice,' he said as he smiled at her, his eyes lingering. She tightened the corded belt around her dressing gown and he bent down and picked up his battered Gladstone bag as she presented her face and awaited his kiss which he dutifully dropped onto her parted, papery lips. They had once been full and yielding and his kisses had once meant more than just goodbye.

'I was asked to help with something else too and I agreed. I said I would be happy to help Sister Theresa make decorations for the Christmas tree on the children's wards next week. I thought we would send a few to Dr Teddy's sister-in-law, Nurse Victoria. Oliver said that she is due to have her baby just after Christmas and I've knitted a matinee coat for it, so I'll send that, too. If I'm not going to have any grandchildren of my own, I may as well knit for someone else's. Sister Theresa called only hours after Mrs Tanner. Such a coincidence. If you hadn't got caught up on the ward and come home before bedtime I'd have told you all about it.'

'Doris…' He looked flabbergasted. It was as though a different woman was seeing him off to work. A stranger.

'What?' she asked defensively. 'I'm not chained to the kitchen sink, you know. I'm not totally incapable.'

'No, no, my darling, of course you are not. Helping with the tree, making the cakes… that's a jolly good idea. You make the best cakes I know.'

'Really?' she asked with an edge to her voice that even she wasn't aware she possessed. 'If that's the case, why do you eat so many of Mavis Tanner's?'

'Right, I'm off,' he said wanting to end the unfamiliar conversation as she reached to open the door. Her job. A small cog in her unchanging and long-established routine. She had stood waving him off to work, once with a belly full with a child, which in turn became a toddler on her hip, a small boy holding her hand, a little man running out of the door at the same time as his father to get into the front seat of the car for his lift to school.

'What about you?' she asked when the door stood open and she folded her arms and pulled her dressing gown tight across her chest to ward against the sudden drop in temperature.

'I've got a clinic, straight after the ward round, and then Sister Horton has asked me to give a talk on the latest antibiotic therapy for the treatment of chronic bronchitis in paediatrics. I want to explain to the nurses about the importance of maintaining consistent antibiotic levels in the blood with the new drugs. Do you know, I happened to be on a ward the other day and it occurred to me that the drug round took over an hour – and that's not good enough for those on the new therapies. The drugs need to be given on the hour. I'm going to talk to Matron about it, see if there is a way the more time-sensitive medications can be given as they should be.'

Her mind was drifting towards the banana bread she had put in the oven. The habits of wartime had never left her and she still lived by the mantra, 'waste not, want not' and had never knowingly put an overripe banana in the bin.

'And when that is done,' he went on, 'I'm having a working lunch in Matron's rooms along with some of the other consultants to talk about the new wards that are being built. Just the usual, darling. Is it lamb chops tonight?'

'If I was the sort of woman predisposed to jealousy, I would feel rather envious about the amount of time you spend with Matron.' She knocked the invisible dandruff from the shoulders of his wool worsted coat, deflecting the true meaning behind her words. She had witnessed their obvious closeness and Matron made her feel inadequate, stupid, like a little woman who knew nothing. She also knew that it wasn't Matron's fault that she felt that way. Matron, the career woman, the professional who spoke to doctors as though they were delinquents in need of a firm hand, had been the other woman for all of her married life.

'Your mistress in blue,' she had once joked, in the days when they did joke about such things, when there was still a sexual frisson, a reason to behave in the coquettish, teasing manner he appeared to enjoy, the days when she hurriedly applied her lipstick as soon as she heard his car turn into the drive. The days when her hair was thick and curled, her breasts as full as her hips, her eyes bright and blue and interested in life. That had been so long ago...

'Here, tuck your scarf in,' she said as she pushed the checked scarf down inside the front of his coat. He laughed and dropped an uncustomary kiss onto her nose, guilt settling on his face.

'You know you've never had to worry. I have always been quite safe with Matron. We both know she has never been interested in men.'

Doris raised her eyebrows. 'So you often say – and I have always believed you. I was never worried that you were going get up to no good with Matron.'

'What is it then?' he asked. 'What does worry you?' His expression full of concern.

'What it is, is lamb chops. It is Wednesday, is it not? It's always lamb chops,' she said. He frowned, about to say that wasn't what he meant as she well knew, but he let the subject drop. If he didn't leave he would be late for his first ward round. 'Do you think you might see our son today and remind him he's supposed to be here this evening for supper too?' She moved the conversation quickly on from Matron and relief flashed across his eyes. He was as married to St Angelus as he was to his wife. His guilt stemmed from the fact that he knew his wife had spent far too many evenings and weekends alone when he should have been at home; but when Matron called, he could never resist. They shared an all-consuming passion for the good of St Angelus, its staff and patients.

'Oh, damn and blast, I forgot to say... Oliver asked if he could bring Teddy home with him tonight and I said yes. Sorry, I forgot.' He gave her a pleading look and she smiled.

'Well, it's a good job you remembered now before I went to the butcher's. I had better make a nice pudding then. Those boys, they love their puddings.'

'Those boys love food,' he replied with disdain. 'They can't keep up with them in the doctors' sitting room. Elsie swears they have hollow legs. She also swears Oliver hasn't stopped growing yet.'

Given that Elsie fed Dr Gaskell as often as Doris did, she assumed she must be the third most important woman in his life... or was that her? Did Matron and her housekeeper come first and second? He certainly spent more hours with them than he did with her.

'So don't you let whoever is volunteering on the WVS tempt either of you with Mrs Tanner's cakes today or you are going to have to be measured for a new suit,' she said.

'Don't be ridiculous. I only bought this one a few years ago.' He looked affronted. 'Our son is operating in theatre all morning but I will make sure I get a message to him, though.'

Their only son had followed in his father's professional footsteps – medical school and straight to St Angelus. He had chosen surgery and the life of a bachelor, much to his parents' despair. 'Mrs Tanner won't tempt me. I'll be as good as gold,' he called back as he half lifted his hat into the air and strode down the path towards the garage where the gardener had already opened the doors and his pale green Humber stood ready to transport him to St Angelus and yet another busy day as one of the most prominent chest physicians and surgeons in the North-West, a living hero on the dockside streets and a man who spent more waking hours of the week in the company of Matron than he did with his wife.

As was their custom, Doris Gaskell stood in the cold and waved until the car turned right at the end of the drive and became swallowed by the privet hedge. She looked up into the grey sky and sighed, remembering Oliver as her little man, recalling a memory of him waving to her at the end of the drive. How her heart had leapt as he dropped his satchel onto the gravel and ran back. 'One more kiss, Mummy, but don't let anyone see.' She took a deep breath. How she had longed for more children, but her husband was always so tired, often away on one course or another, reading case notes or papers into the night, long after she had fallen asleep. Yes, his reputation had come with a huge personal cost. She sighed again, closed the door and hurried back inside to the warmth of the kitchen fire – and to find the brown glass bottle within which lived her little friends, her helpers, the pills that carried her through the day until the evening when her sought-after, popular, God-like husband returned.

Chapter 5

He had brought her breakfast to her room on a tray. 'I thought I had better come and see if you were all right after your funny turn last night. Here's a bit of tea and toast and porridge.'

He held the tray before him and it occurred to her that he was the one who looked nervous. She held the door with her foot and took the tray. 'Thank you.' Just the two words, no further information given.

'Did you sleep well? Do you feel any better this morning?'

'I do, yes. Thank you for your kindness.' She had eaten her meal almost in silence and given him scant information the evening before. The food had made her feel stronger, better. 'I will be leaving for the day, shortly,' she had said.

'Right, well, tell you what, let me make you up a few butties to take with you for your lunch.' She had made to protest, but she was speaking to his hand at first and then his back as he walked away. 'No, I won't take no for an answer. We look after our guests.'

Eva put her sickness down to the crossing from New York. She had spent most of her days in the cabin and thought it was probably sea sickness, but now, on dry land, nothing was improving and the dull ache in the pit of her belly was still there. Just as it had been for months.

She slipped out of the Seaman's Stop unseen and heard Melly's shouting in the kitchen, 'Since when do we make butties for guests? Are you going soft in the head, or what?' She closed the door behind her and did not hear Malcolm's reply. She knew exactly where she needed to be and her first day out and about was spent in the central library. It had taken only an hour for the assistant to find her the newspapers she was looking for.

'Oh, you're lucky,' she had said. 'They don't go into the archives until January. We keep them out the back for a year at a time. All the papers from October, you say? Well, that's easy enough.' The assistant gave Eva a curious look. Why would anyone want copies of the *Echo* which were that recent?

Eva had anticipated her question. 'I'm tracing my family and I want to check the births, marriage and deaths. We were told an uncle died here in October, but we don't know the date. I travelled over to see what I could find out for my mother, his sister. They were separated during the war,' Eva said.

The assistant's expression turned from one of doubt and curiosity to one of complete understanding. 'Oh, I see, yeah, we get a lot of that. Are you from America, then, only you don't sound like a Yank, but we do get lots of them wanting to check the hatched, matched and dispatched. No, you aren't a Yank, I've heard enough to know that. The Yanks, they come in here and they say, "I'm looking for a Mrs O'Hara, she's a relative of mine, would you know her?" Honest to God, it cracks me up every time. They expect me to know who she is, where she lives and what she had for her tea last night.' The assistant gave up. She was getting nothing out of Eva. 'You go to the café next door, love. You look to me as though you could do with a hot meat pie and cuppa and I'll have the *Echoes* up here for you in about half an hour. At least you aren't asking me for the impossible. The last fella who was in here asked me did I know any of the guests at his grandfather's funeral because he was trying to trace his family. He thought that because I get all the papers here every day, I went to the funerals, too.'

Eva managed a smile and headed out towards the café. In her bag, the sandwiches Malcolm had given her crackled in the brown paper they had been wrapped in.

The librarian had been true to her word; the *Echoes* were in a neat pile on a table waiting for her when she returned.

'There you go, queen, did you find the café? You look a bit better.'

Eva smiled. 'I did, thank you.'

'That's good. Today's *Echo* has just come in; it's next to the pile if you wanted to have a look. We always get the first copy off the press here. I'm going to make meself a cuppa and there's a lot to go through there so shall I bring you one back?'

Eva looked at the girl, open-mouthed, and didn't know how to respond. The kindness of the people in Liverpool was something she had forgotten. That, combined with their inbuilt curiosity, would be her undoing if she wasn't careful. The librarian didn't wait for a reply.

'Go on. I'll bring you one over. Sugar?'

Eva nodded and gave a rare smile. She would have to be on her guard. If she said the wrong thing, she could end up in prison and from there she would be no use to anyone. The pains in her belly were low and deep. She had learnt from experience that they would stay that way; she would be safe today. As the tea landed at her elbow, she pushed what she had been reading aside so as not to give anything away and hurriedly opened the first edition of the day's *Echo*; it fell onto the jobs page. As she had thought she would, the librarian looked straight at what she was reading.

'Three weeks before Christmas and people still advertising for jobs. I've just had the matron from St Angelus on the phone, asking me to put a notice on the board.

Half of her cleaners have gone down with a cold and she's looking to take on temporary night cleaners. She wants me to put the word out. I said to her, "Matron, it's not long till Christmas, you won't get anyone now."'

Eva thanked her for the tea and watched as she pinned the notice on the board. Then she waited for the librarian to leave her desk and wrote the number for the job advert down. She had learnt all she needed to know from the newspapers, not least, that the police had been looking for her and, for all she knew, probably still were. As she left the building, the librarian was now busy stamping books.

'Looking for a job are you, love?' she asked.

Eva decided to be bold, and front it out. 'Yes, I'm going to call St Angelus about the temporary night cleaner jobs. Is there a phone box nearby?'

'Oh, St Angelus is smashing and Matron's lovely. Tell you what, come here and use my phone, but don't tell anyone.' She handed the black Bakelite handset to Eva. 'I know the number off by heart; our Madge works on the switchboard there.'

Five minutes later, as Eva was heading up to St Angelus and a job interview which she had every intention of making sure she got, the librarian picked up the phone and spoke to Madge. 'She's a right funny one, something about her... harmless, though, if you ask me.'

★

It had been almost a week and Gracie's delight at having been taken on at the nurses' home as the housekeeper's assistant was only tempered by the fact that, no matter how hard she tried, nothing she did was good enough in Mrs Duffy's eyes, so she was delighted to arrive at work on Monday morning to a note from Matron telling her that, due to a rampant cold having laid off half of the cleaning staff, she would be required to leave the nurses' home at midday and make her way to outpatients A block, a routine she would be expected to follow until further notice.

'Mrs Duffy doesn't want me at the home,' she told her mam when she arrived home that evening. 'I wouldn't be surprised if she told Matron to put me somewhere else in the afternoons. Honestly, Mam, Mrs Duffy hates me.'

'Don't worry, queen,' her mam had replied. 'Once she gets to know you she will be fine – and besides, who wouldn't be delighted to have an extra pair of hands to help them, especially at her age?'

Gracie looked miserable and her mother's heart tightened with the pain of it. Her daughter still looked like a child and, at only fourteen years of age, she *was* still a child, doing a woman's work. Her mouse-brown hair hung in two neatly tied pigtail plaits and the parting in the middle was clean and severe. Gracie redid her plaits twice a day, once before bed and once every morning and her plump cheeks and big brown eyes emitted an aura of innocence. But, despite her appearance, Gracie was smart and her determination to find work to help her mother feed a house full of kids was a testament to her sense of responsibility. How her mother would have loved to have said, 'Stay at home. Let's find you a job you love,' but with a husband who was allergic to hard work, that option was but a dream.

'Anyway,' her mam said, 'her gain is my loss. God, I do miss you being here to help me. Mrs Duffy has no idea how lucky she is in this world. Ask her, does she want to swap with me for a day?'

'Oh, Mam, I'd rather be here. She does hate me and I don't know why. I try really hard. There isn't anything I can't do and haven't been doing here to help you since I could walk. I swear to God, she hasn't smiled once and she bites my head off all the time.'

With considerable force her mother plunged the washing under the water in the huge copper boiler using a pair of wooden washing tongs. The steam made her face sweat and her clothes damp. One of her husband's shirts stubbornly floated on the top, puffed up with air and soap suds, the arms out at the side, resembling a man drowning in Omo.

'If we didn't need the money, Gracie, I'd tell you to tell Mrs Duffy to stick her job, but we can't, love. Not with your da's back being bad like it is.'

Gracie felt the anger surge up and, biting her lip, suppressed it, but as always with Gracie, she just couldn't keep her opinion to herself. 'Funny how his back played up the day I started my new job, isn't it, Mam. Never stopped him going down to the Silly on my pay day, did it?'

Her mother hung the tongs on the nail in the wall and, lifting her apron, wiped her face. 'Gracie, stop it. You can see he's in pain. I told him, I'll call Dr William out if he gets any worse. I've got Granny Ida on my back for not doing it sooner.'

'Oh, he won't get any worse, Mam, and he'll make a miraculous recovery when I get paid today and be off to the pub, then he'll be back in bed again next day. Why should I have to work to give that lazy lump money? Why don't you tell Granny Ida that?'

Her mother looked weary. 'Gracie, your da has his self-respect. I can't stop him going down to the pub with his mates – and besides, it just makes life easier.'

Gracie didn't have time to answer. 'I'm off, Mam, or I'll miss the bus. I've put the milk and sugar in the range oven to warm for the kids' breakfast and the bowls are on the top. I'll see you tonight.' And with that she closed the door to the wash house behind her. She didn't want to hear any more of her mother's protestations. Couldn't bear to. As she reached the wooden gate, she turned back to the house, to the bedroom window that overlooked the yard. Her father was standing there, in his vest and braces, a cigarette in his hand. He threw up the sash and stuck his head out.

'Gracie, I'm dying of thirst up here Where's me tea and where's your mam?'

Gracie knew the large enamel mug was on the table, steaming. If she went back and got it for him, she would miss the bus. If she left it, her mother would get the wrong end of his bad mood all day. She looked at his face and felt like she wanted to ram her fist right into his nose. She lifted the latch on the gate.

'It's on the table; if I get it, I'll miss the bus and lose my job; and if that happens, I'll get no pay and you'll have to go down to the pen tomorrow and line up for work along with the rest of the dockers from around here and sign on for the day, bad back or not.'

She saw the look of horror that crossed his face. 'Don't worry, queen, I'll get it. You get yourself off to work. Don't miss that bus.'

'Mam's in the wash house,' she said, feeling guilty for her thoughts towards her father and her white lie. 'And then she's off to mass. Da, help her carry the washing to the mangle, her back is really bad from bending over the boiler.'

A look of irritation crossed her da's face. 'Not as bad as mine, Gracie, I'm in agony up here.'

'Not as much agony as our ma is in,' she hissed back. 'If she gets any worse, I'll be giving up my job of my own free will to stay at home and help her and you can beg for a pint at the pub door, because there won't be any money from me.' She glared up at him, not knowing where her courage had sprouted from, hoping her look was enough.

Her father's expression changed. 'I don't know where you get your cheek from, queen. All right, all right, I'll come down,' he said as he placed his hands on the sash window to close it, wanting to end the confrontation with his daughter as soon as possible. 'I'm feeling a bit better today – not that you care,' were the last words she heard as the window slammed down shut.

Nurse Pammy Tanner arrived in outpatients A to find Sister Antrobus waiting for her in front of the desk which had a large stack of case notes on one side and a wire tray full of lab reports on the other. Pammy looked as kind as Sister Antrobus did severe. Pammy Tanner's hair, long, dark and shiny, was tied back and neatly tucked under her starched linen cap. Pammy, always being told off for wearing lipstick to work, flouted the rules every chance she got, and outpatients, under Sister Pokey whom she'd expected to see, was one of them.

Sister Antrobus, her steel grey hair scraped into a tight chignon at the back of her neck, glared at her, her horn-rimmed glasses swept up at the sides in an attempt to cling on to a more youthful age. It didn't work and her eyes snapped along to the beat of her sharp words.

'Sister Pokey has gone down with this blasted cold that is sweeping around the hospital, so you have me again. Match each of the lab reports in date order to the patient and insert them inside the case notes before clinic starts so that the doctor can easily see what he needs,' Sister Antrobus barked. 'You have plenty of time. Almost an hour before the baby clinic starts and the chest clinic is light today. Obviously, some of the more chronic chest cases think Christmas shopping is more important than their check-up with Dr Gaskell. They should be struck off the follow-up list if you ask me.'

'Yes, Sister,' said Pammy.

'We only have one more of these before Christmas and then a break until the new year. Hallelujah. I am now about to take my lunch. Oh, we have a new cleaner starting on here today. Half of the cleaners have been hit with a severe cold and I told Matron that we can't possibly have a clinic of forty babies and no mop and bucket in attendance.' An image of a mop pushing a bucket wearing a headscarf flew into Pammy's mind and she suppressed a giggle. Giggling was not something one did in the presence of Sister Antrobus. 'And the Christmas trees are arriving on the morning of the next clinic – can you imagine the mess? That, on top of everything else. Babies and Christmas trees. One an annoyance, the other a permanent irritation.' She gave an involuntary shudder. Sister Antrobus did that a great deal in the baby clinic. 'I told Matron, the passengers on the *Titanic* had less of a flood to deal with than we did in here last week.'

Pammy almost laughed out loud at the memory of the last clinic, but stopped herself just in time. The previous week had not been a good one. Sister Antrobus had grown impatient with one of the new mothers who was undressing her baby ready to be weighed. 'Oh, here, give him to me,' she had barked as she almost pushed the mother away. She lifted the baby into the air, unaware that the mother had already unfastened the nappy pin. The nappy fell away and the little boy, possibly as a result of fright, decided at that moment to relieve himself, all over Sister Antrobus.

'Show her where the cleaning cupboard is and the Lysol, Nurse Tanner. Really, this is the worst day of the week, baby clinic. The little horrors.' Sister Antrobus shuddered again. 'And get that lipstick off your face now, unless you want me to report you to Matron.' And with that parting note, she swept out of the double doors.

Pammy flopped down at the desk, took a handkerchief out of her pocket and wiped at her lips. 'Right, you lot, let's start with alphabetical order,' she said to the pile of lab reports and almost laughed out loud with relief to discover that Doreen, the outpatients clerk, had already done the job for her; all she had to do was insert them into the case notes.

She was almost at the bottom of the pile as her hand landed on the last full blood count. The haemoglobin level was low and she checked the notes that corresponded with the report. They belonged to one of Dr Gaskell's patients. As with all results that could not afford to be missed, she clipped it to the front cover of the notes and placed it on the top of Dr Gaskell's notes. She looked up as the double doors gave the faint swish that let her know someone had arrived. It was Gracie, nervously edging towards the desk. Pammy had seen her at the nurses' home, where she had started work the previous week.

'Gracie, are you the new cleaner on here today?' she asked, puzzled.

Gracie had never felt so relieved in her life to see that it was Pammy behind the desk. 'I am,' she said. 'Matron said I had to come up here at lunchtime on clinic days, to help out. The note also said that someone here would show me what to do.'

Pammy rose. 'Don't look so nervous, Gracie. It's just mop and bucket work. Honestly, it's not too bad. We have the odd accident and the toilets need a regular clean – that goes without saying – and Matron, she's a bit of a stickler. She likes all the chairs and doors to be washed down with a chlorhexidine solution at the end of each clinic.'

Gracie looked confused. 'What's that and why?' she asked.

'It stops infection spreading and babies are the first to be knocked down by it. We have the TB clinics here as well, so we have to be extra careful. Come on, I'll show you around. I'm way ahead of myself, thanks to the clerk, Doreen. She lives in clinic B, which is all surgical, and will come over here to say hello, I bet. Doreen runs all the clinics.'

Pammy walked Gracie around the empty and eerily quiet clinic, opening the doors, showing her which room belonged to which doctor.

'This room gets washed down before and after every clinic,' she said, opening one door. 'The trolleys, the paint-work, the floor, the lampshade, the walls – it's treated like it's an operating theatre. One of the new auxiliary nurses in the yellow uniforms from casualty comes over to do it after the clinic but you will have to do the main surfaces before. That way, Matron knows who is responsible if it's not done to her standard. We never stop cleaning. And none of the babies are seen in this room. Dr Gaskell has a TB clinic here twice a week and no one wants a baby to catch that, do they.'

Pammy turned the handle on another door almost as quickly as she closed Dr Gaskell's. 'Here's the cleaning cupboard with the mops and everything you need. You have to make sure you put everything back properly. You'll have the night cleaners leaving you notes if you don't. They are very particular and you probably know them all anyway. How's your mam? Does she still go to the bingo on Thursdays?'

Gracie felt almost too ashamed to answer. The bingo had been the one treat a week her mother had looked forward to. Unlike the other women, she had never smoked in order to save the pennies her husband barely earnt but there was nothing left for the bingo these days. 'She doesn't have time, not with our lot,' she managed.

'Tell her I was asking about her,' said Pammy, kindly, who knew only too well, how lazy Gracie's father was, not least because her own da Stan was always complaining about him on the days he was in work.

'Oh, I will, I do,' said Gracie, her voice as strong as she could make it, aware that this world, of nurses in uniforms and doctors in white coats, was one she was unused to and fearful of. 'What's that smell?' she asked.

Pammy took hold of the mop handle and a metal bucket on wheels and glided it out of the small cleaning cupboard. 'That smell is Lysol.' Pammy reached up to the shelf and lifted down a large bottle of Lysol. As soon as she removed the cap, the smell almost knocked Gracie out. 'One capful per bucket. It turns a milky white when it hits the water – and if you ask me, the smell alone kills all the germs, never mind the mop full. If I were you, when the baby clinics and paediatrics are on, I would keep the bucket and mop ready. All the mums have to strip their babies down to the nuddy, and every one of the little blighters manages to leave a puddle on the floor.'

Gracie wrinkled her nose. 'I'm only on here for afternoons,' she said.

Pammy smiled. 'Perfect. The baby clinic is on from three until four, every afternoon.' Gracie grimaced. 'Don't tell me you don't like babies as well?' said Pammy.

'I don't mind them,' said Gracie. 'There's enough of them in our house, remember? I'm the eldest and there's been six after me.'

Pammy looked up at the big clock on the wall. 'I lose count of everyone's kids after the third. Look, I have to go and place the notes on the desk in each clinic room. You have a look around. Outpatients' sister will be here soon, Sister Antrobus. If I were you, I would keep out of her way. My advice is: spot a puddle, clear it up as fast as you can. Every half an hour, pop into the toilets. Many of the mothers who turn up with prams have a few other kids in tow and they don't all have the best toilet habits! Just keep the place looking exactly as it is now. With a bit of luck, she may never need to ask you what your name is.'

Gracie smiled. 'I'll take that advice. Oh, look someone's coming in now. I thought it didn't start until three.'

'Oh, that's our Sister Horton with Louis. She has to bring him to the baby clinic to be weighed every week because he was very poorly once. Biddy looks after him in Sister's sitting room over at the school; he has his own playpen in there and Mrs Duffy looks after him down at the Lovely Lane home when she gets busy here – but that is one great big fat secret, so don't tell anyone.'

'Oh, don't worry, I know,' said Gracie. 'Grandad told me when I took the tea out to the workmen and Louis' pram was parked by the front steps and Granny Ida asked me if I'd seen him.'

Pammy felt alarmed, but wasn't quite sure why. Ida Botherthwaite was the kind of woman her mother, Mavis Tanner, described as a scold.

'Hello,' said Emily as she rushed towards them hugging Louis to her chest. 'Can I weigh him now, Nurse Tanner, and could you do me a favour and enter it into his notes? I can't get back at three and I can't wait because I have a lecture so I have to whip him down to Mrs Duffy for the afternoon – everyone is busy here and Biddy has had him all morning.'

'Oh, I know Mrs Duffy,' Gracie blurted out. 'I'm working at the nurses' home in the mornings to help her.'

Emily's face lit up. 'Oh, that's you? How lovely to meet you at last, Gracie. I've asked after you every time we have been. You must be working hard because you are always busy.' Gracie didn't want to say that when anyone called, she was sent off to do a job, out of the way. 'How is it going?'

'It's fine, I'm not sure Mrs Duffy likes me though.' Gracie was immediately embarrassed at having blurt out her predicament.

'Don't you worry,' said Emily. 'She's been managing alone for years and I know her, she will see this as some sort of knock to her competence or authority and really, it isn't. She'll resent you being there for a while but she will soften up and we will help. I'll speak to the nurses and so will Nurse Tanner.'

'Oh, would you?' asked Gracie.

Emily noticed that tears had sprung to her eyes and laid a hand on her arm. 'I'll have a word with Mrs Duffy, I promise. I feared this would happen. She's been there since before the war. You are from the four streets, aren't you?'

'I am,' said Gracie.

Pammy had picked up a stack of notes and was walking in and out of the clinic rooms, checking the notes against a list and laying them on the end of each wooden desk. Emily looked at Gracie wistfully and realised that her own mother, when she had been alive, had known Gracie's.

'It's all going to be fine,' she said, and her tone was so reassuring, Gracie smiled. Emily added, 'It's this one you want to watch out for – absolute dragon, she is, since she came over to outpatients, aren't you, Nurse Tanner?'

'Oh, aye, I am,' Pammy laughed as she rejoined them. 'Come on, then, if we are going to weigh this little lad. Gracie, you're used to babies so let's give Sister Horton a hand and get him stripped off and weighed. Come on, Louis, are you ready?'

Louis, well used to the routine, turned and smiled at Pammy and put out his arms to picked up by her.

'What do I do with the notes?' asked Pammy. 'Shall I put them through as though he attended?'

'Please,' said Emily, looking mildly guilty. 'Look at him, he's piling the weight on and he'll be walking soon. It's just that the year is almost up and the adoption papers all need to be verified. But I can't keep this appointment and I can't miss it either or there will be a gap and I don't want children's services to see it. You know what sticklers they are.'

Pammy wasn't really listening to Emily, her attention captured by Louis. 'Hello, little man,' she said as she lifted him and placed a big kiss on his cheek. 'You come to Aunty Pammy. You go on,' she said to Emily. 'I'll bring him back myself when I've weighed him.'

'Are you sure?' Emily said.

'Of course I am. The clinic doesn't start for ages yet so I've loads of time and Gracie will help me. Go!'

It hadn't been that long since Pammy had been a brand-new probationer and Sister Emily had scared the life out of her. 'Look at you!' Emily grinned. 'She'll be taking over my job as Sister Tutor one day, you just mark my words, Gracie.' She left, smiling.

Gracie took Louis in her arms as Pammy placed a paper towel onto the scales.

'Here, let's put him in here before he soaks you.'

'Oh, he won't do that,' said Gracie. 'I'm holding his nappy against him; I'm used to their tricks.'

They both laughed, but neither of them as much as Louis who began kicking against Gracie and giggling. His brown eyes looked up at Pammy, pools of hidden mischief as she swiftly placed him on the scales. Pammy almost whispered, 'Don't tell Sister Antrobus we've done this. She wouldn't like it. We only need to record the weight on the sheet out there.' She nodded to a pale green piece of paper on the desk, next to the open set of case notes. 'He's a special little fella, is Louis.' She dropped her voice even lower, as though Louis might hear and understand her. 'He was the abandoned baby.'

'Yes, I know,' Gracie whispered back. 'I don't think anyone who lives around here doesn't know.'

Pammy placed her hands over Louis' arms. 'Sit still, Louis, there's a good boy. No, stop your wriggling, you little worm!' The red needle on the scale flew from one side to the other, as Louis kicked his legs and tried to grab hold of the sides of the large cream enamel-coated dish that he was sitting in. 'Oh gosh, he's getting too big for these,' said Pammy. 'Look, I'll hold him and you tell me what the weight is. What do you think that is, twenty pounds four ounces, or is it nineteen pounds?'

Gracie bent her head to look closer. 'It's waving all over the place, I can't tell what it is,' she said and Louis kicked his legs against the enamel dish and blew bubbles at Pammy.

'Yes, I know you can kick your legs,' said Pammy, laughing. 'Would you look at him, I swear to God, he's the cheekiest baby ever. My mam says he'll be speaking before he can walk and it's because he spends so much time with so many adults talking to him. She said he'll be telling his da to bugger off and asking him for a fag and a cuppa if he spends much more time in the porters' hut with the fellas.'

Pammy and Gracie both folded into peals of laughter, and were only outdone by Louis, who laughed with them and began kicking the scales even more violently, making the needle crash loudly from one end of the glass viewing screen to the other as Sister Antrobus swept through the doors.

'What on earth are you doing?' she demanded. 'Clinic hasn't started yet.'

'Oh, I know, Sister,' said Pammy, her voice not as confident as it had been only moments before. 'We're just helping out Sister Horton.'

'Helping out Sister Horton? Where is she?'

'She's gone back to the school, Sister. I said I would drop Louis back.'

'Did you now?' said Sister Antrobus. 'On whose authority? I thought I was in charge of this clinic. Or does Sister Horton think she will assume responsibility for the entire hospital given that Matron lets her do just as she likes?'

Pammy felt her knees go weak beneath her. Everyone knew, Sister Antrobus had wanted the job as nurse tutor. They also knew she had strongly disapproved of Louis' adoption and regarded it as an unforgivable case of hospital staff being unprofessional and overly emotional and had said as much to Matron.

'I don't think St Angelus should be written about in the *Echo* for any reason. No reporter should know that the child is here or that one of the staff is going to take him home,' she had said in Matron's office. 'It makes us look very unprofessional. Strawberry Fields is where orphans belong and no one needs to know about it, either.'

Matron had allowed Sister Antrobus to rant on, un-interrupted, and let her falter to a natural end before she spoke. 'Nonsense. The head of children's services has insisted that the discovery of the child has as much public exposure as is possible. They believe the mother may have delivered him alone and be in trouble. She could have retained products which, as we know, could cause extensive bleeding, infection and almost certain death if left untreated. As far as the child being transferred to Strawberry Fields, don't you think he's been through enough?'

Sister Antrobus had left Matron's office within moments. She knew Matron's mood and was well aware that, on this, she would not be moved.

Sister Antrobus held her arms out to take Louis. 'I shall return him myself, give him here.'

Pammy felt Louis stiffen in response. 'I promised, I would do it, Sister. He knows me, you see. Sister Horton has a lecture and I'm to drop him with Mrs Duffy because he's been with Biddy in Sister Horton's sitting room all morning.'

The colour rose in Sister Antrobus's cheeks. A sister's post with a sitting room was an honour in St Angelus, one she had been denied, all because of one slight mis-demeanour. She felt as though Matron punished her every chance she got, entirely unaware that, in normal circumstances, she would have been sent packing altogether. An affair with a married consultant was not to be tolerated and it was only the fact that Sister Antrobus had very obviously been used that she was pitied rather than scorned for her poor judgement and lack of loyalty to Matron. Sister Antrobus bitterly resented the fact that Biddy, the housekeeper in the school of nursing, waited on Sister Horton hand and foot and now had also become a part-time carer of the child who, by rights, should have been transferred straight to Strawberry Fields children's home and the proper process of adoption adhered to, so she was not about to take no for an answer.

'Thank you, Nurse Tanner, I will take the boy.'

Pammy reluctantly held out Louis to Sister Antrobus and watched helplessly as she marched out of outpatients, Louis over her shoulder, his little hands and arms reaching out to her, crying pitifully. She had let Sister Horton down. Pammy looked around; there was no sign of Gracie who had scarpered within seconds. Very wise, she thought and picked up Louis' notes to write in the weight. Her pen hovered. What was it, she thought, and realised that they hadn't fully decided the correct weight. She would have to guess. 'Fifteen pounds, four ounces,' she wrote in the column and, hurried and upset, failed to notice that the previous weight had been twenty pounds. She hurried over to clinic B where Doreen was in her booth and handed her the notes.

'Baby Louis Horton, Doctor saw him early today,' she said and winked at Doreen. 'When you get the notes back, don't write DNA in them. I've recorded the weight and he's fighting fit.'

'Oh, Doctor has seen him, has he? Really, that's a surprise, because I've just seen him walking straight from the children's ward into the doctors' sitting room,' said Doreen, smiling. 'It's all right, don't look so worried, Nurse Tanner. I know the score. And they don't have much longer to wait. Soon, Sister Horton won't have to do this any more – he'll be all hers and Dessie's officially.'

'We must have a party to celebrate,' said Pammy, 'a big one at Christmas to celebrate our own St Angelus baby. Oh, I've got to dash, left Gracie the new cleaner on her own.'

'Hang on,' said Doreen as she held the notes open at the page the weight should have been recorded. 'Where's the weight sheet?'

Pammy slammed the base of her palm onto her head. 'Drat, I must have left it on the desk. Honestly, it's one of those days today. I'll bring it back over before I leave.'

As Pammy passed through the connecting door between the two outpatients departments, the exit doors were swinging shut.

'Gracie?' she said.

'Yes,' said Gracie from Dr Gaskell's room.

Pammy walked to the door. 'Who just came in?' she asked.

Gracie was wiping down the high windowsills. 'No one,' said Gracie. 'Or not that I know of, anyway. I didn't see anyone. I thought I would start on Dr Gaskell's room now. Is that all right?' She looked worried, as though she had done something wrong.

Pammy looked about her, the floor was wet and the smell pungent. 'No, not at all. That's smashing,' she said as the phone on the desk began to ring. 'Oh, God, I know who that will be. Biddy asking how come Sister Antrobus got her hands on Louis.' As Pammy picked up the phone, preparing herself to explain, she failed to notice that the green weight sheet she had completed for Louis had disappeared from the desk.

Chapter 6

The brown glass bottle was hidden behind the egg cups; given that her husband possibly didn't even know what shelf the egg cups lived on, it was a safe place to keep it. She placed it on the kitchen table, poured herself another cup of the now stewed tea and, unscrewing the lid, flicked out the blue tablet onto her hand. She went to place it on her tongue and then hesitated, looking at her little helper as she sat in the chair.

'You need to get out of the house,' her GP, Dr William, had told her. He was the reason she had attended Matron's party – he had almost forced her to go. 'These tablets will make you more of a prisoner, not less. They will stop you from feeling anxious and nervous, but they won't cure it. I would never have prescribed this chlorpromazine for you – it's just too new, not tried and tested enough. I have no idea why my predecessor gave it to you – and not only you. I have inherited other patients on this drug. Look, why don't you come to the Christmas drinks party Matron is having for us? That will do you more good than one of these things. My wife has been invited, so I am sure you definitely have been. We would only have been invited as an afterthought as I'm just a GP, albeit the one with the highest number of your husband's referrals.'

He had been standing at her back to listen to her heart, one hand on her shoulder. He stopped talking in order to concentrate and the stethoscope, cold on her skin, made goosebumps stand up on her back and arms. 'I'm sorry, it's cold,' he said. Satisfied, he began to fold the stethoscope.

'You have the highest number of referrals because you are a saint who cares for the poorest patients,' she had said as she stood and tucked her blouse back into the waist of her skirt.

He smiled. 'They may be the poorest, but I can tell you this, they are by far the most interesting and rewarding. I'll tell you some of my funnier stories if you come to Matron's Christmas drinks.' He had sat back down behind his desk and grinned up at her.

'I-I can't. I've never been to any of those things. Oliver was only young when she started having her little Christmas soirées for the doctors and their wives and I couldn't go then; I had to look after him and, well, I just never did go. Besides, I think Matron prefers it if my husband is on his own. She's got used to having him all to herself. Quite a pair they are... He can be her company for the evening if I am not there.'

The silence that followed hung heavy in the air until

he broke it with a bark that made her jump. 'Nonsense, I won't hear of it.' He put his hands behind his head and, pushing on his feet, the captain's chair slid back towards the door. Dr William had quickly developed a reputation for himself in the time he had been in Liverpool. Informal, unstuffy and kind, his bedside manner was in almost complete contrast to that of the majority of doctors who came from privileged backgrounds. The previous partner in the practice had regarded the poor as a species to be either despised or patronised.

'Look,' he said, 'I cannot tell you how much I disapprove of you being on this drug. There was an article in the *Lancet* which said that we don't really know yet whether or not this substance is addictive, and there are some who believe it may be. It is true that it has enabled patients with severe malaise, who have been hospitalised, to be discharged back home – but that is not you. I would have asked you to get out of the house three times a day and walk instead. My predecessor was quite wrong – and even if you *were* an ideal case, I would always have sought a second opinion.'

His eyes locked onto hers and he removed the buff slip of card from her notes. She felt a trickle of fear run down her spine; he was going to take her little helper away, the little blue pill that replaced the aching loneliness that lived in her belly with a soft, sleepy fog that she was always so reluctant to wake from, regardless of how many hours had passed.

'Look, can we agree to do something radical? Decide on a plan of action?' He flicked the top off his pen. 'I will write you out another prescription if you come to Matron's Christmas drinks party, is that a deal?' She didn't speak, she just nodded her head. 'Excellent. And with this prescription we are going to replace one of your three tablets a day with a five-milligram for one week, and then replace two tablets a day. After a month, we will hopefully be down to two milligrams three times a day – and then we can wean you off.'

'Take them away?' She looked terrified and he saw it in her eyes.

'Yes, but we will do it together and at your pace, so don't worry.'

He smiled at her and she felt relief wash over her as he wrote out the prescription. He wasn't going to make her stop, not yet anyway. She could have her tablets today.

'Can I ask, er, you won't tell…'

He looked up from writing out the prescription. 'I won't tell your husband, no. Absolutely not – just as long as you agree to work on this with me, which means we are aiming to get to a point whereby you don't have to take these tablets any longer.'

She had breathed a sigh of relief. Tomorrow was another day and she would deal with that when she came to it; for now, she was safe.

She had kept to her end of the bargain, had gone to Matron's drinks party, which had somehow led to her promising to meet Mavis Tanner at Lovely Lane. She just didn't know how. She hadn't expected the knock on her door, but it seemed that Mrs Tanner would not take no for an answer.

'I hope you don't mind me knocking,' she had said. 'It's just that I'm desperate for the help. The hospital is busier than ever this year, what with the new wards going up and Matron full of ideas. I'll be honest with you, Mrs Gaskell, what with running the WVS and everything else, I can't cope.'

'But, w-why me?' Doris Gaskell had stammered.

Mavis didn't hesitate. 'Because every time your husband calls into the WVS for a cake, he always tells me how good yours are and your Oliver, he says to me, "You should get one of my mum's pudding recipes, Mrs Tanner. She makes brilliant ones." You have come highly recommended, Mrs Gaskell, by the two men who eat more of my cakes than the outpatients do.'

Mrs Tanner spun a good line, but Doris Gaskell was not convinced. She had been played and she knew it and she felt ashamed that someone had felt there was a need to do that. It must have been Dr William. I have to do this myself, she thought as she stared into the fire and listened to the familiar sound of cars leaving driveways on their way to work. Soon the Avenue would be quiet. Deathly quiet.

She rose from the table, took a vegetable knife from the drawer and, sitting back down, took her cup from the saucer, patted it dry with a tea towel and then placed her blue friend in the middle. She felt beads of perspiration break out on her top lip and her hands began to shake. She was going to leave the house, meet people, do something useful. She needed her friend for this, couldn't do it without it. She took a long, deep breath and, when she felt calmer, placed the tip of the knife on the indented line that ran across the middle of the pill and applied careful pressure. It snapped in two and she picked up half, placed it on her tongue and threw the other half into the fire before she allowed the panic to return and tempt her to swallow the whole thing. The half of the pill she had thrown away combusted into a small green flame. She would do this herself and that had been the first step. The perspiration stood out in beads, all over her face. And she forced the panic that had returned in an instant and threatened to overcome her, back deep down.

'There, there,' she said as she screwed the lid back on the bottle, 'you did it.' And for the first time in many years she felt a sense of pride. She took a deep breath. 'You have a lot to do today,' she told herself, and suddenly realised that if she could just let herself, she might enjoy her day.

Roland Davenport took the last slice of toast from the toast rack, shoved the corner into his mouth while he struggled to pull his jacket over his arms and all the time his gaze never left his wife, Victoria, who sat at the kitchen table, reading *The Times*, one hand caressing her large full belly. It was a sound he had become accustomed to, the crackle of static between her warm hand and the fabric covering their child; like a wave on the shore, it was soothing and mesmerising.

'There's a frost on the moors,' he said as he glanced out of the window out onto the horizon beyond the large garden. 'You aren't going out, are you? I think it's going to be a bad winter; we need to keep an eye on that, you know, just in case… when the time comes…'

She instantly detected the concern in his voice. 'Roland, Bolton General is only half an hour away and this is our first baby – it will take forever to arrive. I've seen enough come through the doors of St Angelus to know what I'm talking about, honestly, and besides, the little sproglet isn't due until well after Christmas. You must stop worrying.' Victoria smiled up at her husband as her eyes popped wide and she flinched. 'Ooh, that was funny,' she said as her dressing gown parted and she placed both hands on her belly.

'What, what is it?' asked Roland as he fell to his knees next to her, the toast discarded.

Victoria took a number of shallow breaths as the colour rose to her cheeks and she puffed like a steam train. 'Nothing, silly, it's just a Braxton Hicks, that's all.'

'Braxton Hicks? Who and what the hell is that?' he asked as he placed his own hand over hers.

Victoria's face relaxed. 'It's just my body practising for labour, that's all. It's a kind of fake contraction. Happens all the time in the last weeks. It's the muscles, getting themselves ready to push. Oh God, this is really happening, isn't it?'

Roland looked as though he were about to faint. 'Jesus wept,' he said as he rubbed his hand across his forehead. 'Are you sure that's what is supposed to happen? You flushed bright red just then.'

'It is normal, but for the first time I just realised what I've got to go through.'

Roland clasped her hands and pressed them to his chest. 'And I will be with you; you won't be alone.'

Victoria laughed. 'No you won't! You will be pacing up and down outside like a madman. I just want you to make sure that, as soon as it is over, you get in there and get Aunty Minnie out.'

Roland grinned. 'That's right. You leave the difficult and painful task to me, you just deliver our baby.'

They both laughed as Victoria placed both hands on the table and pushed herself up to standing. 'Well, if I were closer and anything *was* going to happen today, we would be fine. I have three very capable nurses heading this way from Liverpool, so please just trot along to your office and leave me to get ready with my Braxton Hicks for company. I know exactly what it is, honestly.'

Victoria began to laugh at the sight of her poor husband as he got to his feet. He was not handling impending fatherhood terribly well. As the head partner in his own law firm, having taken over from his late father at much too young an age, he had heard enough stories from clients on a daily basis to have turned him into a gibbering wreck each night when he returned home. He placed his arms around his wife and hugged her into him. They had married some months before and she had left the nurses' home and moved to the house on the outskirts of Bolton that Roland and his brother, Dr Teddy, had been born in. The wedding had been slipped in, before she had even begun to show, and it had been attended by half the staff from St Angelus, from Dr Gaskell and Matron to the ward cleaners and orderlies and, of course, most of the doctors.

'It's because there's free booze,' Dessie the head porter had joked. But Victoria was more inclined to believe Mrs Duffy, the housekeeper from the Lovely Lane nurses' home.

'It's because St Angelus is all one big family,' she had said. 'Once you are in, you can never leave.'

Teddy had given her away and her only sadness was that her friend, Dana, had left Liverpool and retuned to Ireland after Teddy had broken her heart in the cruellest way. Victoria had still not forgiven him and Teddy's visits back to his old home had been strained to say the least.

Roland kissed her hair and held her as tight as he dared. 'Well, this is one day when I won't be watching the clock, waiting to get back to you, just in case anything happens. And, at the weekend, we have Teddy coming home.'

He felt Victoria stiffen in his arms. Roland had handled her family's estate when Victoria's own father had died and he had told Victoria where Teddy was training. In a roundabout way, Victoria had become a nurse at St Angelus as a result of encouragement from Roland, desperate to follow in her mother's footsteps and to get away from the well-meaning clutches of her Aunt Minnie and be someone who did more than sit around waiting for an equally well-meaning husband to turn up.

Despite opposition and disbelief from her aunt that she would do such a thing, she applied to be a nurse and had been amazed to have been accepted. There were times now, when choosing the wallpaper for the nursery or making Roland his favourite supper, she laughed at the situation she found herself in.

'Is Dana one of your visitors today?' Roland asked.

Victoria leant back and looked up at him. 'She is, with Pammy and Beth. She came back from Ireland two weeks ago. The train gets in at eleven thirty and then they are getting the four o'clock back so I booked a car to meet them through Mrs Stinky Face, just as you said,' she grinned.

'Vic, it's Mrs Strickland, as you well know.'

Victoria pulled a face. 'Yes, I do. Mrs Strickland, your secretary, who hasn't had a nice word to say to me since the day we were married.'

Roland looked uncomfortable. 'Well, she's very old school; she was more my father's kind of person.'

'Yes, I know, and that's why you keep her on, but honestly, you would think I was unclean the looks she gives me. It's not a crime to be three months pregnant when you get married. Anyone would think I had been the first. Matron must have known and she was no different towards me at the wedding – and in my world, her opinion of me counts more.'

Roland looked guilty. 'I know but remember, she knew your parents too. They were my father's clients and she probably feels... oh, I don't know, a sense of responsibility towards us. She is a big softie really.'

Victoria looked doubtful. 'Oh, she's never really liked me. Probably didn't approve of Daddy drinking, Mummy struggling – and suicide, well, that's just a no-no in any polite society. The fact that Daddy lost all the money before that, and then there's Aunt Minnie – well, she takes some adjusting to, even I don't like her sometimes. She's just too bossy and she thinks I'm just like my father and I'm *nothing* like him.'

Roland felt his heart melt as he pulled on his overcoat. 'Victoria, can we talk about the remarkable you? The beautiful, clever, caring, hard-working you? Mrs Strickland is very lucky to know you, Aunt Minnie is lucky to have you as her niece and I am the luckiest of all because you are my wife and the mother of our little sproglet, fast asleep in there. You are very definitely not your father.' His eyes lingered over her enormous belly. It was as if no woman before Victoria had ever been pregnant. 'You, my gorgeous wife, are amazing and you don't have to worry about anyone not liking you – every single person I know loves you, but none as much as I do. Now. I am going to be late.'

He dashed to the door as she shuffled along behind him in her bedroom slippers, her long, ash blonde hair swinging in a ponytail down her back. 'Why did you ask was Dana coming especially?' she asked as she opened the door and leant against it to protect herself from the wind whistling down from the moors.

Roland placed his hat on his head and tapped the top to keep it in place. The moors ran away from the front of the house, the view, broken only by the silver birches and the old oak in the corner of the garden in which could still be seen the remnants of the tree house Teddy and Roland had played in as boys. The front lawn was large and sprawling and the beds manicured, the soil's surface glistening in the morning frost. He took his keys from his pocket.

'Oh, no reason... just that, well, Teddy, you know...'

Victoria sighed and shook her head. 'Roland,' she said, turning his name into an accusation. Dana had been the first of the nurses to fall in love with a doctor at the hospital. She and Teddy had become the golden couple and all had been well until Teddy's road accident. And if that hadn't been enough, in what seemed to everyone to be an act of madness, he had cheated on Dana who, unable to cope with the shame, had returned home to Ireland to ponder her future. 'Do you want me to have a word with her? You do, don't you?'

Roland's face broke into a smile. 'I know it's a lot to ask, but he is just so lost without her. I think something happened to him after the accident and he wasn't himself, but he is so much better now. Oliver Gaskell told Teddy how sometimes it's difficult for people to adjust to trauma and accidents such as the one Teddy had. He told me Teddy would do anything to win Dana back.'

'Oh, I'm sure he would – and that just shows you he has not recovered from his head injury and is completely mad if he thinks she would even give him the time of day. I think that accident affected his brain more than you think.' She flicked back her hair, a sure sign of irritation.

Roland had one more try. 'I know that, darling, but Oliver Gaskell said that when people are incapacitated for a long period of time and they had been close to death in the way Teddy was, the frustration and the anger makes them behave in a way that is unnatural to their personality and do things they wouldn't normally do. Remember, Teddy very nearly died. He was months off work and unable to walk. He did think his career as a doctor was over and to him, well, that was as good as saying his life was over. The poor chap was in a very bad place.' He looked pleadingly at his wife.

'Roland, I know he was incapacitated for months. It was Dana who nursed him back to health and it is as the result of her care and attention that he healed as well as he did. What he did to her was an outright beastly betrayal. The man was a sex maniac. She had to go away into hiding because she couldn't bear the shame. He ruined her life, going off with that tart of a nurse after she had done so much for him.'

Roland burst into laughter. 'Victoria, my brother did not behave well, but you cannot call the poor chap a sex maniac. He didn't get any, that was the point.'

'Roland, stop. Dana even came and lived here and looked after both of you when he was recovering from surgery. Matron was so good about all of that – and then he went and did the unspeakable with that horrible, disgusting woman.'

She almost spat the last words out and Roland knew he was beaten. 'Does it help that the nurse Teddy had his affair with has married a very wealthy surgeon from a London hospital and has left a trail of broken hearts behind her?'

'No, it does not.' Victoria was emphatic. 'Poor Mrs Duffy had to travel all the way to Ireland on a pretend holiday to persuade Dana to come back. It was a good job she had become almost pen pals with Dana's mother. If I even mention Teddy's name, Dana might chew my head off though she's so much better now.'

'Will you at least try?' asked Roland as he opened the

car door. 'I'm guessing if she is coming back here to the house, where she spent happy times with Teddy, she may not still be as angry as you think.' Half in the car, he frowned and got back out again. 'Vic, I've had an idea; why don't we have a Christmas party? We could invite them both, letting them know that they are both invited – and then it's their choice whether they come or not and we can just let nature take its course. Oh, God, stupid me, no we can't, not that close to your confinement. I am such a blithering idiot.'

Victoria sighed, looked exasperated, saw the look in her husband's eyes and instantly melted at the expression of pain that crossed his face. She found the whole situation with Teddy so hard to understand, because she knew in her heart that her Roland would never have behaved in such a way in a million years.

'Roland, you are grasping at straws. Do you think I would want to be anywhere near you if you had behaved like that?'

Roland came back to the door and took hold of her hands. 'Vic, we had a different kind of relationship. That's how we have ended up married so quickly and with sproglet on the way. Dana and Teddy… it was different with them. Dana is strictly Irish and Catholic. For the same reason that we don't wish to be judged for sproglet, we don't judge others' behaviour either, do we?'

Victoria blushed with shame. If people wanted to judge her and Roland, they didn't need to search hard to find good reason and they were mainly with her. A shotgun wedding, her bankrupt, alcoholic father who'd shot himself, and her crazy Aunt Minnie who still thought it was 1930 and life was all about dry Martinis at six and never-ending bridge parties.

'Gosh, is it a fact that pregnancy makes you short tempered and pious?' she said. 'Roland, I'm sorry. I promise that if the moment arises, I will see how Dana feels. You, my darling, are right: life is complicated and none more than mine has been. The party could be a good idea. I'll talk to Mrs Hunter and see if she is up for it. But I'm blooming freezing now, so go on, go and get to work.' She pushed her husband away and blew him a kiss. 'Mrs Hunter will be here in a minute and she is teaching me how to make a lemon and lime Victoria sponge with an elderflower butter cream filling and lime icing for my visitors. We might even save you a slice, if you're lucky.'

Roland grinned. 'You had better,' he said. 'It sounds delicious.'

She blew him another kiss and the car door slammed, the engine fired up and Roland sped off down the long gravel drive. As she closed the door, Victoria pressed her hands against the wooden frame and took a panting breath as her abdomen was seized by yet another sudden tightening. It had been harder than the earlier Braxton Hicks and had lasted for longer. 'Labour, I am not looking forward to you,' she said when it had passed and made her way back to the fire and the last cup of tea in the pot.

Chapter 7

It had long been Mrs Duffy's routine to catch the six twenty to the Lovely Lane nurses' home where she had worked as a housekeeper and replacement mother to sixteen nurses since before the war years. Of late, she had found getting up in the mornings a little harder than usual and, just a week ago, she had confided in her neighbours, Biddy and Elsie, as they waited at the bus stop. It was a conversation she regretted and she had altered her lifetime routine as a result which had left her feeling very much out of sorts.

'Honestly, some mornings it feels as if I have woken in a fog and it won't clear until I've had a second cup of tea,' she had said to Elsie. 'I'm finding it harder and harder to get out of bed. I'm all right once I get going, mind, it's just the getting up.' She had laughed, expecting her neighbours, Elsie and Biddy, to join her in making a similar complaint, but she was bitterly disappointed.

'Isn't it about time you retired?' Elsie had observed

103

over the top of her glasses and beneath the clear, thin plastic rain hat she wore to cover her curlers, which crackled as she moved. The once-white cotton ties beneath her chin, now stained orange with foundation and powder, flapped against her double chin as she spoke. 'You must be cracking on now and no one will thank you if you get taken out of that nurses' home in a box one day. Least of all Matron, the fuss it will cause.'

'Well, it will be a long time before that happens – and I doubt *you* will know about it, because you'll have been long gone yourself.'

This was quite a bold retort for Mrs Duffy, a widow who had made avoiding confrontation in a hospital full of working women, where arguments and spats often took place, her absolute business and, as a result, had managed to avoid a cross word during the entire time she had worked at St Angelus. Mrs Duffy unfastened and refastened the button on her coat in agitation, aware that her heart was beating a little faster.

Ida Botherthwaite broke the moment as she arrived in the bus stop carrying her string bag before her. 'Morning, Ida,' Biddy and Elsie said, but Mrs Duffy was silent, too cross to speak.

'Morning,' said Ida as she extracted a packet of Swan Vesta matches from her pocket and from inside the box, carefully extracted half a Woodbine with a pinched tip, having smoked the first half with her morning tea before she left the house and, striking a match, lit up the second half. Ignoring the three women, she fixed her gaze down the road, looking out for the bus.

Ida worked as the mortuary cleaner. During the war she had shopped Biddy to the Home Guard for not closing her blackout curtains properly. It was a transgression of trust that had never been forgiven nor forgotten and, as a result, Ida was not one of the inner circle of St Angelus staff. The three women, in one subtle movement, turned their backs to Ida. It wasn't just the wartime indiscretion, bad enough as it was. Ida was a complainer and never had a good word to say about anyone or anything. This was not a unique personality trait, but she was the only woman in the hospital who made churlish comments about Matron and no one liked that. When she worked days, Ida sat with the toilet cleaners, the lowest ranking amongst the domestics in a hospital where everyone had a place at morning coffee, and she resented the fact that, despite her husband's position – a man who could hire and fire and therefore hold the fortune of a family in the palm of his hand – she was relegated to the lowest-ranking table in the canteen.

Ida felt wronged and lacking in status. Bertie was not only the foreman of the largest local building company, he was working on the contract at the Lovely Lane nurses' home to build the new nurses' rooms and housekeeper's accommodation. Ida's position as the mortuary cleaner did not reflect well on him and she knew it. He had once told her one of the jokes about a mortuary cleaner that the lads had passed around the site and she had been filled with shame at their laughter.

'I think they meant you, queen,' Bertie had said, without a shred of sensitivity, and every day since then she had smarted at the thought that the men who worked for Bertie were using Ida and her job as a means to diminish his status as their boss.

Ida was very aware of status. She craved it for herself, resented it in others, even her own husband. Mrs Duffy turned to face Ida, wondered should she speak to her as a way of demonstrating her displeasure with Biddy and Elsie, and decided, even in these circumstances, against it. To stand alone was preferable to standing with Ida, but Ida had caught her eye.

'How's our Gracie working out?' she asked.

Mrs Duffy sniffed, this was no reprieve. 'I've no complaints, I'm sure, but I don't need her. Matron must have money to burn, if you ask me.'

Elsie interjected, 'Well, she's keen enough. I saw her running for the six fifty, so she's in before you, Mrs Duffy.'

'I don't know how you manage, looking after all those nurses,' said Biddy to Mrs Duffy. 'I know just how messy they are when they come to the school for their lessons. Lord above, they wouldn't even dream of putting their chairs back under the desks, or cleaning the tea room after them. It's a wonder the wards aren't filthy, messy places. Girls, honestly! Give me boys any day.'

Elsie was not about to let the conversation about

Mrs Duffy's age drop, despite Biddy's efforts to swerve it away onto safer ground. She sniffed and set her jaw in defiance. Ignoring Biddy and speaking directly to Mrs Duffy, she said, 'You need Gracie,' and turning to Ida, went on, 'And for your information, *I* recommended Gracie to Matron, and believe me, it wasn't missed that her own grandmother had failed to mention her, Matron being as desperate as she is for staff. Anyway, what a thing to say, that I certainly won't be long gone. You are very mistaken there. You're older than me, surely, Mrs Duffy. You are just a bit further down the road, that's all.'

Mrs Duffy turned with the speed of a bullet leaving a gun, 'Ex-cu-se-me,' she said, 'you certainly are down the road, every week, in curl up and dye. You keep that hairdresser going the amount of the black stuff they put on your hair. But, I'll tell you what, Elsie, you can't dye out the wrinkles, oh no, they are there for all to see.'

Biddy raised her eyes to the heavens and shook her head. The morning was already ruined and it was only seven nineteen.

'And as for getting on? Getting on? You speak for yourself. I heard you fell asleep on the job at Matron's party, both of you, when you were looking after little Louis. I can assure you, I have never done that, not when he's been in *my* care. Always alert, always on the look-out, I am, never so much as rest my eyes, I don't. I was shocked to my core when I heard that.'

She dug about in her holdall bag to retrieve her purse for the fare just as Ida threw the last shreds of her cigarette to the pavement and ground it out with the toe of her shoe. 'Oh no. You won't ever hear anyone tell you that *I* fell asleep on the job, certainly not when there was a child in my care.'

Elsie and Biddy had both worked in the hospital long enough to know that from the Porter's lodge, to the kitchens, the storerooms to the wards, across the hospital the impending retirement of Mrs Duffy was a keenly discussed topic. The ensuing vacancy was one that would be keenly fought over, not least by Elsie's own daughter, what with Jake being the under-porter and Elsie working as Matron's housekeeper. The new accommodation for the nurses' home housekeeper was being built along with the new nurses' rooms and everyone knew it. Jobs at the hospital were invariably filled by members of family of those who already worked at St Angelus and the new housekeeper's accommodation had been the topic of the canteen for months. Discussions ranged from the central heating that was being fitted, to the tiles on the kitchen floor instead of concrete. No one doubted that Mrs Duffy knew her job was being watched and desired and was holding onto it for dear life in the hope that she would move into the new, self-contained rooms. 'The only way she will leave that place, is in a box,' was a daily comment in the basement kitchens at St Angelus where the head cook herself coveted the job

Snow Angels

and the accommodation and, most especially, the central heating.

'Matron can not only run the best hospital in the country, she can apparently turn her hand to interior design too,' the cook had said.

Mrs Duffy rebutted their observations which always landed in the Lovely Lane kitchen with her own well-rehearsed response. 'I can't retire, there are too many people who need me. Who will look after those nurses if I retire?' Now she said to Biddy, 'Who will look after little Louis when you can't have him in Sister Emily's sitting room? He's a part of all our lives now, that poor little lad, and they need us. If it wasn't for us, she wouldn't be able to work.'

She pointedly turned her back to them both and leant out of the bus stop shelter, her brow furrowed, eyes narrowed, green paisley headscarf tied tight under her chin, brown wool coat buttoned fully to the throat, looking down the road to see if the bus was about to arrive. Her manner announced that the conversation was closed, better than words could have done, but Elsie had other ideas.

'I don't know why you keep your age such a secret. You must be nearing seventy, surely? I don't care who knows my age.'

Mrs Duffy flushed bright red. 'How dare you! I am nowhere near seventy. My hair went white as soon as I lost our Bill in the war, so I just look older than I am.'

Elsie was about to respond, 'Aye, but which war was that?' for they all knew Mrs Duffy had been a childless widow who had lost her husband in the first war and had been alone ever since and Mrs Duffy, who was aware of her own deceit, felt guilty and that just made the situation worse.

'My age is my business,' she said, 'and besides, whatever age I am, I'm a long time off retiring. There's no law against it. You can tell all those vultures over in the hospital what I said, too. My nurses wouldn't want anyone else looking after them. I know their families, I do. Don't you remember how I had to go all the way to Ireland to accompany Nurse Brogan back a few weeks ago? Do you think Matron would send me to do such an important job if she thought I was past it? You can tell them all that, I'm there for a long time yet. Matron, as you know, is very fussy.'

'Oh, I'll tell them,' said Elsie. 'They won't believe it, but I'll tell them anyway.' And then, as if as a reminder, she whispered so that Ida couldn't hear her, 'She's a good girl, Gracie. She will be a good help to you. Be nice to her.'

Mrs Duffy felt anger bubbling up inside. The unannounced arrival of Gracie to the nurses' home had been yet another insult to her pride. To Mrs Duffy's relief, the bus arrived and, for the first time ever, she walked past the row Elsie, Biddy and she usually occupied and no other regular passengers dared to sit on, down to the back of the bus, and sat alone.

★

Later on this grey and cold December morning, Mrs Duffy stood squinting through her glasses, studying the rota on the kitchen wall to see which nurses were on earlies and who she would be expecting in from nights. Not so long ago, she only needed to glance at the off-duty rota once a week on a Friday morning and she would remember it until the next one arrived through the door from Sister Horton's office. Of late, she had need to check the rota every morning.

A voice from the door to the hallway made her jump.

'I've lit the fire in the hall and in the breakfast room, Mrs Duffy,' said Gracie, 'and I've put the water on to boil and lit the grill. Shall I start the floors before the daily maids come in?' Two women came in at ten for two hours to wash and polish the wooden floors that ran through the entire large house and they helped with the nurses' rooms. Gracie, with dirty hands hanging down by her side, daren't move until she had been given permission to do so.

Gracie's mere presence was a reminder that Matron had thought she needed help. How could she prove she didn't, with Gracie marching about the place with a dirty duster hanging from her waistband? Mrs Duffy turned from the rota and looked down at Gracie's hands with disgust.

'Well, I can see you have lit the fire! For goodness' sake,

wash your hands in the scullery. You can't start making the beds like that.'

'I will, Mrs Duffy, but Sister Horton said I was to help you with the breakfast too.'

Mrs Duffy removed her glasses and took a step closer to Gracie, as if to study her more closely. 'Sister Horton? When did she tell you that?' Her voice had risen an octave and Gracie's dirty hands began to tremble.

'Er, when she called in yesterday afternoon to collect little Louis. You were giving the men their tea out the back. She said would I make sure that I helped you with everything, not just the rooms. She said I was to help with the meals too, when I'm not up cleaning outpatients.'

Mrs Duffy's jaw dropped open. 'Well, I never! It's unusual that she didn't say that to me and there was no mention.' She pushed her glasses further up her nose. 'Honestly, no one talks to me any—' She didn't have the time to finish her sentence as the front door opened and Dessie walked in carrying a wooden crate full of milk bottles.

Emily had been sorry not to stay longer when she had been collecting Louis the previous afternoon, but she had taken the time to talk to Gracie. 'How is it going?' she'd asked. Any better since Monday?'

'No,' said Gracie. 'She still hates me. She doesn't want me here.'

'Oh, Gracie, I'll be here tomorrow and I will talk to her, I promise you. She is grumpy with everyone at the moment. I know what the problem is: she thinks we are taking over, making decisions without consulting her and she's right. We are. Are you back up in the clinic tomorrow?'

Gracie had shaken her head. 'No, I've got to stay here and help. They are making cakes in the afternoon with Mrs Tanner to sell in outpatients. I've been told I'm to stay here to help. I'm just glad Mrs Tanner is coming. She's lovely.'

Emily had squeezed her arm. 'Everyone loves Mavis, and everyone loves Mrs Duffy too. Just keep going until tomorrow. I'm sorry, I would stay now, but I have to dash with this little one. Please tell her I'm sorry and I was sorry to leave him in outpatients with you and Nurse Tanner too. We all got on the wrong side of Sister Antrobus for that. It's just a good job Matron is on my side, otherwise I would have been out on my ear, long ago.'

Gracie, smiling, had helped her down the steps with the pram and as Emily almost broke into a run with the wheels bouncing, it occurred to Gracie that she had never seen Emily do anything other than run and rush; she appeared to be always running against the clock.

Now Dessie's voice boomed down the hallway. 'I just know the urn is going to be ready in about,' he turned and took the two steps down into the kitchen and placed the milk crate onto the scrubbed pine table and then looked at his watch, 'five minutes, just as soon as I have checked on those workmen.' He took his cap off and held it in his hands as Gracie, seizing the opportunity, sidled away into the scullery to wash her own hands.

'Dessie, are you checking up on me?' Mrs Duffy eyed him suspiciously. 'Only, Emily was here yesterday afternoon to collect Louis but I didn't see her, I thought she must have been in a rush, and yet she seemed to have found time to talk to Gracie. Is she avoiding me?' She felt hurt; she loved little Louis and felt cheated that Emily had not spoken to her first, especially as she spent a large part of her week looking after him. Her sitting room now contained a second-hand cot where Louis often took his afternoon nap. Dessie looked nonplussed.

'Well, she never told me anything,' he lied, 'but I do know they are coming today to see you, after she leaves the school, because she told me so when she was putting him in the pram.'

Mrs Duffy smiled, her anger forgotten. 'He's grown so fast. He will be too big for that pram soon.'

'You are kidding me?' said Dessie, his eyes wide. 'That Silver Cross is so big and cost that much, I've told Emily I'll be having a kip in there me'self soon. Right, I'm off to see those lazy-arsed workmen and make sure they get going. Those blokes wouldn't have survived on the docks and that's a fact. I don't know what regiment they were in, but the first thing they do in the morning is make a brew. They mustn't have a teapot at home, none of them. I'll tell you what, are you putting a bit of bacon on for those nurses?' Dessie rubbed his hands together and grinned, his eyes wide and expectant, entirely unaware of the irony in his words.

Mrs Duffy blushed. 'Get on with you,' she said. 'Do your work and I'll put a few extra rashers under the grill.' Her humour was restored, she was needed, wanted, appreciated – and that was all she asked for in life, in order to make her happy. Dessie and Emily, the nurses she looked after – *they* were her family. How could she retire? How could she walk away from everything that made her feel worthy and loved? She took Sunday off every week and couldn't get back quick enough on a Monday morning. Her job was her world, it was who she was.

Gracie appeared in the kitchen, hands scrubbed clean. The floorboards above began to creak and muted alarms rang and buzzed down through the wooden floors.

'Come on, Gracie, those nurses will be down here in fifteen minutes looking for their tea and breakfast. If you have to be here, make yourself useful. According to the off-duty rota, Nurse Brogan, Nurse Tanner and Nurse Beth are all off today, which is unusual. They must be out shopping or something. You watch, I'll end up having to take their tea up to them, that lot, honestly.'

Gracie lifted the large pot down from the shelf above the range. She had picked up the routine without any effort. 'They said they were yesterday,' she said, as she rinsed the oversized brown earthenware teapot out under the tap. 'Don't you remember? Nurse Tanner said they were getting the train to Bolton to go and see one of the nurses who got married and they asked, could they have their bacon sandwiches wrapped up in greaseproof paper to eat on the train. They said they would be down by eight.'

Mrs Duffy looked up at the kitchen clock – it was five to eight – and then at Gracie as though she had spoken in French just as they heard three pairs of shoes thundering down the stairs.

'Morning, Mrs Duffy,' said Pammy Tanner as she landed a kiss on her cheek. 'We're going to leg it to the station. Just in time for a quick cuppa first. The bathroom is full and the earlies will be down soon.'

Pammy looked to the table, expecting to see the sandwiches wrapped up and ready. Beth, who was often the first up and had covertly been helping Mrs Duffy in the mornings before she began her shift, took in straight away that Mrs Duffy had forgotten their sandwiches, winked at Pammy and Dana and went straight to the dresser to lift down the cups and saucers, catching sight of herself in the mirror on the way and tucking her thick red, shoulder-length hair behind her ears.

'I've got it, Gracie,' she said as the young girl held the tap on the urn and let the boiling water run into the pot as she spooned in six heaped spoons of loose tea from the metal canister next to the urn. Dana took hold of Mrs Duffy's hand and squeezed it before she turned and, lifting up the crate, carried it to the fridge and placed it on the floor. 'I've got the milk,' she said. 'Pass me the jug, Beth.'

Beth took the large blue and white striped jug down from the press and pushed it across the table. Dana lifted the large enamel plate out of the fridge and slid that down after it to Pammy who took the grill pan out from under the flames and had started taking the rashers off.

'How many for breakfast this morning?' she asked as she glanced towards the off-duty rota on the wall, too far away to see, and squinted her eyes. Breakfast was important. It was all the slips of probationer nurses had between them and the sixteen-stone men they had to bed bath as soon as they got onto the wards.

Gracie stirred the tea, banged the enamel lid into place, plonked the pot on the range and almost pushed Pammy out of the way. 'Go on, get yourself off. You'll be missing your train,' she said. 'I've got it covered here. I've been watching. I know what to do,' she whispered under her breath so that only Pammy could hear her.

'God bless your cotton socks, Gracie,' said Pammy as she allowed Gracie to take over. Dana had emptied the crate and was filling the jug with two pints of milk at once as Mrs Duffy looked on, almost as though in shock. 'Right, that's us done then, eh, Mrs Duffy.' She smiled at Gracie as she popped the milk bottles into the sink and whispered, 'Take no notice of her; give it two more weeks and she will love you.' Mrs Duffy was counting the milk bottles in the fridge. 'See you tonight when we get back. We'll be able to tell you all about how Victoria is doing, Mrs Duffy.'

Each girl planted a kiss on her cheek, ensuring there was no conversation about the fact that the kitchen was running late. As they reached the door, she shouted after them, 'Are you going to see Nurse Victoria?'

Pammy turned back at the door. They had spent the whole of breakfast the previous morning talking about how much they were looking forward to visiting Victoria. 'We are. Have you a message for her?' Pammy asked kindly.

'Wait, just a minute would you?' said Mrs Duffy as she walked to her bag at the back of the kitchen and removed a brown paper bag. 'I remember now,' she said as she handed it over. 'I'm just a bit distracted today, that's all. It's those workmen, the noise and all the commotion. It's enough to drive anyone mad.'

'Can I have a peep?' asked Pammy, who was already peeling back the corner of the bag.

'Of course you can. I crocheted a pram blanket for the baby. It's a lovely lace pattern I've done a few times over the years, for various neighbours and it's always well-received.'

Pammy pulled out the white blanket, edged in lemon and gasped. 'Oh, Mrs Duffy, it's lovely.' The gossamer-thin blanket slipped through her fingers, the intricate lace-worked single ply wool blanket a result of deep concentration and hard work that was plain to see.

'Do you think they will like it?' Mrs Duffy asked nervously and then beamed at the expression on Pammy's face.

'Not half, she will love it, she will. It's so gorgeous. I bet she takes that to the hospital, to bring the baby home in.' Pammy felt her heart constrict at the look of sheer pleasure on Mrs Duffy's face. Pammy planted a kiss on her cheek. 'She will be mad for it, I know she will and I'll tell you this, no one can match that in the way of a gift. You've always been Vic's favourite and you still will be,' she said as she folded the bag and slipped it into her own, glancing out of the door as Dana called from the gate in her soft, west coast Irish accent, 'Pammy, come on! We'll miss the train.'

'I'm coming. Don't forget, Mrs Duffy, Mam's coming at two to use the kitchen to bake the cakes for the WVS. Me da's gutted. He loved the leftovers at home, but our kitchen's too small now, she needs to make that many.'

'I'm looking forward to it,' said Mrs Duffy. 'I'll make sure she takes some back for your da and the boys.'

Pammy turned and looked back as she ran to catch up with the others; Mrs Duffy was smiling and waving, just like any other normal morning, only just lately, every now and then, the occasional morning wasn't as normal as most...

'What took you so long?' asked Beth and Pammy lifted

her bag up from her side. 'Mrs Duffy has given me a pressie for the baby and, honest to God, it's gorgeous. A lovely pram blanket. It was so warm on my hands and as light as a feather. There's nothing much wrong with her if she can do that. I don't know what we're all worrying about. I'm going to tell my Anthony, we need to get a move on, he'd better pop the question soon. This is making me broody.'

'Your Anthony never gets the time to think about anything other than saving lives since he took up the Senior House Officer's post on the receiving ward,' said Beth. 'Seems to me if you are going to marry a doctor, you won't be seeing much of him.'

Pammy looked thoughtful. 'Me mam says that. She said that Mrs Gaskell was at Matron's party and that hardly anyone, apart from Matron, even knew what she looked like. A chest doctor's widow, Madge said she was. Lost her husband long before her time, to Matron and the wards.'

They strode on past the park gates as Dana said, 'Did you see that woman just inside the gates as we walked past? She was there yesterday too – no! Don't turn around!' Dana sounded exasperated as both Pammy and Beth turned their heads to look.

'There's no one there now,' said Beth. 'Did she have a dog with her?'

'I didn't notice,' said Dana. 'But there are a few new dogs in and out of the gates since I got back from Ireland.

I used to know them all from my window. Amazing how much can change in such a short time.' Dana's window overlooked the park while Beth and Pammy faced the gates. 'She did have something in her hands, though, it could have been a lead, she just looked a bit odd.'

'Quick, over the bridge, I can see the train,' said Pammy as she broke into a run, all conversation about Mrs Duffy, women in the park, dogs and leads over.

The meeting with the works foreman, Bertie Botherthwaite, had been more difficult than Dessie had anticipated. 'Make the pathway from the main house three flags wide in that direction,' he'd said flicking the plan in his hands and turning it upside down. 'It faces south and the nurses on their off duty can sit out on some chairs on a nice day. And dig up this section here,' he paced out a section of land, about twelve feet long, 'and then get one of your men to replant Mrs Duffy's precious roses. If any of them don't grow back we all know what to buy her for Christmas. That was the wife's idea; she used to live here when she was a probationer nurse.'

Bertie looked confused. 'Really, what's the point of that? I mean, if you buy her a rose she will want to put it in her own garden at home, won't she? She can't be that far from retiring surely?'

Dessie was measuring out a line on the plans, using his pencil. 'Don't ask me,' he replied. 'I am at the beck and call of two women, Matron and my wife. I learnt a long time ago that the path to an easy life is just to do as they say, not to question why. I know nothing.'

Bertie, who was afflicted with nosiness possibly to a greater degree than his wife, was not going to allow Dessie to shrug off his questions quite that easily. 'Your wife, she's one of the bigwigs up at the hospital now, isn't she? My mother-in-law knew her mam.'

Dessie looked up from the plans. His wife, Emily, had lost her mother and her two small brothers in the war when their house had taken a direct hit as Emily had run to the shop for her sick mother. Mavis Tanner had been in the butcher's queue with her as they heard the sickening sound of the bomb falling. Emily's mam had been a patient of Dr Gaskell's and he would sometimes, when Emily least expected it, remind her of that and, unintentionally, bring her mother into her day. The flimsy bonds of belonging wrapped around the community and held them together, each one aware, knowing and understanding another's loss, pain and happiness too.

Dessie sighed as Bertie continued, 'Aren't you the ones who adopted that baby who was in the *Echo*, the one who had been left for dead in an empty garage last Christmas?'

Dessie felt his skin prickle. He and Emily had had no luck trying for their own child and had both fallen in love with baby Louis when he had been admitted to the hospital as a very thin, neglected and abandoned baby almost a year ago. The thought of him being transferred to Strawberry Fields children's home had broken everyone's heart in the hospital and the children's services department at Liverpool Corporation had been only too delighted to oblige by allowing a senior sister like Emily to foster Louis while they went through the adoption process.

'Aye, that's us.' Dessie and Emily had hated the fact that children's services had insisted the story of Louis be placed in the *Echo*. Mrs Casey, the head of children's services, had been insistent. 'We have to demonstrate that we have made every effort to locate his actual mother,' she had said. 'Honestly, you will thank us in the long run when we can prove beyond all reasonable doubt that we have done our best. It will work in your favour.'

Thanking Mrs Casey was not at the front of Dessie's mind right now. It was almost a year since he and Emily had brought little Louis home with them and there was one more round of interviews followed by an assessment until the papers could be signed and, just in time for Christmas, he could officially become their son and they could register his name as such. Dessie already had the forms ready to take to the town hall and hand over to the registrar the first moment possible. Bertie pulled out a cigarette from behind his ear and waiting patiently for his answer from Dessie, lit up. There was more Rizla than tobacco and glowing red flecks of paper and tobacco floated down onto the plans. Irritated, Dessie flicked them away with the side of his hand. The studied silence did not deter the foreman.

'They said you've had to wait while they try to trace the mother; that must be tough on you. I saw the little lad in the pram outside on the front steps yesterday when your missus called in? He doesn't look like he had been half-starved. Looked fine to me. Most of them types go straight to the children's home, don't they?'

Dessie lifted his head and forced a smile. 'Yes, he's bouncing fit now, thank you for noticing.' There was an edge to Dessie's voice which Bertie appeared not to have picked up on. 'Very soon he will be legally ours – and when he is, everyone can stop commenting on his development as though he is a museum piece.' Dessie wanted the conversation to end right there and then, but Bertie had other ideas.

'Oh, well, not sure that's quite right is it, matey?' Matey? Dessie's back stiffened as he slowly lifted his head from where he was trying, without success, to make sense of the plans Matron had shoved in his hand as she told him to oversee the building works at the Lovely Lane home. Bertie ploughed on. 'Not according to the paper anyway. You had to wait a full twelve months to give them time to find the mother. Is it nearly that now? I'm sure that's what I read that the judge had said. Hang on, I might have it wrong mind, yeah, you could be right. Doesn't time fly?'

Dessie took a deep breath. 'Do you remember everything you read in the papers?' he asked.

Bertie beamed from ear to ear. 'I do,' he said proudly. 'I read the *Daily Post* from front to back in my break at work and then I start on the *Echo* when I get home. Pride myself on never forgetting the detail, I do. You need an eye for detail to be a good builder, I always say.'

Dessie laid the plans on top of the bricks that were sitting on a wooden pallet in the middle of what had been the large garden, but was now effectively a building site. 'Do you know, Bertie, I am very sure Matron would rather you were getting on with building these new rooms for her new nurses coming over from Ireland and Mrs Duffy's accommodation than reading the paper. I mean, I am very sure that's not what she thinks she's paying you for.'

Bertie looked offended. 'Hang on, you're joking, aren't you? I'm allowed to do what the 'ell I want on me break.'

'Which break is that?' Dessie asked. 'Because I asked Matron could I have a look at your contract and in there it says one morning tea break at ten thirty for thirty minutes.'

Bertie adjusted his cap and furrowed his brow. 'Aye, that's right. That's when we have our break, at ten thirty, so it is.'

Just then one of the workmen called out from what had been the old wash house in the garden, 'Bertie, your brew is ready and the lad is back from the shop with your paper.'

Bertie had the good grace to blush and look embarrassed. It was still before nine.

'If you don't mind,' Dessie said in a voice loaded with the upper hand, 'we will just take a look at these plans first.'

'Aye, of course we will, boss,' said Bertie, red-faced and flustered as he ground his heel down on the last of his cigarette stub and, lowering his head, matched Dessie's interest in the sketches, all conversation about Louis thankfully forgotten. But the process until the day Louis became officially theirs was ingrained on Dessie's brain and was counted down, day by day. Only Dessie knew he would never truly breathe freely again until the fully signed-off adoption papers were in their hands. They loved Louis as if he was their own flesh and blood, more even, and surely if anyone was going to step forward to claim him, they would have done so by now. The prospect of police involvement, for having so badly neglected him, would have provided a deterrent.

'No mother who left her baby strapped in a pram, alone, starved, in a dark garage is ever going to show her face,' Dessie often said to Emily to comfort her when, in the small hours, she woke, checked on Louis and then had one of her panic attacks. 'If she ever turns up, she will end up in jail for abandoning him. He could have died. No one is going to let her take the little lad from us.'

'Is that true, though? I've heard so many stories,' Emily would say into his chest as he held her tight. 'Mothers who come back just days before the papers are due to be signed having changed their minds.' She would look up to Dessie's face and scan his eyes, looking to find the same fears and doubts that she harboured, always relieved to see none.

'Emily, those are the healthy babies, born in the mother and baby homes. Whoever gave birth to Louis, and I refuse to call her a mother, she is long gone and very soon he will officially be our little lad.' There would be a silence while they both thought on his words. A cock might crow from a yard down near the docks, a tug hoot on its way out to the bar to collect a ship and guide it in on the morning bore and a lone cow might be lowing in the dairy shed at the end of Admiral Street. 'I love it when he calls me da,' Dessie would say, pulling his wife closer into his chest. 'Makes my heart burst it does.'

He would look at Emily, already fast asleep in his arms, and there she would stay until they were woken by the noises they were still unused to, the noises that drowned out the tugs and the seagulls – the shouts and demands for attention coming from little Louis' room.

Chapter 8

Teddy leant on the hatch in outpatients chatting to the outpatients' clerk, Doreen.

'Do you prefer it over here to Accident and Emergency?' he asked.

'Oh, yeah, I do. A change is as good as a rest, isn't it?' Doreen smiled up at him. 'Tilly, who took my job, she's loving it over there. She's so ambitious. I reckon she will be running the place soon – next stop, Matron's office. How are you now? I've got to say, you look much better these past few weeks, it's like you are back to your old self.'

Teddy flicked open the front of a set of case notes. 'I am. I am back to my old self, Doreen.' He closed the cover and sighed. 'I don't know what happened to me. I mean, I know I had a car accident and lost the use of my leg, but I think I lost my mind too.'

'What did Mr Mabbutt say?' Doreen asked.

'Oh, you know what Mabbutt is like. You have to pick between the bloodies and then search around under the bad temper. He's a top surgeon, but it's a good job his patients, of whom I am regretfully one, are asleep when he operates and they can't hear him and the way he carries on. The new maid in the consultants' waiting room was so scared of him she apparently walked out yesterday.'

Doreen laughed. 'The rumour is flying around that she became so upset she burst into tears, flung her pinny in his face and ran out – but not before she threw his crab sandwich on the floor and stood on it. He was distraught, apparently; not that she had run out, but that the crab, which he had brought in himself in a tin from Lyons, was ruined. And Dr Gaskell was even more upset because everyone had to make their own tea.'

Mr Mabbutt's temper was legendary in St Angelus. 'It's a shame,' Teddy said. 'People really don't understand him. He's just a man who is a surgical perfectionist and he wages this constant fight against infection which he takes personally. I sometimes wonder if paranoia is creeping in. I caught him telling Matron that he wanted the theatre walls – and all the grouting in the tiles – washed down before every single operation and he wants the mops and buckets throwing out every time they are used. Matron looked at him as though he was mad. He shouts at his patients too, those who don't do as he says and I should know. Anyway, he was very sympathetic when it came to my actual physical injuries, but it was Oliver Gaskell who really helped me.'

'Really?' said Doreen, surprised. 'Dr Gaskell junior, the ladies' man?' Unlike his father, Oliver Gaskell was not taken terrible seriously.

'Yes, he put me on the straight and narrow. He said I had not adjusted and he thought I had suffered a kind of mini breakdown as a result. And you know, talking to him about it, well, it kind of transformed everything. I don't think we pay enough attention to how injury affects people's minds as well as their bodies. I know I hadn't and I was putting myself under such pressure to return back to work on the wards that I was in a panic. I kept having nightmares and reliving the accident. The thing with an accident, Doreen, is that everything is out of your control and it's so frustrating, so hard to adjust to; and I reckon the people who cope worst with accidents must be doctors and nurses. There is truth in the saying that we do make the worst patients.'

Doreen grinned. 'You don't say? Who would have ever guessed that!' Her irony was lost on him as he closed the case notes he had been studying with a flourish.

'This one is a DNA, it's half past now.' He flicked the buff-coloured case notes into the red plastic-coated wire tray on Doreen's desk.

'Oi, you,' she said as she picked up the folder, opened it onto the right page and wrote, DID NOT ATTEND, in capital letters on the page that had been allocated and slipped it into the notes for the appointment and then placed it back in the tray. She was so busy chatting she failed to notice the name on the front cover or that the notes belonged to baby Louis.

'I don't suppose you have seen Nurse Brogan around, have you?' Teddy's face was pleading, his manner desperate.

Doreen gave him an apologetic half-smile. 'I haven't,' she said. 'But Sister Horton is starting the rehearsal with the nuns for the ward singing. Matron wants the carol singers to go round the wards between the seven to eight visiting each night for the full seven-night countdown before Christmas and I know Pammy Tanner and some of the others are going so Nurse Brogan might well come along too. She has a lovely singing voice so I don't think she will be allowed to skive off because you know what Sister Horton is like; she loves her carols and the nuns, they make the hairs on my arms stand up and put tears in my eyes, they sing so beautifully.'

Teddy looked hopeful. 'Shall I join them when are they rehearsing? I can croon a note or two.'

Doreen didn't look convinced. 'I don't think that will be a good idea, not after what you did. I don't think if you were Father Christmas himself Dana would ever forgive you, Teddy.' Her voice was gentle, her eyes kind. She felt sorry for him, but knew there was no point in letting him get his hopes up. 'If you are looking for a girlfriend, I think you had better look elsewhere because there is no way Dana will ever take you back. She had to come back to finish her training and I think she's very brave. You are so lucky Matron didn't tear the skin off you, treating one of her nurses like that.' Doreen, standing, began to tie her bundle of case notes together. 'You are done here, now,' she said. 'That was your last on this afternoon's list. You start on Dr Gaskell's chest ward tomorrow, don't you?'

'I do, and I start on his wife's cooking tonight. They've invited me for dinner – or rather, Oliver has.'

'That's nice,' said Doreen. 'I'm going home to me mam and da and, as it's a Wednesday, it'll be sausage, mash and onion gravy for us. I imagine if you are going to Dr Gaskell's you'll be having something fancier than that. They say his wife is lovely, if a little left behind.'

Teddy thrust his hands in his pockets. 'Left behind? What do you mean by that?'

Doreen took her red coat down from the peg, slipped her arms in and shuffled it up over her shoulders. 'Oh, you know, she's like a ghost. No one ever really sees her – and when they do, she never really speaks. Mrs Tanner has apparently got her making cakes down on Lovely Lane with Mrs Duffy. It's a Christmas miracle that she agreed, but you know Mavis, she can get anyone to do anything.'

Hope sprang into Teddy's eyes. 'Fabulous, I'm glad I'm going for supper tonight. She makes the best bread-and-butter pudding. I wonder… should I ask Pammy to help me with Dana? Do you think she takes after her mother?'

'Dr Davenport, do you ever give up?' Doreen pulled

the belt on the mac tight across her slim waist. 'Have you even been listening to a word I said? Move on. It is never going to happen.' And then, with a note of distraction, she said, 'I need a new winter coat. They say the temperatures are going to drop like a stone from tomorrow. I mean, I put this on for the rain, but it's not really warm enough...'

Teddy wasn't listening, his mind on another thought. 'Doreen, why haven't you got a fella, a lovely young woman like you?'

Everyone knew Doreen's story. Attacked and raped, she had been admitted into casualty, the department she had worked in and Teddy had been one of the admitting doctors who had looked after her. When he had been run over, she had spent the day and night looking after his brother, Roland, not leaving outpatients until she was no longer needed and they could cope. She had run as fast as her legs would carry her, around the back of the hospital to the path lab to fetch the blood that was needed to save Teddy's life. As a result, there was a familiarity a doctor wouldn't normally have with a clerk. If it hadn't been for Doreen, her quickness of mind and fast legs, he might not be here now. They had their own unique bonds of attachment and they knew it.

'You know my story,' she said. 'You were there, and thank God you were. No man wants soiled good, does he?' She raised her eyebrows and lifted the wooden hatch to walk out over to medical records.

'Doreen, don't be daft. It wasn't your fault and none of that stuff matters any more. No one cares.'

Doreen let the hatch fall for the last inch so as not to catch her fingers and then slid the bolt across before she turned to him. 'The priest does... and anyway, who is there? I'm twenty-five already. On the shelf, that's me. I'm not pretty like Pammy Tanner or your Nurse Brogan with her blue Irish eyes. I'm just plain old Doreen and I'm used to it now. Now shift – you're keeping me from my sausages and mash with onion gravy, and who needs a man when I've got that waiting at home for me? You've never tasted onion gravy until you've had our mam's. She puts a drop of the Golden Knight in it, her secret recipe. Now, I'm off to the school to see if Biddy Kennedy wants to walk down with me. A good friend to natter with and me mam's cooking is better than any man and that's a fact.'

Teddy roared with laughter. 'Well, if you put it like that, Doreen... I'm partial to a bit of onion gravy myself, so any chance of an invite? Tell you what, tell your mam I'll have a listen to her heart while I'm there. She loves the attention and it always beats a bit faster when I'm around.' He stood aside to let her past and Doreen laughed at his audacity.

'Teddy Davenport, do you have no shame? You'll do anything to get a home-cooked meal! I'll tell Mam, I'm bringing you home, next onion gravy night.'

Teddy grinned and watched Doreen as she pulled the

belt on her gabardine mac tight and walked towards the interconnecting door. She had let her hair grow down to her shoulders and it suited her generously plump cheeks and lips. Teddy thought she had a funny face, not pretty, but striking, not least because the blue of her eyes was flecked with distinctive large patches of dark brown and she had a cute button nose. He knew very well why she was calling to collect Biddy. Just like the night she had been attacked, it was winter, dark and wet. Ever since that night, she hated to walk home alone and always looked for someone to accompany her. As she disappeared through the door she almost bumped into Sister Horton heading towards her. They stopped and chatted and so before Sister Horton made her way over, Teddy disappeared. She was another woman in the hospital not speaking to him because of what he had done to Dana, and he couldn't face her ire today. His remorse ran so deep, sometimes, it threatened to overwhelm him. He could think only of Dana and the future he had thrown away. As he marched towards the doctors' sitting room to meet Oliver he spotted a young woman hovering by the main entrance. She was peering intently through the doors, watching Sister Horton. She was clutching a thin coat tightly to her chest. Being of a naturally helpful disposition, he stopped and spoke to her.

'You look lost, can I help?' The breeze was fierce and lifted his white coat by the hem as it billowed about him and he plunged his hands into the deep white pockets to hold it down, his stethoscope dangling precariously about his neck like a noose.

The young woman recoiled from him and stood back from the light which flooded out of the windows. She had folded her arms across her and appeared to avert her face from his gaze. She was dressed like any other woman from the dock streets and looked the same, poor and cold. She carried no bag, but he noticed that a small block of wood protruded from her pocket. She was too thin, as many of the local women were, the result of hard work and putting others first.

Teddy knew that many mothers on the dock streets would miss a meal in order to feed their children more. He watched them as they piled out of the gates of the processing houses and factories, faces gaunt, cheekbones sharp and jutting. Many war widows hurried home to cook a meal, only to go out again to a second job, cleaning. Those who had husbands were no better off as they watched the reward of their efforts handed over the bar at one of the many street corner public houses. Most mothers around the dock streets would allow their own clothes to fall from their backs before they would let their children go without a pair of shoes and have to miss school.

Observant doctor that he was, his skills developed under the close eye of Dr Gaskell, this woman caught his attention as he waited for her to answer. Something was wrong. She was far too thin.

'I, er, no, thank you. I wasn't sure if I had the right...' she said and then turned and made to run down the path towards the main entrance. He had noticed the accent and she was not from Liverpool. She fell, only it was more of a collapse than a fall. Teddy was by her side within seconds, helping her to her feet.

'Here, let me help, come inside. You look frozen. Did you trip?'

Once she was on her feet, she shook his arm away. 'No, I don't want to go inside. I'm looking for the main administration block.'

She brushed down the front of her legs and her coat. She was on the verge of becoming distressed and Teddy, having spent his fair share of time on casualty, had met this before. He pointed to the side of the main entrance.

'There's no sign but it's at the top of the steps that lead up from the main entrance, next to Matron's rooms. But, seriously, can I just check your blood pressure at the very least?'

'No thank you, I just caught my foot. I'm fine.' He strained to hear her words which were weak and carried away on the wind. Her headscarf covered all of her hair and was tied under her chin, the collar of her coat up against the breeze. 'I have to go.'

But before she turned away, she looked at him for a second too long. He got the impression that she might have been about to ask him something, but changed her mind at the last moment and turned on her heel and hobbled away. Odd. Very odd, thought Teddy, who plunged his hands back deep into the pockets of his white coat to protect them from the cold as thoughts of the hot currant, puff pastry slices that were served in the doctors' sitting room at five o'clock, just as the operating lists finished, filled his mind and quickened his step.

Eva stood at the foot of the steps and caught her breath. The pain had been bad. She could barely walk when it was at its worst, but at least it had gone now, before the interview with Matron.

She made her way up the stairs and joined the other women waiting to be interviewed. It was obvious Matron had expected more to turn up for the block interview for cleaners and Eva was soon aware that she had a stronger chance of being taken on as a result of being only one in three to attend.

'The job is only temporary. Three weeks, just to get us over the Christmas period,' Matron had said to all three of them and each woman nodded, desperate for money and hoping to make a good impression in order to be taken on permanently. 'Excellent. Please report back here at seven this evening with aprons and your pairs will meet you.' To Eva she said, 'You will be with Ida Botherthwaite, mortuary and school of nursing.' She moved on to the other applicants, but Eva wasn't listening. 'School of nursing', was all she heard. That was where she had seen the pram; that was where Emily Horton worked, where Eva wanted to be.

He had almost made it to the doctors' sitting room before he met her. They were both walking with their heads down against the wind, neither looking where they were heading.

'Oh, I'm sorry,' he said as he looked up, about to apologise further before it felt as though he had received a punch to his heart. Dana!

She didn't speak. She had her cape fastened tight across her, her hands holding the edges tight together from the inside. She pulled it tighter, as though to protect herself.

'Dana, I'm sorry!' Teddy blurted the words out.

She blinked, her blue eyes flashed, there was an almost imperceptible shake of her head as she said, 'Excuse me' and pushed past him. He watched her back as she went, her starched hat, threatening to fly away, aware that the only emotion he had been able to identify on the face of the person he loved more than life itself had been disgust.

Chapter 9

Biddy had tied a muslin cloth around the basin and then wrapped newspapers around the outside before she nestled the basin at the foot of the pram, under the covers. 'Don't want to burn your feet, do we little fella,' she said as she tucked the blankets around it. 'That's for your tea later, and your mam and da. Now, let's get your pram coat on, the one Mrs Duffy knitted for you.'

Emily burst in through the door. 'Oh, is he ready? I've got to run. The lady from children's services is coming to the house. There's all the final paperwork to fill in.'

Biddy pulled Louis' arm through and blew a raspberry at him and grinned as he fell about in peals of laughter. 'He's all ready for you and so is your dinner, in a basin in the pram. And the chocolate cake you asked Elsie to make is in a tin on the pram tray underneath, so don't go bouncing it off.'

Emily placed her arms around Biddy's shoulders. 'I don't know what I would do without you lot. Is it cook's scouse?'

'It is, and she had that much left over, I made sure we got it up here because I know it's Dessie's favourite.'

The door opened as Jake arrived. 'I'm here. I'm looking for a little footballer in a pram, ah, there he is.' Jake launched at the pram and bounced the handle as Louis roared with laughter and began kicking his legs.

'Oi, stop that, you'll tip the scouse up,' said Biddy.

'Come on, little fella, before I get into big trouble,' said Jake. 'Let's be on our way. Emily, Dessie said I was to tell you that there was no way you could be late tonight because you have to make a good impression.'

'Oh, get Dessie,' laughed Emily as she took her coat down from the peg. 'He's the daddy so he has to make a good impression too.'

'Is she coming to the house?' asked Biddy.

'Yes, she is. Tonight. I had to put her off today – there was no way I could make it with the exams.'

Biddy smiled at her. 'No one could be bringing up a baby better than you and Dessie are. I mean, look at him now, that child isn't short of admirers, as long as you don't count Sister Antrobus in there. I reckon, despite his bad start, that lad will be speaking soon and walking. Have you thought about a party for him, when it all goes through?'

'Yes, and we will even invite Sister Antrobus.' Emily frowned. 'Was she cross today?'

'She made a good show of being cross, but somewhere between outpatients and here that little lad had worked his magic. I only heard her chatting to him as she brought him up the stairs and by the time she got through that door, she didn't want to hand him over, I kid you not,' Biddy placed both hands on her hips as she leant slightly backwards to ease the pain in her lower back. 'Go on, on your way now, don't be late and make your Dessie nervous.'

Biddy watched as Emily grabbed the bannister and ran down the stairs after Jake and her son. Biddy took a deep breath; she was worried about her Emily. She felt closer to her than her own daughters and there was no doubt in her mind that she would play a part in the lives of Emily, Dessie and Louis until her dying day. But it seemed as though, for a very long time, Emily hadn't stopped to catch her breath. The social evenings she used to attend with the staff had ended abruptly and everyone understood why. She had a huge responsibility, taking on Louis, and she appeared anxious almost every day. As though she was waiting for something to go wrong.

As Biddy dashed out of the door, she was met by Elsie coming the other way. 'She reminds me of a duck on a pond, that one,' Elsie said, nodding her head towards Emily who was pushing the pram out of the back gates. She looks so serene on the surface, but is really paddling away like mad underneath.'

'She's waiting to fail,' said Biddy. 'It's not like she had any time to get used to him before he arrived and she's learnt everything she has from the likes of us and Mrs Duffy. I mean, let's face it, it's us bringing him up, or as good as. We've taught her everything she knows.'

Elsie shook her head. 'I hate to think of her worrying; the pair of them, they're smashing parents and they love that baby to bits, anyone can see that. No one could do any better, not his own mother, whoever she may be, if she'd had a mind to, rather than abandoning the poor boy. Are you going straight home?'

'No,' said Biddy, 'I'm calling in to see if Malcolm is all right. I haven't seen him for a week.'

'What are you like?' said Elsie. 'You take on everyone else's kids and problems, you do, and I'll tell you this: no one else would go out of their way to visit Mr Grumpy, not even if his mother was the Virgin Mary. Old before his time, that man is.'

'I can't help it,' said Biddy as she took her transparent plastic head covering out of her handbag, flicked it open and placed it over her headscarf. 'When you make a promise to a dying woman as I did, you have to keep it and that's all there is to it. Besides, he's not that bad. One day some woman will open her eyes and see what a good catch he is.'

'Pity we're not twenty years younger, eh Biddy,' Elsie laughed.

Malcolm looked delighted to see Biddy when he opened the door and surprised to see Doreen with her.

'I've brought you your favourite,' she said as she fished

around in her holdall. 'There you go, raspberry and almond slice with a sprinkling of desiccated coconut on the top. Everyone is going mad for that on Mavis Tanner's WVS stall and I thought to myself, I know who I need to take some of that for. I mashed some up and fed it to baby Louis on a spoon today too. God, he loved it he did.'

Malcolm's eyes lit up as Biddy took the small tin out of her bag. 'Biddy, do you feed half the Dock Road?' he said.

'Aye, sometimes I think I do,' she said. 'Between me and the hospital kitchen, that's how half the families around here survive. Me and Doreen are on our way to the bingo, aren't we, Dor, but I thought I'd drop this off first and besides, we're a bit early.' They both stood silent as they heard Melly's high-pitched laugh coming from the Silly next door.

'I'll tell you what, it would be a lot easier if someone came and closed that place down, then all the drunken sods wouldn't be peeing their pay up the entry wall and I wouldn't need to feed half the Dock Road,' Biddy said.

Malcolm opened the door wide and stood back. 'Come on in, Biddy, Doreen; park yourselves in the sitting room. It's six o'clock so I'll light the fire and fetch us a drink and a plate for the cake.'

'Is it fish pie for your tea?' Biddy asked, her nose wrinkling in the air.

'Yes, how did you know?' said Malcolm, genuinely surprised.'

'Because it's Friday, soft lad, and your house smells of hake. Since when have you not had fish pie on a Friday?'

Malcolm laughed. 'Biddy, you know me so well. Sit down, Doreen.' Malcolm pulled out a chair for Doreen who took in the room. It was orderly and nothing gave Doreen more pleasure than order. It was homely, too, and Doreen thought what a lovely room it was and how she would happily miss the bingo to spend the night in the big leather armchair. Malcolm was holding the gas poker into the fire and as the firelighters burst into flames she tried to guess his age now. She had known him all of her older life, since he had returned from the war and guessed him to be in his late thirties.

'Right, I'll fetch us a bottle of stout each up from the cellar.'

'How old is he?' Doreen whispered as they heard Malcolm descend the cellar steps.

'In the head, sixty, in the body, not yet forty,' said Biddy. 'Too much responsibility too soon, it makes people old before their time.'

Doreen kept the rest of her thoughts, or rather, feelings to herself. She wasn't the only person on the shelf – a little further along sat Malcolm and she had only just noticed.

Biddy was having the same thoughts at the exact same moment. Why had she never had the notion to bring Doreen with her before? Then they heard the front door open. Biddy craned her neck to peer through the hatch and see which of the sailors it was – she had got to know many of the regulars over the years – and was shocked to see a woman close the door behind her and walk down the corridor. The woman wasn't aware of Biddy but bumped into Malcolm as he emerged from the breakfast room, carrying a tray on which perched three bottles of stout and two glasses.

'Oh, there you are,' he said. 'Did you see who it was you wanted to see up at the hospital.'

The woman nodded her head. 'I did, thank you.'

'And were they pleased you had gone to so much trouble?'

Biddy noticed that there was no answer and Malcolm sounded uncomfortable as he spoke again. 'Sorry, love, I didn't mean to pry. I told Melly to put extra in the fish pie for you and it's in the kitchen when you are ready, no extra charge.'

No extra charge? Biddy couldn't have been more curious – she was sure they were words Malcolm had never before spoken. She rose to her feet, slowly and peered further through the hatch.

'Are you sure I can't pay?' said the woman, her voice hesitating, making it clear she might refuse the meal if she had to pay.

Malcolm snorted. 'Heavens no. I mean, it's not like you're one of the sailors and can walk into the pub for your dinner and sit on your own, is it? And I know the hospital only has a canteen for the staff, not for visitors.

Where else could you get food from at teatime? A woman can't live on Jacob's Cream Crackers alone.' He saw her frown and felt like a fool. 'Sorry, Melly saw the packet in your room. She's put them in the kitchen cupboard for you. It's your kitchen too while you're staying here and we will do your tea for you. It's Saturday tomorrow, scouse night.'

The wind howled outside the door and the woman didn't speak but, Biddy noticed, that didn't deter Malcolm who carried on talking. 'Listen to that and they say there is going to be snow soon, so you need an extra layer on you to keep you warm, you're that thin, and the scouse will do that for you. My mam used to say, "When you're a bit under the weather, there's nothing like a pan of scouse to stick to your ribs."'

'Aye, she did that, I can hear her saying it now,' Biddy blurted out. 'Oh, I'm sorry, I didn't mean to but I couldn't help but overhear. Hello, love.' Biddy stepped into the hallway and grinned, her hands clasped before her over her ample belly, her headscarf still on, but received no warm smile in response as the woman, her eyes wide and looking as though she had seen a ghost, backed towards the stairs.

'This is Eva, Biddy. Eva, this is Biddy. We are just going to have us a bottle of stout, would you like to join us?'

Eva shook her head. 'No, no thank you. I'm going to go and have a wash and a lie-down, thank you.'

Malcolm looked mildly confused. 'Yes, you go and

rest; your pie is on top of the range keeping warm when you are ready. Always at seven o'clock on the dot, no extra charge.'

Biddy's eyes opened wide; he had said it twice, no extra charge. He had barely finished his sentence and the woman had disappeared up the stairs.

'Did you just hear that noise?' Biddy said as he stepped into the parlour and placed the tray on the table.

'What noise?' said Malcolm.

'That one, that whizzing sound.' Biddy held her hand in the air as if to silence Malcolm as she listened hard.

'I can't hear anything,' said Malcolm, as he found the bottle opener on his large bunch of keys.

'Can't you? I can. It's your mother, God rest her soul, spinning in her grave. She was my best friend when she was alive, Doreen, but she was as tight as a duck's arse. So who is that, then? Was she sent by the Pope? I can't think of any other reason why you've gone soft in the head,' asked Biddy as she sat back down in the chair.

'She's a lost soul, that's who she is,' said Malcolm. 'I can't make head nor tail of her.' He stood at the side of the table and poured his own stout while Biddy's settled.

'Well, what's her name then?'

'Now that I do know. Her name's Eva. Mind, it is about all I do know. A proper secretive one, she is. But that's all right by me. I like people who don't gossip.'

Biddy sipped the foam off the top of her drink. 'Hmm, I don't, they're no use to me,' she replied.

'Anyway,' Malcolm said, 'I have other things to worry about, Melly has given her notice in. She's taken the right hump to me taking in a female guest. Says she doesn't like the fact that she's being expected to cook for someone who is no better than she thinks she is.'

'I know what she means,' said Biddy.

'Well, I'm glad you do, Biddy, because I haven't a clue. I'm not worrying, though, I'm sure she will change her mind. So there's a bit of gossip for you.'

Biddy looked shocked. 'Malcolm, that's not gossip, it's your life. Different altogether. What I like is a proper bit of gossip. Now, if Melly had left you already without a word of warning and was off down to the docks, looking for a bit of business, that would be gossip – and don't go raising your eyebrows at me, you know she's done it before. It's how you got half of your customers here when you first started, or did you think it was just a coincidence that they were all such good friends of Melly's?'

Doreen blushed as Biddy threw her head back and laughed. 'Come on, Malcolm. There's nothing wrong with a bit of gossip. What is there to talk about if you don't have any? Now, where is that Eva's accent from – it's not from around here, is it?'

'I don't know and I'm not asking. All I know is that she's lost, Biddy, and I don't think she's well, if you ask me, which is why I'm feeding her up too. She says she's visiting someone at the hospital, but I think it's a doctor she's seeing because she's definitely not well.'

'Do you want me to do a bit of sniffing around?' said Biddy.

'No, don't do that. It's not my place to enquire – that *is* none of my business. Truth be known, I'm enjoying having her here. She ate with me last night and I'm thinking that whatever it is that is wrong with her, it can be helped with a good feed and a bit of looking after; and it's nice to have someone to talk to. I'm thinking that when she realises I'm here to help she will tell me all I need to know.'

Biddy knew only too well what he meant about enjoying company over a meal. The suppertimes and evenings and hours at home lasted twice as long for her as they did for those who had husbands and company, of that she was sure.

'Well, you be careful, Malcolm, that's all I'm saying.' But Malcolm was in his own world as he sipped on his stout, ignoring his favourite cake on the plate, a small smile lifting the corner of his lips. She studied his face as she picked up her own glass and thought to herself that it was the first time she had seen him this way since he came home from the war. Mr Grumpy had disappeared and she wasn't quite sure who had taken his place.

'Drink up, Doreen,' she said to her silent companion and was alarmed to see a look of acute disappointment settle on Doreen's face as she stared into the roaring fire.

Chapter 10

'Oh, get us,' said Pammy as the train pulled into the station and they passed a man in a peaked cap, standing on the platform with a piece of cardboard in his hand which had written on it in bold black letters, *Nurse Brogan and friends*. 'There's a welcoming committee. Or a man in a peaked cap, anyway.' She was standing at the window, with her head as far out as she could manage, clinging onto the window frame. Her dark hair was loose and fell over her shoulders, in contrast to Beth, who wore hers in a bun on the nape of her neck, exactly as she did when she was in uniform. 'Did you know Victoria was sending a car for us, Beth?'

Beth had placed her bag on the overhead rack above the seat and stretched up to pull it down. She couldn't reach and, slipping off her shoes, stood on the velvet-padded seat rather than ask one of the other girls for help. She grabbed at the rack with one hand as she aimed for the bag with the other. Beth was as proud and independent as she was organised and efficient.

'Oh, come here, shortie,' said Pammy as she reached up and lifted the bag down with ease.

'I did know she was sending a car, actually. And you would too, if you'd bothered to ask me, Pammy.'

'I knew too,' said Dana, grinning. Her red hair appeared to shine even more so on a dull morning such as this was. 'But that's all right, Pammy, don't you be worrying yourself now – it's what we are all here for, to make your life easier.'

'I always thought that was my job, Dana,' said Beth. 'Seriously, Pammy, one day you will write something down or make a list – and when you do, it will be as if you can see for the first time.'

Pammy shook her head. 'Honest to God, Beth. I don't have to make lists and things, because if I did, you would have nothing to do. Now, stop your moaning; and Dana, don't you dare start going all Beth on me. Isn't one of you list makers enough? Let's get off this train and into that car.'

Victoria was waiting at the window of her front room as the car pulled up and could barely contain her excitement as she ran to open the door almost before it had stopped.

'I've been that impatient, waiting,' she said as the girls clambered out. 'It's just too long since I last saw you! Come in and tell me all the news.' Victoria linked one arm through Dana's and the other through Beth's. 'I do love living here, it's so peaceful, and being married and huge with child, but gosh, I do miss all the laughs, and Mrs Duffy – how is she?'

Lunch passed in a babble of chatter, each finishing and interrupting the other's sentences until suddenly the pace and ferocity of the chatter calmed along with the cutting of the cake as their eyes, fixed as one onto the triple-layered elderflower-flavoured buttercream-filled Victoria sandwich cake.

Ten minutes later, sated, the silence was broken. 'I have never in my life heard of such a thing as an elderflower buttercream,' said Pammy as she licked the sweet-smelling butter from her fingers. 'It's gorgeous. Can I take the recipe for Mam? She's always looking for new ideas for the WVS. Mind you, it's all about the mince pies, just now, with Christmas just around the corner.'

'You can, if Mrs Hunter lets me have it,' said Victoria. 'She brings a recipe book in with her and then takes it home at the end of each day. She's so protective about her recipes. Those kind of women always make me laugh. It's like a power thing, they have to be the only ones with the secret knowledge, like it was invented by MI5. My mother, she would stop whatever she was doing and write a recipe down for anyone, so it's all alien to me. I have missed you lot,' she sighed. 'Though I have to be honest, I do not miss the seven a.m. bedpan round on men's medical.' They all groaned and screwed up their faces at the memory.

'Well, that's a revelation and a half,' said Beth with a wry grin.

'Do you miss us though?' Pammy leant forward with her elbows on the table, her hands cupping her chin.

'Do you miss nursing?' asked Dana.

'Oh, I do. I really do, all of you and nursing too,' said Victoria. 'I miss the patients, Dr Gaskell, Matron – just the smell of the place, even. I am adjusted, though. I thought the days would drag with me being here, Roland at work and me not working, but I have so much to do every day, they are just flying by. Add to that, the fact is that I just pass out fast asleep every afternoon for well over an hour.'

'How are you feeling for the rest of the day, then?' asked Beth. 'Have you had your bloods checked? You aren't anaemic, are you?'

'The doctor says not, but he didn't actually check my blood. He says he can tell by my eyes. I told him I thought that if you could tell by my eyes, it was pretty extreme, as in I would be very anaemic by that point. He didn't seem to agree. He's the kind of doctor who doesn't like to be told what's what by a woman.' They all groaned in unison.

'If you are having a girl, Vic, I hope that will have all changed by the time she is our age. Men can be so pompous and just downright... downright...'

'Wrong, is the word you are looking for,' said Victoria.

'Yes, that's right, *wrong* – and yet we believe every word that comes out of their mouths, don't we?' Dana held out her plate for the slice of cake Victoria was offering and the others held their breath. Dana had said very little since her return about her break-up with Teddy, even to Victoria, who would have become her sister-in-law and, as the house had been left to both the boys, might also have been the one hosting in the vast kitchen they were now sat in.

'Well, they aren't all wrong,' said Pammy tentatively. 'My Andrew is wonderful. He's never said or done anything I haven't agreed with. To be honest, he just does as he's told and he never argues.' Pammy had been dating Dr Anthony Mackintosh for over a year and was madly in love.

'Now, he may, but just like a worm, one day he will turn; all men do,' said Dana and there was a sharp edge in her voice.

'Well, my da hasn't and me mam says all men behave as long as you don't come between a man and his footie.' The three girls stared at Pammy, not knowing what to say. Her hands flew to her mouth. 'Oh God, I'm sorry, Dana. Your Teddy, he didn't even like footie, did he?'

Beth groaned. 'Will someone throw Pammy a shovel?'

To their immense relief, Dana laughed and buried her face in her hands. 'Pammy, if I hadn't come back to finish my training, I would have come just for you to make me laugh again.'

Pammy looked relieved. 'Seriously, Dana, none of us have wanted to say too much in case we set you off crying.'

Dana picked up her almost empty cup and sipped on

her tea. 'I'm done with the crying. Honestly, I'm over it. Oh, I'm not saying that your brother-in-law is my best friend, Victoria, and that I wouldn't slip arsenic in his tea if he was here, but my heart has stopped aching and I have stopped crying. I don't wake up consumed by anger any more and I have realised that the best thing for me now is not to wallow in the past, but to look forward to the future.'

Beth looked like she was about to cry. 'Dana Brogan, I am very proud of you. That is *exactly* what you should do.'

Victoria remembered Roland's words before he had left for work and felt her heart sink. There was no way she was ever going to be able to broker a reconciliation between Teddy and Dana. She would not insult her friend in that way and yet she felt sad. She thought of Christmas and christenings, birthdays and summer parties. Apart from Aunt Minnie, the girls before her were all the family she had. She decided to change the subject because she could see that Dana had had enough of talking about the past, but she was not going to ban Teddy from the discussion. He may have been the most stupid idiot ever to walk the earth, but he was her brother-in-law and she did love him.

'Anyway,' she said now, 'Teddy brought me some ferrous sulphate tablets and I've been taking those one a day. They do make me a bit sickly, though.'

'How far is it to the hospital?' asked Beth.

'Over half an hour – and that's another battle I'm having with the GP. He thinks I should be having the baby at home and Roland won't hear of it – he wants me to be wherever there's medical staff and equipment at hand. He's such a fusspot and Teddy, being the doctor in the family, has told Roland, no home birth for my sister-in-law.'

If Dana was at all bothered by the mention of Teddy's name, she wasn't giving anything away.

'What a pity you don't live nearer to Liverpool – the new maternity ward at St Angelus has opened and we could all have been there and helped,' said Beth, who looked excited at the mere prospect.

Victoria rose to fill the kettle again, but, 'Here, let me,' said Pammy and took it out of her hand. Victoria sat down gratefully in the chair.

'I'm afraid you would have to fight Aunt Minnie off. She is coming back to Bolton from London in time for Christmas and the birth – and on the subject of Christmas, listen: Matron's drinks party gave me an idea. I want to throw a Christmas party, but I need everyone to be free on the same night, so I was thinking, the Saturday before Christmas, what do you think? If it's not your off duty, you have time to request it.'

The girls looked up, excited. 'Gosh, I've never been to a proper Christmas party,' said Pammy as she refilled the pot and placed it back under the tea cosy on the table. 'I mean, we've had parties in the church rooms and Father

Christmas comes to the bingo hall for the dockers' kids at the bottom of our street, but nothing posh like this in a big house. And the house is lovely, Victoria. What will we wear? Oh, girls, I wonder if there's time for Mam to make us all something?'

Victoria watched Dana the whole time Pammy was talking. 'Dana, I know what you are thinking – and if you won't come because you know Teddy will be there, then I won't have the party.'

'What?' said Pammy in a voice loaded with acute disappointment. 'Dana's over all that now, she just said. Got his comeuppance, he did, didn't he, Dana?'

They all looked at Dana who smiled and they could see it was genuine. She was not upset. 'Victoria, you have your party, sure, don't be worrying about me. I'll work. We can't all be off, can we?'

It appeared as though Victoria hadn't heard as she said, 'You can all stay here and Roland will make sure everyone is back for the following day. Dana, I'm not listening because I refuse to allow you to let anyone stop you from enjoying yourself and you just said yourself, you are looking forward, not back. In fact, Beth and Pammy, you come with Teddy in his car, but Dana, can you get the two days off and be here the day before? I need someone to help me deal with Aunt Minnie or she will just take over.'

Victoria looked at Dana, challenging her to take the final step to freedom.

'Actually,' Dana said, 'Sister Horton said that we will all be off the weekend before and working all over Christmas, now that they have married nurses. They are allowed to have Christmas off because they have children and husbands. It's like single nurses are orphans and don't have family.'

'Doesn't seem very fair to me,' said Pammy.

'It means we can all come to the party though,' said Beth. 'There is an upside.'

Dana took a deep breath; she actually liked Victoria's Aunt Minnie and it did mean she wouldn't be the only single woman in the room and she was closer to Victoria than anyone else at St Angelus, but... 'Vic,' she said in a pleading voice.

'Vic nothing. Tell you what, come and help me the day before if you don't want to be here on the night and I will make sure we get a car to take you back to Lovely Lane. Dana, I'll be thirty-four weeks-ish by then, I *need* you.'

They all saw the moment Dana relented. Her shoulders dropped, her face relaxed and a smile crept to the corners of her mouth. 'Oh, all right then – as long as you let me go back to Lovely Lane if I want to.'

Victoria clapped her hands in glee. 'Fabulous, all settled. Oh, my gosh, let's start planning. I'll get a pad and pen.'

As Victoria waddled out of the room, Beth asked the others, 'Do you think she's taking too much on? She's huge.'

'That's why I said I would come,' said Dana. 'I'll do all the running around and make sure she sits down.'

'Phew,' said Beth. 'Now all we need to do is see if your mam can make our dresses in time, Pammy – and hide the arsenic in case Dana has a change of heart when she sets eyes on Teddy.'

Chapter 11

Ida Botherthwaite glanced at the clock on the mantel-piece before she leant over the fire and applied her pillar-box red lipstick in the mirror. Her wire curlers were lined up along the mantelpiece and errant orange hair escaped the wire prongs like springs from a broken mattress. This was one of only three occasions a week when Ida removed her curlers. Bingo on a Thursday, the pub on Friday night and for mass on Sunday morning. She slipped the top on the lipstick and it clicked shut with a satisfying snap. An orange line, resembling a minor country road on a map, ran all the way under her chin. A pronounced demarcation between the area of her body to which she had applied Coty foundation, in her preferred shade, Sienna, and that which had none. She sniffed at her reflection and buttoned up her coat, glancing at the clock again. It was four minutes past seven. Bertie was four minutes late and she had to leave at seven fifteen on the dot. That was her routine and there was nothing Ida hated more than a change in her routine. She heard the latch drop on the back gate, the gate click shut and her husband walked up the yard with the *Liverpool Echo* tucked under his arm. Order had been restored.

'You're late,' Ida said as he walked through the back door into the kitchen.

'Stop your moaning before you start,' he replied as he hung his cap on the back door. 'I had to collect my winnings from the bookies, didn't I?'

As if a magic fairy had waved her wand, Ida's mood changed. 'What, you won today? How much?'

Bertie grinned and took a brown envelope from his pocket and placed it on the table. 'I only went and won ten quid, didn't I.'

His wife snatched up the envelope deftly before he had the chance to blink. 'That's two weeks wages for me,' she said as she glared at him.

Bertie could have kicked himself for telling her and lunged to snatch it back. He was remarkably successful and, his manhood restored, he suddenly felt overcome with generosity. 'You can have ten shillings,' he said as he extracted a note from the envelope.

'And the rest, Bertie. You have a son with a bad back and he won't get to enjoy his Christmas if I don't get any money to him.' She stood, feet solid, arms folded, face set to ferocious.

Bertie looked from her to the envelope, then over her shoulder to his dinner keeping warm on a pan of boiling water. The house was filled with the smell of Ida's buttery pastry, baked to perfection and containing his shin of steak, slow-cooked all afternoon in onions and potatoes before it was popped into the pie crust.

'The envelope, Bertie. If it isn't in my hand by the time I count to ten, your dinner is going to land in the dog's bowl.' Bertie licked his lips and looked at the envelope, but Ida never made idle threats. He knew it was hopeless and he handed it over.

'Thank you very much, Bertie,' said Ida tartly, as though she were speaking to a badly behaving four-year-old, 'and here you go; you can have the ten shillings back for spends and, as a bonus, you can have your dinner too for that. Think yourself lucky you have a wife as generous as me.'

She took the money out of the envelope and threw it onto the fire. From the corner of her eye she watched Bertie as he went through his homecoming routine. He turned on the taps in the scullery and, as the water thundered into the enamel bowl, pulled down his braces and unbuttoned his shirt and undid the belt around his waist.

'Don't pee in the sink,' Ida shouted as she tucked the notes into her purse.

The smell of Wright's Coal Tar soap did battle with the beef and lost and the dog, who had risen from her old army blanket at the sound of her master returning home, sat hopefully by the oven door, looking up to the pan. Ida clicked the purse shut, placed it in the bottom of her bag, underneath her packet of egg sandwiches wrapped in greaseproof paper and pulled the zip all the way around. She knew the purse would be safer in her bag at work than it would be at home, with Bertie.

'Are you going to the bingo before work?' he shouted from the scullery. She had picked up a tea towel and was removing the plate from the pan and laying it on the kitchen table.

'Don't I always,' she said. 'God willing, we can make it a double win and have a good Christmas. With your winnings and my club money, we're doing all right this year, so far. How was work? Was the boss man, Dessie, on your back again?'

'Aye, he was. I don't know why it is Matron thinks she has to keep sending him down. I told her, we've got a job to do and we know what we're doing. I mean, I wouldn't tell him how to go about the head portering, would I? Imagine if I turned up at the theatre doors to wheel one of the patients back to the wards? He'd have my guts for garters. What makes him think he can do my job, eh?' The rest of his complaint was drowned out by the sound of his own head being placed under the tap and his hair washed as his stream of words became an incomprehensible splutter. Ida buttered a slice of bread and placed it by the side of his plate.

'Was our Gracie there?'

'Yes, and she's a hardworking girl our Gracie. She's the one you want to be giving the money to, her or her poor mother, not that fat lazy arse of an oaf who I am ashamed to call my son and who lies in his bed all day long.'

Ida slapped another slice of bread and butter on the plate. 'And was that baby there again?'

'What's that?' Bertie came out of the scullery, upper clothing removed, apart from his grey string vest, rubbing his still-dark hair with a towel.

'The baby, was he there? Did Sister Horton just dump him on Mrs Duffy again? They'll be making our Gracie look after him next, because that Mrs Duffy's too old in my book to be looking after a child so young. So, was he there?'

Bertie frowned. Ida asked him about the baby every day, as often as she asked him for details about the new accommodation that was being built for Mrs Duffy. Tonight was no exception and these conversations irritated Bertie beyond belief. He liked to read the obituaries while he ate his tea. Bertie was a man who listened to noise all day long, drills, hammers, saws. 'Is a bit of peace and quiet too much for a man to ask for?' he had once asked when he was trying to eat and read. It was the first and last time he ever complained because his paper ended up on the fire. He reluctantly lifted his head from his plate.

'He was, as always. And I'll tell you what, if that woman didn't have that baby being left with her every day, his Lordship wouldn't be coming down to check up on me every five minutes. It's not me he's checking up on. It's her. That's why he's in and out all the time. A nuisance it is. No one helped us with our kids – you had to give up work so why should they have their cake and eat it? All my working life I've been able to work to my own pace and now I'm looking over my shoulder all the while.'

'It's not right, that isn't,' said Ida as she fastened the ties on her rain hat. 'A baby who went through what he did needs to be looked after by one person, his own mother, preferably – and I did work during the war, at the munitions factory. It was my mam who looked after ours and that's how it should be, family or no one. If I'd just left our kids with any old person, we'd have been a lot better off, but I didn't, because it's not right.'

Bertie pulled out the wooden kitchen chair and scraped the legs across the tiled floor to reach the salt on the other side of the table. The sound made Ida's teeth grate. 'It was shocking too,' she said, 'seeing them out with the pram last Friday night when I walked home from the bingo. The night air is bad for a baby's chest. No child of that age should be out in the dark. He'd have been better tucked up in his cot and she should have stayed in and looked after him not out gallivanting late at night. You never saw me down the pub, when ours were little.'

'Thank God,' muttered Bertie under his breath as he poured the salt into the palm of his hand. In the early days of their marriage, the pub had become Bertie's second home out of a necessity to escape Ida and the kids – and that was one thing he had put his foot down about in the days when he still could, that the pub was his place of sanctuary, and the kitchen, Ida's. 'The adoption must be happening soon. I almost told Dessie Horton what you said as well, about them having the baby out at night, too.'

'Don't do that,' said Ida, her voice sharp as she stopped dead on her way towards the pantry. 'I don't want him guessing it was me.'

'You don't want him knowing what was you?' Bertie looked confused.

Ida sniffed, looked around the room as though she was checking to see if anyone was listening, glanced at the Virgin Mary on the wall, ignored the disapproving frown and reached a decision; she would tell him because the burden was killing her and confession hadn't worked one little bit; in fact, she strongly suspected that father was cross with her and not on her side. She had almost worn her rosaries out with the penance.

'Bertie Botherthwaite, don't you dare tell anyone what I am about to tell you, now.'

'What?' said Bertie intrigued. 'Since when have I ever repeated to anyone what you tell to me?'

She looked at him defiantly. 'I've written a letter of complaint.'

'A letter of complaint? About what and to who?'

'To the Liverpool children's services, that's who. That baby is being pulled from pillar to post, out in that pram at all hours and they went after the publicity, they wanted it all over the papers and on the telly, so now they have to live with everyone having an opinion, don't they.' Ida drained the dregs of cold tea from a cup she had left earlier. 'It was disgraceful,' she said as she banged the cup on the saucer. 'It should all have been kept confidential, out of the way of nosey beggars.' Bertie nodded his head in agreement. 'Tonight, Biddy almost ran over me, she did, running along the road with the pram, taking him back home. She said he had been in the school with her at the hospital and now she was taking him home for his tea because Emily had new nurses on the wards she was checking up on. I bet that lad doesn't know where he lives half of the time.

'Well, life might be a lot easier for us soon. She isn't fit to look after that baby – and if he isn't at the nurses' home, I reckon they won't want Mrs Duffy there any more; it'll be time for a new pair of hands and I have as much chance as anyone of getting that job. So, you make a good job of that housekeeper's accommodation, because it could be us living there. But no one must know it was me who sent that letter. I didn't sign it, of course.

'Right, I'm off to work. I have a new cleaner working with me while Noleen is off; Eva her name is, a right odd one. Imagine, I know nothing about her other than she talks funny and, what's more, she knows nothing about me, because she's never asked, not a single question – not where I live, if I have a family, a fridge, a twin tub, nothing. That's not normal, that isn't. Very secretive she is, hiding something. Make sure you wash up and put everything away spick and span before you go down to the pub or you'll feel the frying pan on the back of your head in the morning and I won't bother to wake you up first.' Ida's good humour had disappeared as quickly as it had arrived.

The back door slammed shut. 'And that is normal, is it?' asked Bertie, but no one heard him, other than the dog, who licked his fingers as he dropped them by his side for her to lick clean so that he could open the *Echo* without staining it.

As Ida reached the back gates of the hospital, dusk had fallen, but she could still make out the wisp of a figure ahead of her, half running, half walking.

''Ere, Eva, wait for me,' she shouted. Eva did not appear to have heard her and continued at her brisk pace, so Ida shouted louder, 'Eva, stop.'

Ida spotted Emily Horton pushing the pram towards the back gates, the wheels bouncing on the cobbles, at the same time as Eva did. Emily didn't see either Eva or Ida, she was too busy peering in over the canopy, singing to Louis. Ida could make out his little white fingers, gripping on to the side of the pram. Eva had stopped dead and had as good as shrunk into the gate post. The gates, long since taken to contribute to the war effort, had never been replaced. Ida was almost out of breath by the time she had reached Eva.

'What the hell are you running like that for?' she asked as she caught up.

Eva wasn't listening, she was staring at Emily and the pram. Little Louis was wearing a hat, knitted by Biddy, which he was trying to remove with one hand as he gripped the side of the pram with the other. Emily, secure in their own world, was laughing.

'Oi, you little monkey, leave it on. You'll catch an ear infection if you let the cold get into your ears.'

Emily's protests were neither understood nor heeded as the hat landed on the cobbles beside the pram and Emily, too late to stop the wheels, was already a yard ahead by the time it hit the floor. Eva could not help herself; she lunged forward, crossed the path and, retrieving the hat, held it out to Emily to take, while her eyes never left baby Louis, who stopped smiling, and stared in the eyes of the strange woman who stood at the side of his pram.

'Oh, thank you so much,' said Emily. 'He's such a wriggler. Here, come on, little man, it's going back on – thank goodness it's not wet. Thank you, love.' Emily spoke to Eva without looking at her as she slipped the hat on and fastened the chinstrap over the side button. Then, bending down, she cupped Louis' face with one hand as she hugged him and placed a tender kiss on his cheek and briefly hugged him into her. All the while, Louis' eyes were locked onto Eva's, his expression sombre. He was no longer struggling to remove the itchy hat and Eva could not breathe, felt for sure that her heart was breaking in two. As the tears filled her eyes so that Louis became nothing more than a blur before her, she turned back to the gate. Ida slipped her hand through her handbag and shrugged it up onto her elbow and, in an unusual act of kindness, slipped her arm through Eva's as she approached her.

'Come on, love, I don't know what's up with you. You look like someone in a trance. I've no complaint with your work, mind. The mortuary floor has never been so clean as it was last night after you mopped it. Now, we've got fifteen minutes to spare before we collect the mops and buckets. Matron, as miserable as she is, leaves a table for those coming on nights. It's for all night staff, porters too, in case anyone didn't have time for their tea before they left for work. Let's me and you go and get a cuppa to put a bit of colour in your cheeks.' As Ida guided Eva away, Eva stared over her shoulder at the sight of Emily pushing the pram away and down the path. 'Oh, never mind that one,' Ida said. 'You won't get any more than a curt thank you from her. Right up her own arse, she is, and I wouldn't even mind, only it's not really her baby.'

Ida poured the tea and sat Eva down at the empty table. There were a few women in the hall, eating the left-over barm cakes with whatever had been put up for supper inside. Matron hated waste and she knew some of the women would have gone without food to feed their own brood and had insisted on something being made of everything that was left over. The offerings were always appreciated. 'Oh, lovely,' they heard one woman say from the counter, 'dripping, sprouts and stuffing with the bread tonight, girls. Better than what I gave our lot.' The sound of cackles filled the air along with the gentle hum from the bubbling urn.

'Get that down you,' said Ida. 'Do you want me to fetch you a barm?'

Eva shook her head. 'No, I have eaten already.'

'Put sugar in your tea then, you look peaky.' Eva stirred her tea and didn't object to the two sugars Ida heaped into it. 'Now, I thought you became very upset back there, when you picked the baby's hat up. You looked like you had seen a ghost. Lost a baby of your own, have you, love?'

Ida thought she was bang on the money as Eva almost spat out her tea. But recovering, she shook her head. 'No, no, not at all. I'm just not feeling very well,' she said.

Ida took out her tobacco tin; she knew Eva was lying and decided she would bide her time. 'Of course, love, never mind, I don't mean to pry,' she lied. 'We'll have our tea and this ciggie and then we'll crack on.' Ida watched Eva drink as she exhaled a plume of blue smoke over her. She was a patient woman who would bring all her skills into play. Eva would crack, soon enough.

Chapter 12

Dr Gaskell knocked on the door of Matron's office, then popped his head around the door. 'Are you free?' he asked.

'I am indeed,' she replied as she looked up and gave him a distracted smile. Her desk was placed in front of the window, Blackie, as always, asleep in his basket at her side and behind her, a curious seagull perched on the red sandstone windowsill, peering in, almost expectantly.

'Have you been feeding that seagull?' he asked as he closed the door behind him.

'No,' she answered, slipping a paper knife into an envelope she was holding. He could tell she was being less that truthful.

He marched over, took a biscuit from a plate that had been pushed to the end of her desk and moved closer to the window. The seagull began to patter excitedly from one end of the windowsill to the other and began tapping the glass. 'Really?' he mocked.

'Oh, here,' she said as, vexed for having been caught

out, she jumped up from the chair and lifted up the sash window. 'Don't tease her.' Dr Gaskell noticed the way Matron looked at the gull and saw that they had a moment of tenderness as the gull stood still and calm, knowing what was about to happen next. The wicker of Blackie's basket crackled and a growl emanated from somewhere within the woollen tartan blanket. Matron placed the biscuit deep into the ledge in front of the gull and the gull looked at her adoringly, before pattering towards her. She shuffled the biscuit along to a place she felt safer and then began to peck away at it as Matron made soft clucking sounds. Matron shut the window carefully so as not to frighten the gull away. Dr Gaskell walked over to the fire, poked it and stood with his hands behind his back as she sat back down at her desk.

'So, do tell me: I saw a message on the noticeboard, asking staff not to feed the gulls and let me think, who was it who had signed that letter?' He rubbed his chin as though deep in thought. 'Oh yes, it was you.'

She threw him a look of utter disdain. 'Yes, well, that one is injured. I couldn't just sit here and watch her starve to death, could I? She needs to build up strength to fly again. She loves porridge.' She picked up the paper knife and a letter.

'Oh, well, that's fine then. So you won't mind if I feed the stray cat that hangs around the consultants' sitting room?' She looked up, exasperated, and he grinned. 'You carry on with your correspondence.'

'Oh, would you look at that,' she exclaimed, as she pulled an embossed invitation out of an envelope, 'an invitation to a Christmas drinks party in Bolton.'

'Ah, yes, to the Davenports'?'

'It is, did you get one too?'

'We did. It's a rather long way to go, however, so we were thinking of booking accommodation nearby. Would you like to come in the car with Doris and I?'

Matron thought hard. She was unused to leaving her hospital. Hated doing it. She often remained, the sole person in charge, sailing the ship day and night.

'Let me think about it. It is very short notice, only ten days away.' She opened another letter and leant back in her chair. 'Oh, dear, this isn't good news at all.' She leant forward and, laying the letter flat on her desk, smoothed the sheet with her hands. 'It's a letter notifying me that the head of children's services has left and has been replaced by a Miss Devonshire – do you remember her? She was a busybody on the trust once.'

'Devonshire? I think I do. Was her fiancé a major? Fell in the war?'

'He was – she just acted like one. Anyway, if that wasn't bad enough news, not only has she taken over children's services, but she will be personally taking over the adoption process for little Louis because, apparently, they have received a complaint.'

'A complaint? Who from? And a complaint about what?'

'It says a complaint that Emily is working full-time and rearing the child using the assistance of casual non-family members.'

'Is there a problem with that?'

Matron looked up and peered at him over her glasses. 'Not as far as I am concerned. Emily had permission to continue working and adopt which is unusual, I know, but they did allow it. I specifically checked with Emily when she said she and Dessie wanted to adopt him and she told me that Mrs Casey had said it was absolutely fine; and as Emily herself said, how would we have won the war if women hadn't gone out to work? I'm afraid they are going to have a tough time with this Miss Devonshire. I'm not sure that if *she* had been the head of children's services when Louis was discharged, she would have allowed them to take him straight from the hospital to home. She was a right stickler, do you remember? She tried to block the building plans for the new maternity unit, said that in her experience, babies should be born at home.

'I smell trouble, I can tell you. It also says that Emily has him out in the pram, late at night. That's just not true. Well, apart from the night they were at my party. Oh my goodness, it must have been someone who was at the party who has written the complaint! Who on earth can that have been? I need to see Emily immediately.' Matron picked up the phone on her desk and dialled the switchboard. 'You had better go and find Elsie,' she whispered to Dr Gaskell, 'we are all going to need some tea,' and then, 'Ah, Madge, can you get me Sister Horton on the telephone, please, I need to speak to her urgently.'

Madge sounded very apologetic. 'I'm so sorry, Matron, I can't. She and Louis have already left, and Dessie too. Big night tonight – they are completing the paperwork for the adoption. Someone from the adoption services arranged to meet them at the house, so they left early. Nervous as a newborn kittens they both were.'

'Oh Madge, I was dreading that!' Matron sighed and made no other comment realising that she had probably said too much already and hastened her goodbye. 'Thank you, Madge.'

'I can call in there on my way home if you would like,' said Madge, her voice anxious.

'No, no, Madge, I will catch her in the morning, thank you,' she said and replaced the receiver, looking in dismay at Dr Gaskell. 'Emily and Dessie have already left, because they have a meeting with children's services – oh dear, they are going to be in for a bit of a shock when they discover someone has made a complaint.'

'Complaint?' Dr Gaskell snorted. 'I don't know a baby better raised than that child. Did they see what he was like the day he was admitted to hospital? Do they know he had been abandoned and left to die?'

Matron shook her head. 'I am sure that is all in the case notes and the former head, Mrs Casey, was very well aware and they have probably gone home thinking it is she who is coming to see them.'

Dr Gaskell shrugged. 'Well, as I said, no child's better reared so there won't be any problem at all. One look at him and Miss Devonshire will be singing their praises. This is a storm in a teacup, nothing for us to worry about.' She made to speak but he raised his hand and cut her off. 'No, really, you must not worry. Can you imagine Emily tolerating that?' He pointed to the letter. 'She will handle it perfectly well. She's worked in this hospital all of her working life. She knows how to speak to people from dockers to that Minister who came from the Government when you made the proposal for the new unit – and then there's Dessie, a man of great tact and diplomacy; he won't put a foot wrong. Dessie is so devoted to that baby, he makes me feel ashamed that I left all the raising of Oliver when he was a baby to my wife. All will be well. Personally, I am looking forward to seeing them both tomorrow and hearing how they dealt with the old battleaxe. Now, where is Elsie? I'm half dead with thirst.'

Emily ran all the way from St Angelus, taking shortcuts through the cobbled back alleys as fast as she could move while pushing the pram. 'Where are you two off to in such a hurry?' asked Mavis, stepping out of her back gate as Emily almost collided into her with the pram.

'Oh, Mavis, I'm sorry. We've got Mrs Casey coming from children's services to fill in the final paperwork for the adoption. We had exams at the school today and… well, you know what's it's like.'

Mavis peered over the top of the canopy at little Louis. 'Do you know what, none of us know how you've managed to do it, Emily. Hold down your job and bring that little fella up as well as you both have. I said to the others at break yesterday, thank God she has that sitting room and kitchen over at the school, and Biddy, she'd never be able to manage otherwise, but if anyone was going to do it, it would be you.'

Emily blushed under the rush of unexpected praise. 'I've had a lot of help, Mavis. Dessie is well-trained – and who'd have thought I'd ever say that? And, you know, I don't have to work weekends. I feel as though this little lad is being brought up by a big family, which is funny, really, considering I don't have any family at all.'

Mavis placed her hand on Emily's arm. 'You've got us, love.'

'And I don't know what I would do without you all, honestly. Biddy, Elsie, Mrs Duffy… you all love him as though he is one of your own. The biggest blessings in my life, you all are.'

Mavis smiled. 'I'll tell you what, queen, I've never known Matron so soft since he arrived. Did you know, the other day when she was taking Blackie for a walk around the park, she tied his lead to the handle of the pram and took Louis with her? I saw her going past the window and I'm not sure she's ever pushed a pram before. It's like she was trying it out, bouncing it up and down, she was, and she did smile.'

Emily laughed. 'I saw her myself. Elsie had taken him over to Matron's kitchen and apparently he joined in a meeting between her and Dr Gaskell and spent the time being bounced up and down on Dr Gaskell's knee.' Emily shook her head, smiling. 'Honest to God, I don't know how Dessie and I get away with it. And Matron was so excited about the Christmas tree for her flat this year – she's bought presents for Louis to go under it.'

She stretched out across the pram and pulled up the blanket that Louis had pushed down before sleep had claimed him through the rocking and bouncing of the pram over the cobbled road. No one knew his true birthday, he had never been registered before his admission to hospital – the abandoned child who had been so emaciated when he arrived on the children's ward it had been touch and go. Left in the garage of an empty house, he had barely ever cried, having learnt from a very young age that there was no point: no one ever came.

'She has a heart of butter, does Matron. She just doesn't like us to know, that's all,' said Mavis as she shuffled around in her bag, removed a packet of cigarettes and lit one. 'You want one for the journey home, love?' she said to Emily as she held out the packet.

'No, neither of us smoke around Louis.'

'Why not?' asked Mavis. 'The only thing it will harm is his pocket when he gets older if he takes a liking to it.'

'Oh, I'm not sure about that,' said Emily. 'Anyway, I need to polish the parlour before Mrs Casey gets there. Dessie is on his way now too, but I should just make it before him. Thank God Louis is sleeping.'

'I wouldn't worry about her, no one can judge you, Emily, not unless his name is St Peter.' Mavis took one last peer over the top of the canopy, blowing her smoke into the pram, as they parted. Emily waved her hands and tried, without Mavis being able to see, to waft the smoke away from the face of her peacefully sleeping child.

'Hello, I'm Miss Devonshire, no relation to the Duke, just in case you were wondering.' Her laugh cackled, forced and rehearsed for the frequent times she used her unfunny explanation to accompany her officious introduction. Emily and Dessie were speechless in front of the total stranger and ushered her into the house, past the sleeping Louis in his pram and invited her to take a seat in the front parlour of their terraced house. They looked at each other with amazement as they watched the stranger march down their hallway.

'Who is she?' mouthed Dessie to Emily as he closed the door.

'I've no idea,' Emily mouthed back.

Miss Devonshire had failed to remove her gloves as she shook their hands, her own so thin Dessie could feel the hard bones beneath. He had disliked her on sight. 'What Duke?' he mouthed to Emily now as the woman took in the layout of the parlour with one sweeping glance, ignoring them. Much older than either of them, her forbidding style of dress, pickled in pre-war aspic, made Emily feel flippant and very unmotherly in comparison. Miss Devonshire wore a mid-calf length tweed skirt, a frilled high blouse, a hand-knitted heather-coloured cardigan buttoned up to the neck and a cameo brooch securing her blouse peeped out over the top. Her hair was dark, worn in tight short pin curls tucked under a bottle-green felt hat with a feather pinned in the side.

'Is Mrs Casey poorly?' Emily asked, her voice tentative.

'Poorly? Not as far as I know. She has left and I have taken her post. I am the person you will be dealing with from now on. Yes, I thought it was you.' Miss Devonshire peered at Emily over her glasses. 'I used to sit on the board of trustees at St Angelus.'

Emily racked her brain and then she remembered her, a difficult, uncompromising and stubborn woman who had voted against her application to train as a nurse. A woman who was easily impressed by an applicant with an address in the right neighbourhood of Liverpool and quick to discriminate against those who came from around the dock streets.

'Here, let me take your coat – you'll feel the benefit

when you leave,' Emily said, trying to make her voice sound as helpful and cheerful as possible.

Miss Devonshire slipped the open, thick worsted wool from her arms. 'Thank you so much,' she said as her eyes took in the room. She missed nothing, from the dust on the brow of the plaster cast of the Virgin Mary to the teacup stain on the Formica coffee table. Emily noticed that the clothes and detritus associated with Louis, which she had shoved behind the sideboard, were peeping out, right in Miss Devonshire's line of vision.

Whilst Miss Devonshire appraised the parlour, Emily took a peep at the label on the inside of her coat – Andrée of London it read and Emily thought Miss Devonshire must be a wealthy woman. What would she make of their terraced house in the middle of a row with no garden and only a back yard? Emily wriggled slightly as she walked back in from the hall and pulled her skirt down, aware it was not as long as Miss Devonshire's and afraid of being thought a victim of fashion, rather than a devotee to her son. Miss Devonshire turned her attention disapprovingly towards Emily as she sat on the sofa opposite and clasped her knees together and turned her legs in one smooth manoeuvre, over to the right. Miss Devonshire acknowledged the attempt with a raise of her eyebrows as she bent to retrieve a folder and pen from her bag on the floor. She examined both Emily and Dessie over the top of her spectacles in the manner of unusual specimens under a microscope.

'Can I get you some tea, before we begin?' asked Dessie.

Miss Devonshire looked at Dessie as though he had grown two heads and then at Emily, the tilt of her head asked the question: isn't that your job? That alone had been enough to get Dessie's back up, before she had even refused the offer.

'No thank you,' she said stiffly.

Emily frowned; she knew the drill, having written the St Angelus manual for training nurses preparing to move from working at the hospital to the district herself. *'Refuse all offers of drinks from homes where general levels of hygiene are below standard and there is a perceived risk of contracting gastroenteritis or a potential risk of cross-contamination when entering the next home on your visit list.'*

She thinks our cups aren't clean enough, Dessie thought to himself, or that a man is incapable of making a brew. He made tea in the porter's hut for the men all day long. Especially the younger lads, who often reported for work in the morning without a brew or a crust in their bellies. Despite his usual even and placid personality, it was obvious to Emily that his blood had begun to simmer. It was a rare sight.

'Obviously, the child is well and sleeping,' she began.

'His name is Louis, thank you,' said Dessie, who sounded as though he was giving instructions to an underporter as well as stating a fact. The 'thank you' hung in the air, a command, waiting to be obeyed. Emily caught her breath when he spoke again. 'His name is Louis. I thought you would have known that, from the notes in your hand. The night sister on the ward when he was admitted, she named him. It's all part of his story and in his notes. We don't know what his real name was, or even if he had one... Mrs Casey knew the background.' Dessie felt challenged and uncomfortable. He sensed danger, but had no idea why.

It was apparent that Miss Devonshire was not terribly interested in the detail and frowned. She turned over a page in her notes, glanced down and said, 'Ah, yes, Louis. Now, under normal circumstances, he would have been transferred straight to the Salvation Army home in Strawberry Fields. But with your position at the hospital, as the head of the school of nursing at the time, before you stood down, and with yourself being a porter—'

'Head porter,' Dessie interrupted. And then, as if to make sure she understood, he said it again, 'I'm the head porter.' Then he fixed his incredulous gaze on his wife. Stood down? Before Emily stood down? Stood down from what? Miss Devonshire's words ran riot in his brain. But he had no time to comment as Miss Devonshire lifted her eyes to his.

'Er yes, indeed, *head* porter.' It was apparent that she had little regard for the variation of rank, once rank had fallen so low. She continued, 'It has been some months now and his mother has not been traced so it is time for us to complete the paperwork for the child. However, there are a number of problems and I'm afraid one is quite serious and does cast a question over your reliability and trustworthiness and, therefore, your suitability as a mother.' She had turned her gaze and her attention fully onto Emily.

'Louis, his name is Louis,' said Dessie, his voice tightly controlled. She had done it again; it was as if the identity of Louis didn't matter to her, he was just a commodity, a name in a cardboard file.

He's guessed something is wrong and I must know what it is and I haven't told him, thought Emily. She knew he had been about to tell Miss Devonshire that Emily had not stood down as sister tutor at the school of nursing, that she was very much still in post and in charge, but something had stopped him. Emily took in a sharp breath; she knew her Dessie and she had never once seen him lose his temper, but she could sense that in just the few moments since Miss Devonshire had walked into their house, she had upset him; and added to that, he was confused.

Miss Devonshire had the good grace to flush pink as she realised she had failed to remember Louis' name, only seconds after being reminded and half folded the notes over, her face set. She looked far from happy, not a woman who enjoyed having been found wanting and corrected. Oh, no, thought Emily. This is all wrong. We are going to lose him. She doesn't like us and she knows, I can tell, she knows. In a flash, a thought came into her mind.

'Dessie, I would love a cup of tea, would you make one for me, please? Miss Devonshire, are you sure that you won't join me? We don't have many opportunities to get out the best china since Louis arrived, do we, Dessie?' Miss Devonshire squared her shoulders as her back stiffened. 'And Matron's housekeeper, Elsie, she knew you were coming today, she lives down the road,' she added hurriedly, 'and called in just half an hour ago. I saw her yesterday down at the shops and told her you were coming.'

Dessie's head swivelled. *Down at the shops? Called in half an hour ago? No she didn't. You have seen her every day this week at work.*

'Elsie said that she had told Matron about your visit and that Matron asked her to make one of her best chocolate sponge cakes so that we had a lovely cake to offer you.'

Dessie stared at Emily, speechless. She was talking too much, too fast. Elsie hadn't called in, Emily had brought the sponge back herself from the hospital in a tin on the tray on the bottom of the pram. Why was his wife saying such things?

Emily shuffled to the edge of the sofa cushion and, with her hands in her lap said, 'So Matron's housekeeper has made a chocolate sponge with a chocolate buttercream filling covered in melted glazed chocolate – she melts the chocolate with cream and it is divine. It's her speciality, just for you. Dessie is desperate for a slice, aren't you, Dessie?' Emily gave Dessie a look with a flick of the eyes towards the kitchen. It was a look that told him exactly what he needed to do. 'Elsie's cakes are as light as a feather. You will never taste any lighter, unless of course, it's one of Mavis Tanner's.'

Dessie hadn't moved. His face set, his eyes never leaving Miss Devonshire. He was clearly displaying an expression that Emily knew would normally have been reserved for an audacious cockroach that had strayed under the skirting board into the parlour. She glared at Dessie to help her, but no help was forthcoming. Miss Devonshire, though, smiled, her expression softened, Emily took a second to wonder at the magic held in the mere mention of the word 'chocolate'. 'I just know that Elsie will ask me if you enjoyed it when I next see them, her, when I see her, her, Just her. She will be asked by Matron you see and without your accepting a cup of tea...' Emily trailed off, suddenly realising herself she was talking too much.

'Well of course, I would not want to disappoint Matron,' said Miss Devonshire. 'It sounds delicious. How generous of her. My mother was a patient of Dr Gaskell's during the war and was nursed by Matron herself. A small slice would be most agreeable.'

Emily smiled and her shoulders, which she hadn't

realised were as stiff as a board, began to relax. Matron
had won the day, but then, didn't she always? The clock
struck four on the mantelpiece as the plaster statue of
Our Lady appeared to shed a tear from her place on the
wall. Never before had Emily felt her presence in the
room as she did at that moment. It had been brought
back from a trip to Lourdes and, in the firelight, Emily
often thought she caught her smiling – but at that moment
Emily felt as though the Virgin Mother was weeping for
her and Dessie.

As she heard Louis shuffle restlessly in his pram, Emily
licked her dry lips. No, she told herself, they were making progress. They would find common ground over a
slice of heavenly cake and she would find the divine
inspiration she needed to get out of this hole. She placed
her hand on the wide leather arm to rise and make her
way to the kitchen, then the next question hit her like a
slap on the face.

'Tell me,' Miss Devonshire said, 'I am very curious and
I do have an official obligation to be satisfied with regard
to your answer. You see, I am not satisfied and I am
aware that you are not telling me the truth.' She pinned
Emily back onto the chair with just her look alone. 'Just
how is it you think you can continue to run the school
of nursing at St Angelus and rear a child who has had
such a dreadful start in life, given that the two roles
are entirely incompatible and the one of childrearing,
very much a full-time job? We do not allow working

women to foster or to adopt – and giving up work was a condition of your having Louis. Mrs Horton, you have lied to us on your forms, and you knew you were lying, didn't you?'

Dessie rose from his chair as fast as a bullet from a gun. 'I'll go and make the tea and fetch the cake,' he said.

Emily rose just as fast. 'Yes, I'll, er, I'll fetch the plates. She looked up at the Virgin Mary and, in her head, whispered, 'Please, help me...' as Miss Devonshire's voice droned on. Then Emily laughed. It sounded like glass breaking. 'Of course it is a perfectly reasonable question – and I haven't lied at all. I have been trying to leave, honestly I have, but you know Matron and how busy the hospital is. Anyway, I'll just make the tea, Miss Devonshire – these men, they like to think they can do everything as well as we can, don't they?' She let the door close tight behind her before Miss Devonshire could reply.

Once she was in the kitchen Dessie hissed in an urgent whisper, 'Emily, what the hell is going on? What does she mean, you've been lying? You have never given up work, you've never tried. Matron thinks they allowed you to work with Louis. Matron thinks it's because you worked at the hospital and had such good medical knowledge and contacts that we were allowed to take him with so little fuss. Please tell me what's going on. How do we get out of this?' Emily stood, stock-still, one arm folded across her chest, the other, across her mouth as though trying to stem a flow of words wanting to rush out. 'She's quite obviously never going to buy us taking him into work for Biddy to look after and using Mrs Duffy and Elsie when you are stuck. She's not the type to go for that in a month of Sundays.'

Emily looked crestfallen. 'I don't know, I haven't had time, I didn't think of that one... Oh, Dessie I meant to give up work. I know I said to them that I would, but we've managed, haven't we? And the time went so fast and it's all working so well. I know there's a bit of juggling but, he's thriving on it.'

Dessie looked into his wife's face. Her eyes were darting around the kitchen as though expecting to find the answer to her dilemma in the tea caddy or the bread crock. 'Emily, you are going to have to tell her and you are going to give up work or we are not going to be allowed to keep him. Did you think someone just like you was going to walk through that door? Someone with your imagination and energy and the work ethic of Matron? She has already questioned your character, as good as called you a liar.'

Emily's face fell; her colour drained away into her boots and her bottom lip wobbled. Dessie grabbed her by the elbows and looked into her face. 'Emily, do not doubt yourself. You are one of those few rare people who knows how to save lives, to raise a child, heal the sick, to get things done. You have been looking after people and solving problems all your life. That woman in there? She has a list of rules she has written down in a book – she is *nothing* compared to you. But unless we tick every one of her blessed rules, she will not let us keep Louis, not even if we had a testimonial from the Pope himself, never mind Matron. You are going to have to tell her you have given up work and you will have to do it.'

He let Emily go and wiped his brow with his hand as he broke out into a sweat. 'God in heaven, she might take him with her now! You've lied to Matron and she may sack you anyway – and me into the bargain. Emily, what have you done?'

Emily felt strangely strong in the face of Dessie's meltdown, her own entirely forgotten. One of them had to be strong at all times, there was too much at stake. She squared her shoulders and walked over to the kitchen cupboard and took down Elsie's large tin with a picture of a small boy with chestnut curls cuddling a golden labrador on the lid. She looked down at the smiling face of the boy and took a deep breath. It occurred to her suddenly that he looked just like Louis. We must get him a dog... the thought randomly flitted across her mind. She was used to dealing with a crisis, she would not let this one beat her. Chocolate would be her unbreakable sword of courage. She removed the lid from the tin and almost immediately, the kitchen filled with the intense aroma of dark and velvety cocoa. Emily smiled as her face transformed from panic to pleasure. It was like a drug.

She looked defiantly at her husband and said, 'I can't and I won't leave my job, Dessie. And I will not give up Louis either.'

'Jesus wept.' Dessie ran his hand through his hair and turned away from her to face the door. He had removed his cap to receive the visitor, an unusual event in itself as it only normally came off for bed. He felt exposed on a number of fronts. His heart tightened with fear as he realised how much little Louis already meant to him. He turned back to his wife. 'Emily, you are going to have to lie again because we are in trouble here. Why didn't you tell me and Matron that giving up work was a condition? Look at her, she is never going to let a working woman foster and adopt him. She will have him out of here and through the gates of Strawberry Fields in a flash.'

Emily bit her lip. 'Well, may God forgive me, because that is *never* going to happen. Not unless it's over my dead body. Trust me, Dessie, I can sort this.' She blessed herself, muttered a prayer and minutes later they both walked back into the parlour and laid two trays on the table, one laden with the teapot and cups, the other with the chocolate cake which Emily placed closer to Miss Devonshire. Emily noticed that Miss Devonshire couldn't help herself – she leant forward and inhaled the smell of the chocolate. There was a particular type of woman of a certain age, who had become acquainted with a limited supply of chocolate, only to have it taken away from them throughout the war years and rationing and Emily had noticed that they were all the same, hooked on the magic of the cocoa bean. Chocolate was the drug of peacetime and there were some who couldn't get enough of it, couldn't resist it, would have sold a baby to get their hands on it...

As Miss Devonshire inhaled, Emily noted the faint beginnings of a smile lift the corners of her mouth and her cheeks flushed slightly. Louis made urgent cooing noises in the pram – it was as if the aroma of cocoa had wafted over and slipped under the hood to alert him.

'Here, let me cut you a nice big slice,' said Emily as she crouched on her knees beside the table.

The tip of the bone-handled knife pierced through the glazed chocolate and, as she slowly depressed it, shards of chocolate slivers tumbled onto the plate, then the cake itself broke to the pressure as the knife slipped down through the layers of moist, dark-chocolate sponge and whipped, cocoa-loaded buttercream. Emily could have wept with gratitude as she placed the cake slice onto her best Old Country Roses Royal Albert china, placed a floral-handled cake fork on the side and handed it to Miss Devonshire. Elsie, I love you, she thought as Miss Devonshire's breath quickened, and a moistness appeared on her top lip.

However, she was obviously a woman used to denying herself and metering out the pleasures in life. She teased herself, licked her lips, and in a slow and definite act of denial, placed the plate on her lap, lifted up her folder and said, 'Now, let's at least answer a few of these questions before we try this wonderful cake. I am very sorry to have to tell you that we have received a letter of complaint informing us that you have been leaving the child with a variety of carers, that his upbringing is chaotic. That you have not given up work to care for the boy as agreed and you have even been seen out pushing the pram, late at night. Is this true?'

'Louis,' said Dessie, who was pouring the tea. 'His name is Louis. Who was this letter from?'

Emily glowered at Dessie whose tone was cold and controlled. She could see he was white with anger.

'I'm sure you are both aware that the case of this little boy is known all over Liverpool. It was in the news, on the television. Not that I approve of that, but there are people out there who have written in from time to time enquiring about his welfare, concerned members of the public. Of course, we don't give any details away in our replies, other than to say the boy is well cared for. It is obvious that someone has taken it upon themselves to ensure that all is above board, proper and correct.'

Emily couldn't help herself. She shot forward in her chair. 'How dare they! There is no child more loved or cared for in Liverpool than Louis. He has more people looking out for him than you can imagine.'

Miss Devonshire smiled. 'I am very sure. However, we do have to satisfy ourselves that the conditions of adoption are met and we do require a certain level of integrity and honesty from our potential parents – and I am afraid to say that we do have an issue here regarding your statement that you had given up work and the facts as they are today. Mrs Horton, you do not comply with our basic criteria.'

Emily lifted her teacup, sipped, took a breath, prayed to the statue of Mary bearing down on her from the wall above and let the steam provide a filter for her lie, a cover for her blushes. She swallowed hard. Her first visit in the morning would have to be to Matron's office to tell her what she had done. The baby she already thought of as her own would not be abandoned a second time. She had to tell Matron that she had lied to her and would have to give up work that very day. If this dragon insisted that she had to give up her career as Sister Tutor in order to comply with the rules, then so be it. She had reached a wall.

Emily was the one who had had her cake and eaten it. But it was a price she would have to pay and the person who would suffer as a result would be Louis. Not only did they need her money, but she was very sure Louis was the happy, bouncy well-adjusted baby boy he was because of all the external stimulation he enjoyed from the people who had supported her and Dessie in raising him. Emily placed her cup on the table as Miss Devonshire bit into the cake.

'Oh, this is just delicious,' she said. 'Matron's house-keeper you say? She knows her cake.'

Emily smiled and rose to meet the impatient call of the child she now thought of as their son. They were both so full of love for him, it exhaled on their breath and filled the room. It ran through their veins and rested deep in their heart as much as it would have for any child they had conceived and given birth to.

'I'll help,' said Dessie. 'You can meet the most important person in the house, now,' he joked, his voice brittle as he followed Emily but Miss Devonshire wasn't listening as she heaped another fork of chocolate cream into her mouth.

'What a waste of cake,' Emily hissed to him.

'And what a whopping lie you told,' he whispered back as she scooped Louis up into her arms, his gurgles of delight masking their voices. 'I can't believe you lied to Matron. You will have to confess, first thing in the morning. Emily, what were you thinking of?'

Emily lifted Louis who began to jump up and down in her arms and, throwing his arms out to Dessie, made excited squealing noises of sheer pleasure.

'You may just get away with this, but you will need Matron on your side and this affects all of us, our family,' mouthed Dessie as he grinned at Louis to distract him. 'Come on, little fella, does that nappy need changing? I can do it as well as make the tea, can't I? Your da is a man of many talents,' he said in a voice loaded with a false brightness.

Emily looked crestfallen, her shoulders slumped. She

had let them all down. When they had first brought Louis home, children's services had been delighted, almost no questions asked, but she did remember the final paragraph on the form and her final conversation with Mrs Casey, where she promised to give up work. She remembered the conversation with Matron, the day she lied and told Matron that Mrs Casey was happy for her to continue working. Her fingers had been crossed behind her back – but, right now, that gave her no comfort. The words on the forms she had signed, swam before her eyes, *all adoptive mothers are expected to devote themselves fully to the raising of the adopted child. No adoption can be approved in a home where a mother works either full- or part-time, not even for pin money.*

Emily remembered the words 'pin money'.

At the time they had brought him home, Matron had sorted it all, answered all the awkward question, attended the interviews with the police and children's services had been only too happy not to have to deal with such a high-profile case. This meeting was a very different to the ones only a year ago.

'Who wrote that letter of complaint, Dessie? His – his real mother?'

He could see her mind working and shook his head in despair. 'No! Not his real mother, Emily, because she's here, looking after him, charming the snake sitting in our parlour eating Elsie's chocolate cake who thinks we aren't good enough.'

Emily grabbed at his sleeve, a look of desperation in her eyes. 'But Dessie, who else could it be? Do you really believe that people have been writing and asking about him? Mrs Casey was always so nice and she never said that. I-I feel as though I'm being watched.'

Dessie transferred Louis to his side and wrapped the boy's legs around his waist. His hair had only just begun to grow. They had joked that he would be in his first cap before he could walk or visit a barber. Emily reached out and stroked back the thin and fine curling tufts of hair that were beginning to cover his scalp.

'He's my son,' she looked up to Dessie with tears in her eyes, 'and someone is trying to get him taken from us. It *must* be her.'

Dessie threw his free arm around his wife and almost violently pulled her into him. 'Emily, he's our son and no one is taking him anywhere.' He kissed the top of her head and hugged his wife hard again and then let her go. 'Come on, pull yourself together now, we have a job to do. We will both go and see Matron in the morning and ask her what we should do. The worst of this is the complaint. But he's ours and he's staying here with us.'

Emily extracted a handkerchief from inside her sleeve, blew her nose hard and, taking hold of her son's foot, blew a raspberry on his toes, made him giggle with delight.

'I'm fine, I've had my wobble,' she said and Dessie knew what she meant. His Emily was strong and able, but fell down her own emotional manholes every now and then and he had seen it happen so often, he knew just what to do. His job was to pull her back up. She smiled up at him and his heart stopped racing with fear.

'Thank God for that. Tell you what, when that one has gone and this is over, I'm off to the pub and I'll bring us back a pint and a gin and orange to have in with our tea.'

'Ssshhh,' said Emily with her finger on her lips and a smile she could not suppress – and grinning, Dessie called out in a falsely bright voice and with a wink to his Emily, 'Here we go. Here's our little Louis and he's dying to meet you!' He walked ahead of Emily into the parlour, saying, 'Right then, Louis, you come along and meet Mrs Duke.'

Bertie arrived at the pub ten minutes earlier than usual, buoyed up by the extra ten shillings in his pocket and the knowledge that Ida wouldn't be back until the morning. He was free. No wife to nag him and no Dessie on his back, just him and his pint and his paper. Sometimes life wasn't too bad at all. As soon as he opened the bar door, he was dismayed to see Rex, his own son, a lazy man who feigned illness and lived off his daughter's benevolence and his wife's understanding, sitting at the end of the bar in Bertie's usual. Bertie was ashamed of Rex. He was a man who begged pints from others, something Bertie had never done and he had never put his hand in his pocket for anyone else. Rex caught Bertie's eye before he had a chance to slip around to the other end of the bar.

'Dad, how's me mam? Off down the hospital on her night shift, is she? I told our Gracie today, get Matron to give you more hours, queen. We could do with a bit extra in the bread bin. I said, ask your nan, she'll sort it.'

The area around Rex was clear and, as a consequence, the remainder of the stools further down the bar were full. Another source of shame to Bertie – his son was shunned by local men. Bertie wasn't the only one who preferred to avoid him. Reluctantly, Bertie slipped onto the only vacant stool, placed his folded copy of the *Echo* on the bar and called out to the barman, but didn't ask for his drink by name. He didn't need to. The barman nodded his head in acknowledgement and Bertie knew his pint would appear by his side shortly.

'Doesn't our Gracie work enough hours?' said Bertie. 'She's still only a kid. I see her in the nurses' home every morning and Ida tells me she's up in the clinics in the afternoon.'

Rex sipped at his almost empty pint, his belly protruding out over the top of the belt of his trousers and barely contained by the fabric of his stretched shirt, the recently relocated buttons as close to the edge as they could now sit. Rex swallowed the last dregs in his pot and peered pointedly into the bottom as he placed it on the bar with an exaggerated thud.

'Aye, well, she could do a few in the evening as well.

She's only helping her mam with the tea for the kids and the dishes when she's at home and that doesn't bring anything in through the door, does it? She knows I can't work with my back, can I, Dad?'

Bertie swivelled the bar stool so that it slightly faced away from Rex and opened the *Echo* out onto the page with the football news. He removed his tobacco tin from his jacket pocket and extracted a roll-up he had made before he left the house, just for this purpose and then counted out the change for his pint and laid it on the counter in a neat pile of pennies with a silver sixpence on top.

'You haven't got a spare one in that tin have you, Dad?' asked Rex, his face a picture of hope as Bertie lit up. Bertie sighed, looked in his tin, extracted a Rizla, shredded some tobacco into the fold and handed it over.

'Here, roll it yourself.'

Rex's eyes lit up.

The pint arrived, the money was scooped up by the barman and Bertie took a much anticipated and very long pull. Rex lit the cigarette and failed to say thank you.

'Our Gracie said she saw you this morning, down at Lovely Lane. It's going on a long time that job, isn't it?'

Bertie would rather not have engaged in conversation, but it appeared that Rex had other ideas. 'She did that, she makes a lovely cup of tea, does our Gracie.'

Rex snorted. 'Someone wants to tell our Gracie, charity begins at home. I'd have to pay her to get her to make me a drink in our house; either that or beg, she has no heart that girl. All about her mam and the kids, she is. I may not as well exist.'

Bertie tugged on his cigarette and blew the smoke towards Rex. He wondered if Gracie ever wished that Rex didn't exist, because as shameful a thought as it was, he knew he did. He tried to think of something that Rex had ever done that was useful and nothing at all came to mind. He blamed Ida for spoiling him when he was a kid.

'Well, she makes tea for us in work and I suppose she is paid to make it. She can turn out a nice cake, too,' said Bertie as he smoothed the pages of the newspaper flat with the edge of his palm.

Rex looked hurt and Bertie felt guilty. 'She's never made a cake for me.' He was a man who was more stupid than he was unthinking and Bertie knew that and felt filled with shame. His evening was not going as he planned. 'Did you get to speak to her then?' asked Rex. 'Did she tell you about the woman she keeps seeing hanging around the nurses' home and the hospital? She thought she must be a mate of me mam's because she saw them walking together through the back gate of the hospital the other night.'

Bertie flicked the page over, he was only halfway down the obituaries, already disappointed that he hadn't yet come across anyone he knew. After the obituaries, he would move on to the football. Often keen to read even the first few lines as soon as the paper landed in his hands, he never succumbed to his own temptation. He saved the best until last. It was a mark of his strength of character that only Bertie knew about and appreciated. The best until last, when he was sat in the pub, his pint in one hand, his cigarette in the other and the football pages laid out before him. That was as close as Bertie could get to heaven on earth – and right now, his own son, the laziest man in the neighbourhood, was spoiling his moment. He glanced up, irritated.

'No, Gracie never said anything to me other than would I like her to fill up the sugar bowl in our hut.' Bertie looked back down at his paper. He hoped his tone had been sharp enough to deflect any further questioning, but Rex was having none of it. He had come to the pub to talk and a man of very few manners, he ploughed on.

'I thought it's nice that my mam had a friend now. It's not like she's Mrs Popular, is it?'

Bertie took a deep breath. He had read the same lines three times. He had been out of sorts since Ida had left the house, had felt as though there was a stone in his gut since she'd told him she had written the letter of complaint about the abandoned baby because it didn't feel right. He had seen Mrs Duffy with the baby boy when he was at work and she acted as kindly and with as much affection and pride as any grandmother would have. His Ida wasn't Mrs Popular and she wasn't Mrs Nice either – and he felt a strong sense that this time Ida had crossed the line in her interfering.

'No, Rex, you're right. Your mam isn't Mrs Popular, in the same way, you aren't Mr Hardworking and that poor wife of yours, God love her, she must be the most hard done to and unluckiest woman in the dock streets to have got herself married to a lazy git like you.'

Ida might be meddlesome and unpopular, but when it came down to it, she was his Ida and he would have to undo the harm she had done. Tomorrow, he was going to get her to write another letter to the children's services. He saw the baby every day and despite his grumbles, he was a well looked after little lad. He could not deny that and he could not stand by and see Mrs Duffy heartbroken either. He would tell Ida how unhappy he was with her letter and to try and undo any harm she had caused. He placed the lid back on his tobacco tin, picked up his pint and looked around the bar. The corner of the bench seat was free.

'There's a draught coming through that door. I'm off to sit by the fire,' he said and before Rex could say another word, he had moved. As he finally settled into his paper, he realised he couldn't concentrate and it wasn't just the letter Ida had written that was bothering him, or his son, grumbling in the corner and cadging a pint from an unsuspecting stranger who had just walked in. And then he remembered. He had seen a woman himself at the park gates, across the road to the nurses' home; she had been there every morning when he arrived. Bertie had noticed her because he was always the first to arrive and he had to wait for Mrs Duffy to open the side gate for him after he rang the bell to let her know he was there. Was that the woman Ida was friendly with? Ida wasn't really friendly with anyone. Even her daughters avoided visiting whenever they could.

Bertie moaned – all he wanted was a quiet life – and making complaints to the authorities didn't seem to him like a good way to go about achieving that. He sensed something bad might come about as a result of Ida's interfering. 'What's up with that woman?' he muttered to himself as, giving up, he neatly folded his newspaper.

'Another pint over there, Bertie?' called out the barman above the noise.

Bertie slipped his tobacco tin back into his pocket. 'Not tonight, I'm off back to our house,' he shouted back, and made his way back home along the edge of the Mersey and wondered why Ida had to make his life so complicated.

Eva sat in her room on her bed and turned the pages of the *Echo* the librarian had given her a spare copy of to take away. 'We keep ten of each one, just in case someone wants one, so go on, take it.' As she turned each page, it felt like a lead weight as she struggled to take in the words, while still able to breathe. Her son had been almost dead by the time he had been found. The police were involved, the case left open – and they were still searching for the mother. She read every last word again as she'd done every evening and when she had finished, she composed herself. No, there was no road to redemption. Only one way forward. She would have to summon every ounce of bravery she had but it would be no hardship. At the end of it, her son would be in her arms and he would, once more, be her own.

Chapter 13

Mavis Tanner, Doreen and Mrs Duffy were in the kitchen in Lovely Lane nurses' home, scrubbing down the large square pine table, ready to start the WVS baking that had had to be postponed because so many people were down with colds and flu.

'They were all on earlies today, so no one to help me to clean down after breakfast,' said Mrs Duffy, apologising regardless of the fact that none were necessary.

'Didn't our Pammy help?' asked Mavis.

'Your Pammy always helps, they all do. I've never had such good probationers to look after.'

Mavis rinsed her cloth out under the tap and looked delighted with Mrs Duffy's answer. 'What about Gracie? Where's she?' she asked over her shoulder.

'Gracie is turning out all the bedrooms. I've told her to get the beds out from the wall and give them a good brush and mop behind – that should keep her occupied and out of my hair until it's time to go up to the hospital and do her stint on outpatients.'

'Mrs Duffy!' Doreen looked cross. 'You mustn't be mean to Gracie, she's a hard little worker.'

Mrs Duffy looked sheepish, but was unrelenting. 'Doreen, I don't need her. I manage very well. Didn't I just say, I have the best nurses to look after, anywhere? This is their home while they are with me. They don't want strangers poking about in their things.' She was as aware as anyone of how ungracious she sounded and felt cross with herself. She had no explanation as to why she resented Gracie as much as she did.

Mavis changed the subject. 'I'm surprised our Pammy is a good help, to be honest, her head is so full of her and her Anthony. I swear to God, they'll end up married those two.'

Mrs Duffy beamed with pleasure. 'A wedding, and to a doctor too! Wouldn't that be wonderful, Doreen?'

Doreen was in the fridge, removing packs of butter. 'It would,' she said, 'only if I get to be bridesmaid, though. That's me, always the bridesmaid, never the bride.'

Mrs Duffy gave Doreen a second glance; something was wrong. 'Are you feeling all right, Doreen?' she asked her.

'Oh aye, I'm just fine,' said Doreen and she loaded her arms and closed the fridge door. 'Never mind me, what I want to know is why is Mrs Gaskell coming here today?'

'Oh, that's my fault,' said Mavis, 'I invited her.'

Mrs Duffy was in the larder, bending her knees as she

picked up the huge flour bin with two hands and walked with it, banging against her thighs, back into the kitchen which was a hive of activity. Doreen walked over to the Roberts' radio on the sideboard and began to fiddle with the dial.

'There's going to be a Christmas party and then a christening for Victoria and Roland's baby before we have a wedding,' said Mavis who was laying out enamel baking trays on the sideboard. 'I couldn't make these cakes in my house, even if I wanted to because I've got four dresses on the go and a tailor's dummy stood half-dressed in the larder for the party of the year. No wonder our Stan never comes home and spends all his night in the pub – there's nowhere safe for him to sit without getting a pin stuck in his backside.'

'Have you had your invite, Mrs Duffy?' asked Doreen.

'I have and I've decided I'll be going on the train with Emily and Dessie. Biddy is having Louis at her own house – he's staying there overnight and Elsie is going to help her. Dessie has booked us into a little pub, just down the lane from the Davenports' house and I'm so excited. It's a little holiday, and just before Christmas, too.'

Mavis frowned. 'Well, I hope it keeps fine for you. You know what the weather can be like over there – they're right by the moors and it can turn awful nasty in an instant.'

Music began to fill the air, crackling at first but then it rose to fill the kitchen.

'Doreen, how do I get that back onto the world news when you've gone?' said Mrs Duffy, frowning.

'Don't worry,' said Doreen grinning, 'I'll do it for you. Now, you never answered my question, why is Mrs Gaskell coming here today? I'm sure she's not your best friend, Mavis, so who asked you to invite her?'

Mavis was now back at the table and she could just about reach the centre of the table if she stretched long and hard and flicked her cloth with the end of her fingers. 'There, gotcha,' she said as she scattered errant bread crumbs towards her. 'Emily Horton did, almost put my arm up my back. She said it would be a good thing if we asked Dr Gaskell's wife to get more involved in things and I have no idea why. I mean, I've never even heard Emily mention the woman's name before, have you?'

Mrs Duffy looked slightly put out. She was close to Emily, was virtually Louis' surrogate grandmother and Emily ran most things past her. 'I have to say, I'm very surprised she didn't say anything to me. The first I heard was when Dessie mentioned it this morning.'

Mavis placed her hands on her hips and sighed. 'You don't mind, do you, Mrs Duffy? I suppose I should have asked first, I just assumed Emily would have.'

Mrs Duffy placed a pile of brass weights on the wooden table. 'Well, I'm not putting up with any lah-di-dah, just because she's a doctor's wife.'

'Nor me, said Mavis as she lifted down the heavy set of brass scales from the shelf. 'The amount we have got on between now and Christmas, there's no room for any more parties or big ideas. I told Emily, she needs to sit on Matron if she comes up with any of her fancy notions. The drinks party went straight to her head and I don't just mean the sherry. We have the carol concert. One member of staff with a voice like a nightingale and she thinks we can all sing like angels. I thought the mince pie and sherry evening in her flat for all the doctors and their wives was enough, oh but no, not Matron. She wants a cake sale at the WVS the week before Christmas now and sherry and mince pies giving out to everyone at the concert – and have you noticed, there is one theme running through all of this: bleeding cakes and baking – and who makes them all? Muggins here. And you, I couldn't manage without you lot of course.'

Mavis lifted her apron out of her wicker basket which stood on the draining board, gave it a flick and began to fasten the ties around her waist. 'Right, well, Mrs Gaskell, she's already late and I haven't got time to waste. Let's get cracking on the mini Christmas cakes for the WVS.'

Mrs Duffy was already peeling the greaseproof paper from the butter.

'That's a shame. I hope she still comes, I was looking forward to meeting her myself,' said Doreen.

Mavis lifted the bags of dried fruit from her own basket. 'Well, I was myself when I went to knock on her door,' said Mavis. 'I have to say, she's not one of us. Very timid, I would say. Like a frightened mouse she was when she answered the door – and you know, Madge thought it was very odd when I told her Emily had asked me to call on her. I got the feeling Madge knew something, but she wasn't letting on.'

'Madge, not letting on?' said Mrs Duffy. 'Are you kidding – she can't hold her own water that one; why Matron has her in charge of the switchboard, I'll never know.'

'I've though that many a time,' said Mavis. 'It's because she can put a voice on, not like us, eh. Where're the glacé cherries, Mrs Duffy? And will someone put that flamin' dog outside? He's just nearly had the butter.' Scamp was as familiar with the terminology 'flamin' dog' as he was his true name and in a streak of grey and flying hair, he left the kitchen in a flash with the butter paper hanging from his teeth. 'What am I going to grease the trays with now!' shouted Mavis, giving chase.

Doris Lillian May Gaskell stood on the steps of the nurses' home and stared at the brass knocker of the front door. The unfriendly looking and gleaming lion's head glared at her. Her heart was pounding in her chest like a trapped bird. She could hear the sound of music and laughter and a loud shout and no matter how hard she tried, her hand would not move from her side to lift the large knocker. She had found it impossible to refuse Mavis Tanner when she had knocked on her front door, but saying she would help in the safety of her own kitchen was one thing, being out here now, in this strange and unfamiliar setting, was another altogether. She turned as she heard the squeal of the brakes on the bus and thought of running down the steps and jumping on, but then, what would she say to him when she got home and he asked her why she hadn't gone, after saying she was? She felt beads of perspiration on the back of her neck, her hands wringing in front of her.

'Do it,' she said to herself, 'just do it.'

She stared again at the knocker and then at the bell pull – and although it was only inches away from her, it could have been miles. Her hands and arms felt like lead. She heard the laughter from inside rise and float out around her. It should have sounded welcoming; instead it felt intimidating and threatening. She had thought it would be only Mavis waiting for her, but there were definitely four or five voices inside. She almost jumped out of her skin as she heard the sound of metal banging and, looking to the side, she saw a young girl, emptying a metal pail of rubbish into a bin.

'Hello,' she said. 'Just turn the handle, the door isn't locked during the day.'

'Oh, I'm sorry,' said Mrs Gaskell, 'it's my first time here and I, er…' She looked around for a reason why she had been staring at the door knocker like a madwoman. 'I-I know the little boy, Louis, is here quite often and I didn't want to wake him.'

Gracie placed the pail and dustpan on the ground and walked towards her. 'Oh, well, his pram is always in that room there,' she pointed to the window on the right of the doorway, 'or because Mrs Duffy likes him to get lots of fresh air, since they began the building at the back, he's often on the top of the steps out here. To be honest with you, nothing ever wakes him up.' Gracie laughed at just the thought of Louis. 'He's a little terror,' she said as she reached the steps.

Neither of them turned at the sound of a small cough from behind the hedge, thinking it was just someone walking towards the park. Gracie looked at Mrs Gaskell and then at the door and, walking up the steps, opened the door for her.

'Here you go. I'll come in with you.' Gracie walked on ahead. 'Mrs Duffy, you have a visitor,' she called out.

Mrs Gaskell was rooted to the spot; her feet still wouldn't move and her heart beat like a runaway train. Her eyes filled with tears and she felt ridiculous, childish, trapped. Do it, move your feet a voice screamed in her head. She felt physically sick. God, was this who and what she had become? Where was the carefree, beautiful young woman who had walked down the aisle all those years ago? The young woman who had happily given up her job at the Blue Star Line offices down on the docks to raise her family.

'I'm going to become a lady of leisure,' she had laughed when she had handed her notice in. And that was what she had done. So much leisure, there were some days that felt as though they lasted for two and the hours that weighed so heavy she dragged herself through each one, never quite finishing the tasks she had set for herself, as she sat and waited for the time to pass. When had she become this pathetic specimen who didn't even have the confidence to go outside the house, unless it was to places she knew well, like the butcher's or the greengrocer's? What morning had it been when she no longer wanted to leap on the bus into town and go shopping, finding excuses to stay at home? She had persuaded herself so often that to go out of the house was an effort, to stay indoors a pleasure.

'Oh, I enjoy staying in. There's nothing wrong with that, it's just what I like. We are all different,' she had said so often to her husband as she packed him off out of the door to attend yet another social function, alone. 'Too much effort. I can't leave Oliver. And it's you everyone wants to speak to.'

Her excuses rang in her ears. She had no idea when or how she had changed. She only knew that she had slipped so far, that knocking on the door of the nurses' home had become an impossible thing for her to do.

'Oh, my gosh, you scared me,' she said as she almost physically jumped again as a scruffy grey dog came and sat at her side. 'Where did you come from?' she asked looking around. The grey hound, stared up at her and then he whined and looked pointedly towards the sidedoor to the garden, and then straight back at her. She laughed. 'Goodness me, you are telling me where to go,' she said. He gave a little bark and then placed his paw firmly on the top of her foot. 'Look at you, even you have more confidence than me,' she said and was overcome with an urge to bend down and throw her arms around his neck. 'Will you take me in?' she whispered. He bent his head and licked her hand. He was the scruffiest-looking dog she had ever seen in her life. Steel grey fur, flat on his back, in tufts around his neck and ears.

'His name's Scamp,' said a friendly voice she didn't recognise and before her stood a gentle-looking woman with soft white hair, drying her hands on her apron. The dog barked again, in obvious excitement. 'He gets excited,' said Mrs Duffy. 'He just ran off with the butter wrapper in his mouth out of the back door. Scamp, would you stop and go away, now? Hello, you're Mrs Gaskell, aren't you? I do apologise for that scruffy great lump meeting you at the door. Watch your coat, there'll be grease all over his face.'

From the gloom of the unlit hallway, Mavis appeared at her side. 'And she's not talking about Gracie, either.' Mrs Gaskell blinked, somewhat surprised, as Mavis began to giggle and elbowed Mrs Duffy in the ribs. She looked over her shoulder and then whispered conspiratorially, 'Only kidding, it's just Gracie's not Mrs Duffy's favourite, is she, Mrs Duffy?'

Mrs Duffy had no time to answer as Scamp, for no

known reason, began to bark at the hedge at the bottom of the steps and then leapt down the steps almost in one spring, still barking furiously. Mrs Gaskell heard a muted scream and, without waiting for further instructions, ran back down the steps and after Scamp. She called out his name and, miraculously, he stopped and ran back to her. Mrs Gaskell bent down and took hold of his collar before he thought of making a second run for it. She looked up and saw the back of a woman disappearing through the gates of the park.

'Well, at least you stopped, you are a naughty boy,' she said. 'Come along.' She half-walked and half-stooped back to the nurses' home to be met by Mrs Duffy at the bottom of the steps.

'Oh, thank you,' she said as she glared at Scamp. 'That dog living here is the divil's own work. We were so nervous about you coming and embarrassed that you would have a bad impression of us and look, Scamp did it all for me. What will you think?'

For the first time Doris Gaskell smiled. 'You were nervous of me? I was nervous about coming!' she blurted out.

Mrs Duffy looked surprised as she marched Scamp up the steps as Mavis reappeared with Doreen who had Scamp's lead in her hand. Gracie hovered behind.

'Too late for that,' said Mrs Duffy, 'Mrs Gaskell here got him. What or who was it he was after? I bet it was that cat from the funeral parlour.'

'I saw the back of a woman going into the park, but I'm not sure he was after her, I think he just scared her because she ran in through the gates.' She placed her hand on Scamp's head and stroked him. 'There, there, shhh, don't bark.'

Mrs Duffy bent down and clipped the lead to Scamp's collar. 'Scamp, where have you been. Honestly that dog, some days he goes missing for hours. It's a good job the parkie knows where he lives! It will have been Gracie's fault, leaving the side gate open. She opened it this morning. Honestly, she is a liability.' She stood and Mrs Gaskell felt a stab of envy at how sprightly she was. 'Welcome to the mad house,' said Mrs Duffy. 'I hope you don't go back home and tell your husband you got an awful welcome here. Let's get into the kitchen and close the door, before Scamp starts chasing cars down the road and taking chunks out of the tyres – and I don't know about you, but I'm desperate for a cup of tea.'

Mrs Gaskell, without a word spoken, fell into line behind Mrs Duffy and took a deep breath. This was not going to be as bad as she thought. The whistle of the kettle and the sound of Mavis beating eggs and sugar together guided them towards the kitchen.

'Oh, you made it! I wouldn't have blamed you if you had got back on the bus with all that commotion,' said Mavis. 'Come on in, we've been expecting you. Let Dr Gaskell's wife past, Doreen.'

There it was again. 'Dr Gaskell's wife.' That was how

everyone at Matron's drinks party had introduced her. She had a name and no one ever used it. Was that when she had lost the essence of who it was *she* was, when people stopped calling her Doris and used the moniker, the doctor's wife, instead?

'The kettle has just boiled and while you lot have been faffing about outside, I've got the first batch in. This is going to be just great, isn't it, Mrs Duffy? We'll have the WVS ready for Christmas in no time at this rate. I've never had so much help. Sit yourself down, Mrs Gaskell. You've been on the bus, so tea first for you before we put you to work.'

Doreen was at her side now and held out her hand. 'Pleased to meet you, I work in outpatients and I see your husband every day. I'm always telling him to go home, I am.' She smiled, and it was such a gentle smile it calmed Mrs Gaskell's rapidly beating heart.

'Oh, I think he's mentioned you, Doreen,' she said and she knew in an instant that Doreen could see the thin film of perspiration on her top lip, knew that her heart was racing madly.

Doreen winked. 'Here, let me take your coat,' she said and Mrs Gaskell allowed her coat to slip down her arms, watched as Doreen walked out of the kitchen and hung the coat in the hallway. Only she knew that in the pocket sat her little friend, waiting, in hiding, just in case... Mavis arrived at her side, holding a clean cup and saucer and slipped her arm though hers.

'Now I really want to know – are your mince pies as good as your husband says they are? He tells me your baking is amazing and your Oliver, he's always winding me up, he is. "I'll just test if it's as good as my mum's." he says when they call in after outpatients – and honest to God, you would think a plague of locusts had passed through on their way to the Holy Land, not just the St Angelus housemen, by the time they finish. Mind you, I shouldn't complain; our Pammy and her Anthony – he's a doctor at the hospital too – they eat me out of house and home every Sunday. That lad was that thin he was when he and our Pammy began dating; he didn't know what a good roast dinner was until he came to our house. At least you can see him now when he comes in through the door. You know, I think he's mates with your Oliver. He's a lovely lad, isn't he?'

Doris took a deep breath, she was going to be okay. She realised Mavis could talk for Liverpool and she wouldn't have to contribute much as a result. She had felt Doreen touch her soul with her smile and Mrs Duffy, she had no sides to her and her only obvious beef appeared to be an irritation with the young girl who had disappeared, Gracie. Other than baking cakes, and that was something she could do very well, without any effort at all, these ladies were not going to demand anything from her. As she sat in the chair, Madge leant over and poured her tea.

'Do you know any of the ladies who work up at the

hospital?' she asked, pointedly and Mrs Gaskell shook her head. 'Oh, that's a shame,' said Madge, and pulled out a chair opposite her, 'they are a good lot. Don't know where I would be without them, I live on my own, you see.'

Mrs Gaskell felt overcome with an urge to reply, 'So do I.' It wasn't true and would sound barking mad if she did, but that was how it sometimes felt.

'Anyway, Mrs Gaskell,' it was Mavis again, 'about your mince pies…'

'It's Doris,' she said and the room fell quiet until Doreen broke the silence.

'Doris. That's my mum's name, that's nice.'

Doreen sprang up to the sideboard and came back with a pen and paper. 'Right, ladies, let's make a list. We have promised to take mince pies to Victoria's party and we need them for the carol concert and outpatients too, so we had better start on numbers. Doris, thank God you are here because really, I don't think we could have managed without you.'

Doreen began to write out the list, Doris picked up her teacup and realised, for the first time in a long while, that she felt happy.

Emily Horton flicked the brake on the pram as she reached the bottom of the steps to the Lovely Lane home and peeped over the top of the canopy. Louis was fast asleep, his arms raised above his head, his face turned to the side, a half-smile on his lips as the corners twitched up at the sides. Her heart melted and she spent longer looking at him than she knew was normal.

'It's because he's such a surprise,' she had explained to Dessie who only that morning had asked her why she stared at their young son for so long. 'He just turned up in our lives and I didn't have the nine months before to get used to the idea. It's a miracle he's here. Sometimes, when I'm looking at him, I feel as though I've been holding my breath.'

Dessie had stroked his wife's hair and smiled down at her. He felt as though he had been holding his breath for every minute of every month he had been theirs, but he would never say so. Emily had been so blinded with happiness when they had first brought Louis home from the hospital that she had been oblivious to his many notes of caution, his words of warning, his desperate attempt to prevent his wife – and him – from falling too deeply in love with a child who was not their own and would not be until all the checks and paperwork had been completed. It had only occurred to Dessie in the past few weeks that the burning love they felt for Louis had been essential. How else would they have found the patience needed to bring him back to health? To nurture the flesh on his bones to fill out and pad him enough to stop them fearing they might accidentally break a bone when they changed him, to conjure a smile to appear on his face – and more than anything, to see the light that appeared in his eyes which in itself told them the worst was over. He was safe.

But while Dessie fell more and more in love with their son as each day passed, just recently he had kept one eye over his shoulder because he knew he had not imagined the woman he had seen at the top of their street outside the fish shop and then, from the bedroom window, outside their back gate, hovering in the entry, her manner furtive. His first thought had become a question he had asked himself over and over: is that Louis' mother? For there was not a man, woman or child he did not know on the dock streets. He had served with most of the men, attended the christenings of the children and mourned the fallen at mass each Sunday. But the woman in the entry was a stranger... He decided to say nothing to Emily – why worry her more than she was already?

Emily had no trouble in bouncing the pram up the steps and tugging at the bell pull. She had slept badly, her mind running riot. Miss Devonshire had agreed to speak to Matron before she made her decision, but for the first time ever the prospect of Matron's intervention did not fill Emily or Dessie with courage.

'She's just going through the motions, before she takes him off us,' Emily had cried in the early hours of the morning, and for the first time ever, Dessie, wrapped in his own thoughts of impending doom, was entirely unable to comfort her.

Mavis hadn't hesitated for even a second when Emily had asked for her help in finding ways to get Doris Gaskell out of the house and involved.

'Look, I can't say why, and this has to be strictly regarded in a professional capacity, but I need your help,' Dr William had said to Emily, and Emily had repeated almost the same words back to Mavis.

'Dr William needs our help, and it has to be strictly between us.'

Emily knew that Mavis had no bonds of patient confidentiality to tie her – and as Mrs Gaskell wasn't a St Angelus patient, neither did she. She was aware that there would be some discussion amongst the domestics and housekeepers, however, in St Angelus, but Dr Gaskell was as close to God as any living person could be and there would be no unkindness or animosity – everyone would want to help.

'What can I do, I just run the WVS? Our Pammy might be a nurse, but I'm no doctor,' Mavis had said.

'I know, Mavis, but we just need to get her out of the house, Dr William said. You know what Dr Gaskell is like, he's always so busy. Anyway, is there anything you can do?'

Mavis had been a wonder and hadn't hesitated. 'Are

you asking me could I do with an extra pair of hands to get this hospital ready for Christmas? You do know, don't you, that I'm running all kinds over here and have an army to feed?'

Emily had taken her hand. 'I know and I can't say why, because I don't know why, but all I do know is that we are needed to help someone and that's enough for me. We have to get her out of the house, give her a purpose, make her feel part of the St Angelus family. Can you help?'

'Well, Emily, she's not one of us, is she? I mean, she's a doctor's wife, isn't she?'

Emily understood; Mavis was unlikely to meet a doctor's wife down at the bingo. 'She is, but she's still a woman in need and she is a part of us, so is there any way you can think of getting her involved?'

'Are you serious? I've got no end of jobs I can give her to do. Eh, I'll tell you what, Dr Gaskell is always telling me she's a smashing baker. Why don't I ask her to help out with the baking? And I'm not kidding, Emily, I could do with it. It won't be us helping her, it'll be the other way around.'

Now Emily, inside the Lovely Lane kitchen, marvelled at the magic that was Mavis.

'Well, would you look at this, Louis,' said Emily as she sat on the armchair in the breakfast room. Her voice was timorous and trembling, but no one noticed. 'It's like a cake factory in here.' Louis was perched on her knee as she slipped his pram coat down his arms and Doris Gaskell was standing on the other side of the table measuring currants into a bowl. She stopped what she was doing for a moment to look over and smile at the baby she knew as much as anyone about. She remembered the newsreader on their small television reading out the details from his sheet of paper, and the headlines in the paper had screamed THE MYSTERIOUS ABANDONED BABY.

'He's well-loved,' she said to Emily who beamed at her.

'Thank you, he is. He really is.' And she pulled Louis into her and held him tight. Too tight, Doris had thought. It was as if she thought someone was going to snatch him from her arms. Mavis was placing a tray with the first batch of small individual Christmas cakes into the oven and Mrs Duffy was pouring Emily a cup of tea.

'What will I get for the baby, Emily? Have you a bottle in the pram?' Emily reached down to the bag she had unclipped from the base of the pram handles and dropped at her feet and retrieved a glass bottle of formula milk. At the sight of it, Louis pulled himself free and began to bounce up and down on her knee excitedly. 'Hang on, little fella,' Mrs Duffy said, 'just let me warm it up in a jug of hot water first. Oh, would you look at him! Remember when we used to give him his milk on a teaspoon? No one would believe it now, would they?'

Emily pulled Louis into her again and Doris saw the tears running down her cheeks. She hesitated, unsure, and looked to Mavis who was squinting at the knobs on the gas cooker.

'God in heaven, Mrs Duffy, I think I preferred the range. It's like Churchill's war rooms in here with all this equipment.'

Mrs Duffy was twirling the glass bottle of formula around in a pot jug. Doreen had gone to find Gracie, who they had all forgotten about, to tell her to come into the kitchen for a break, having first persuaded Mrs Duffy that it was the right thing to do, that taking a tray to Gracie was the wrong one. So Doris Gaskell placed the mixing bowl on the table, wiped her hands on a tea towel and, taking a hesitant look about her, walked over to Emily.

'Here, let me take him,' she said gently as she put out her arms and lifted Louis, who was more than willing to be picked up. 'Mavis, you are needed here,' she said, with a little more urgency in her voice. She lifted Louis up onto her shoulder, and because Emily was so obviously distressed, she pushed down the smile that had wanted to jump onto her lips. The smell of him, the feel of him, the love in him as, pressing his knees into her chest, he looked into her face and smiled. *This* was what used to make her happy. Caring for Oliver. That was the last time she had felt truly wanted or needed or even worthwhile.

'What's up, love?' Mavis looked sharply at her and following the direction of her eyes down to Emily, flew from the cooker to Emily's side.

Doris took Louis over to Mrs Duffy and bounced him on her hip as she watched Mrs Duffy tip the bottle and test the temperature on the inside of her wrist.

'Oh, he's there,' said Mrs Duffy as she looked up – and immediately knew something was wrong. 'What's up?' she asked.

Doris nodded to where Mavis stood with her arms wrapped around a sobbing Emily. 'Here, give me the bottle,' said Doris. 'You see to Emily and I'll look after him.'

Mrs Duffy didn't argue and rushed to Emily's side. Doris pulled out the old wooden rocking chair, adorned with two almost threadbare, feather-filled tapestry cushions from next to the cooker, and sat down with Louis. No encouragement was needed as, familiar with the chair, the rocking and the routine, Louis almost threw himself onto his back and put both hands up for the bottle. He reminded her so much of Oliver.

'Here you are, little man,' she said as she placed the teat in his mouth and his hands grasped both sides. He sucked hungrily, his eyes locked onto hers. She took one of his hands into hers and kissed his fingers, sighing as she did so. She didn't know how she had found herself here, in the warm kitchen of Lovely Lane, a beautiful baby in her arms. And on top of all that, she even had an evening to look forward to: Oliver was coming home and bringing Teddy with him. Oliver needed a wife and she would love nothing more than a grandchild, she thought as she tipped the bottle slightly to release more milk.

Doreen tiptoed up, pushing Madge before her. 'What's up?' she mouthed, glancing over her shoulder towards Mrs Duffy and the others.

'I don't know?' Doris whispered back. Both looked anxious at Emily Horton's obvious distress, but began almost immediately to coo over Louis.

Gracie had heard Mrs Duffy blaming her for leaving the side gate open and Scamp's escape and had slipped out of the back door to check it was locked. Bertie was talking to one of the carpenters who was making a window frame and walked over to her.

'Penny for your thoughts, queen,' he said to her back as she pulled the bolt across the green-painted door.

Gracie turned sharply around at the sound of his voice. 'Oh, Grandad, I'm just bolting the gate before I get into any more trouble,' she said.

Bertie took the rag hanging from his belt and wiped his hands on it. 'Did you get the blame for the dog escaping?'

Gracie smiled. 'Don't I always get the blame for everything around here? I came and opened the gate for Emily Horton, to bring the pram around the back, because she sometimes does and she told me last night she would be here early this morning. I thought I was being helpful. I forgot about the noise you made with the hammers,

Grandad.' She looked so forlorn, Bertie felt sorry for her. 'And, anyway, if that woman hadn't been hanging around the hedge again, he probably wouldn't have run out. Do you want me to fetch you a mug of tea?'

'What woman?' Bertie asked.

Gracie flicked her ponytail back over her shoulder. 'The woman who was waiting on the other side of the door by the hedge. I thought she must have been waiting for one of your men because I've seen her here a few times and I think she must work up at the hospital because I saw her with Nanna Ida.'

'Did you now?' said Bertie. Wives did sometimes come to the site, to collect pay packets before they walked into the pub, but none had been to this site for weeks and certainly Ida was not friends with any of them. 'When did you see them?' he asked as he tucked the rag back into his waist.

'I was finishing in outpatients and I saw them in the canteen so I'm sure it's the new woman who Nana is cleaning with.'

Bertie furrowed his brow. 'Honest to God, your nana. Sometimes I think she leads a secret life.'

Gracie detected the concern in his voice. 'Why, Grandad, what's she done now?'

Bertie felt an overwhelming need to unburden himself. He had barely slept the night before and Ida's words kept running around and around in his brain. He gave a big sigh, looked over his shoulder and then up at the large red-bricked house before him with the tall sash windows. 'She's only gone and written to the children's services, complaining about how that little fella, Louis, is looked after.'

Gracie's hand flew to her mouth. 'Grandad, she never did!' she gasped.

'She did,' he replied, and now that he had said it out loud, he regretted it. He felt worse, not better. 'What do you think will happen?' he asked.

The blood had left Gracie's face. 'They might take him off her and she loves that baby. I think she would die if that happened to her.'

'What do I do?'

Gracie didn't speak for a moment or two but he could almost see her mind working. 'I think she has to go to children's services and say she was sorry, that she wasn't telling the truth.'

Bertie snorted. 'Don't you think I haven't thought about that? Come on, Gracie. Your nan say she's sorry?'

He met Gracie's gaze and as the realisation dawned, watched the hope fade. 'We can't do anything then,' said Gracie. 'I need my job, Grandad, it's all we have.'

She looked so worried he regretted telling her. 'Aye, you're right, queen. Go on, we'll say nothing to anyone – but you keep an eye out for that woman and ask her what she wants next time you see her,' said Bertie. 'She might be wanting to rob the baby.' They both began laughing at the absurdity of his statement and felt better as a result. 'Can't have you getting the blame for every-thing, can we? Tell you what though, I won't blame you if you fancy making me a nice cuppa?'

'I will Grandad, as long as you don't tell me da. I'll keep your secret, you keep mine.' Gracie smiled and dis-appeared up the back stone steps with a heavy feeling in her heart.

'I have got into a terrible mess,' Emily sobbed into Mavis who cradled her in her arms, stroking her hair, as Mrs Duffy stood to her other side, her hand on her shoulder. Madge, silent, rolled out a sheet of shortcrust pastry and continued with the baking. Madge was never com-fortable with tears, her own or anyone else's. 'I lied on the adoption forms and I knew I was doing it. I said I was giving up work to adopt Louis, and I never have and I never wanted to. I love my job and I knew I could bring Louis up *and* work. I looked after my mother and the boys in the war, before the bomb and mam was so sick. I thought that if I could do that, then I could bring up a healthy baby and work with no problem. But now they are onto me and I have no choice. They won't sign the final papers unless I give up work and Matron confirms it. And someone has made a complaint about how I look after Louis. Said they saw me pushing the pram at night with Louis inside.'

'Who won't sign?' Mavis looked confused.

'Who made a complaint?' Mrs Duffy looked angry.

'The children's services won't sign. The battleaxe of a woman, Miss Devonshire, she is adamant.'

'Does Matron know?' asked Mrs Duffy.

Emily's tears flowed afresh. 'No, because that's the worst of it – I lied to her too. The forms said quite clearly that adoptive mothers must be full-time mothers and – and I told her I had been given an exemption.'

Mavis fell to her knees and threw her arms about her as Emily laid her head on her shoulder. Mrs Duffy opened the drawer on the press and removed a clean white napkin and handed it to Emily. 'Here you go, love,' she said and Emily wiped her eyes and blew her nose as they all watched her.

'And had you,' asked Mavis, 'been given the exemption?'

Emily shook her head. 'No, and what is worse, I haven't only lied to Matron – I didn't tell Dessie what I had done. Now I have to tell Matron and this – this will be my last Christmas with you all. They won't let me carry on as we do. You should have seen her, the old battleaxe. She would take him away from us and not feel a bit of shame.'

'I don't understand it,' said Mrs Duffy. 'They weren't that fussy when my next-door neighbour took in the kids from number twelve when the mam died.'

'Yes, but they had family to help too. Dessie and I, there are no parents, no sisters or brothers.'

'Nonsense! What are they on about? You have us.

We are all your family. Hardly a day goes by when we don't see Louis and we all help to look after him.'

'It's not enough,' wailed Emily. 'If I don't leave, I can't keep him and that is all there is to it.'

They all looked over to Doris and Louis who had finished his bottle and was happily lying across her lap as she patted his back. A loud burp filled the room.

'You haven't lost your touch,' said Mavis, 'thanks for doing that.' She nodded her head towards the bottle and Doris smiled. A genuine smile of happiness, her anxiety forgotten. For the first time in a very long while she had been needed, had done something truly useful – and it felt so good she couldn't keep the smile from her face or the stinging tears from her eyes.

Chapter 14

Eva closed the front door to the Seaman's Stop as quietly as she could. She had tried to make her escape unseen earlier in the day and had failed. She had crept down the stairs, stood on the bottom step, listened for any noise and there being none, had tiptoed along the hallway, but as soon as she reached the hatch he was there, as if he had been waiting to catch her. The palms of her hands were as damp as her mouth was dry as her thoughts froze. She had spent what felt like her entire life running, hiding afraid of being caught.

'You off then?' Malcolm had said, surprised, and her heart hammered in her chest as she wondered, should she lie? It was so easy to do, she had done it all her life, from the day her parents had bundled her out of the house in the early hours of the morning in Poland and handed her over to their friends to take her with them to England. 'Melly says you ate all your tea tonight. You can say what you like about Melly, and I do, God knows, for I have to put up with her every day of my life, but she can make good grub. Did you enjoy it?' He pushed the pencil he had been writing with behind his ear. 'I'm just filling in the laundry book,' he said. 'I need to put it on top of the laundry bags by the back door.'

He was making conversation, she was not, and despite the fact that she didn't answer him, he was unperturbed. He thought her pallor sallow, like a wax candle and his immediate alarm was dispelled by the fact that Melly had told him she was eating everything she put before her. Her eyes were fixed on the clock and the only thought running through her mind was that she had to get away. The hospital gates were a ten-minute walk up from the docks and she could not afford to be late because to be late meant she'd be noticed and she never wanted to be noticed.

'Are you off to the hospital?' Malcolm still had his glasses on and peered over the top at her.

'Yes. I told Melly that I would clean my own room because I sleep during the day now and I will change my own sheets.' She didn't add that she was glad that removed any possibility of Melly rummaging through her belongings.

'You are a funny one,' said Malcolm as he shook his head. He wanted to say that a night cleaner's job wouldn't cover the rent and ask where was the rest of the money coming from. But she dropped her head, lowered her lashes and looked forlorn so he would not push her. When she was ready, she would talk. 'Well, don't you be worrying. Your breakfast will be on the range, ready and waiting for when you get back as you know.'

Eva felt a twinge of guilt. She didn't need the money, she had money, but how could she tell him? She had run with enough money to start a new life. Lovely Malcolm... he was the most thoughtful person she had ever met; if she had known a man like Malcolm before, things would have been very different. But she had a secret to bear and it was one she could not share with anyone and especially not Malcolm because Malcolm knew Biddy and she hadn't expected that. She had wanted to wait for the right moment, to reduce the chances of being caught, but Biddy had seen her, met her, and Liverpool women were as inquisitive as baby kittens and as sharp as knives. That Doreen had never taken her eyes of her, had weighed up her every word as she had spoken, did not like her; she had sensed that immediately. She would have to act fast. She had got the job as a night cleaner with almost no effort at all and this was exactly where she needed to be, in the hospital, on the inside. There would be a way, an ideal time, and she would find it.

She felt the pain begin, just as it always did. Low down and slowly, like fingers splayed and stretching, it reached out across her abdomen and with it, she knew, the heat would come and the light-headedness.

Malcolm pushed down on the desk with his hands as he rose. 'I need to fill the coal bucket,' he said as he picked up the laundry book to deposit by the back door.

'Can you feel the change in the air? Look at that. It'll be white with frost out there in no time. Maybe we might have a white Christmas after all.'

She breathed in deeply and then held her breath, her only weapon against the pain, and then she counted in her head, *one, two, three*. She could hardly hear a word Malcolm said as he prattled on, not noticing her as he pulled the string on the laundry bag.

'I've got a tree being delivered tomorrow. I always have one. Me mam used to make me da carry one on his shoulders all the way back from St John's market every year until the war and I've still got all the baubles and bits and bobs we used to put on it.'

Four, five, six. It was at its height. This was the point at which she often passed out. *Swallow, breathe. Remember to breathe... seven, eight, nine. Hold on, hold on.* The blackness began to creep into her peripheral vision. *Oh no, no, I can't.* Her legs began to shake and the pain, the pain, was rising higher, spreading further; breathing became almost impossible as the heat flushed into her face and burnt her cheeks.

'I know the night shift doesn't start until after visiting is over, so let me light the fire and make you a cuppa before you go. Most of the night cleaners will still be at the bingo.' He opened the door and hauled the bag onto the step and tucked the laundry book under the string. 'There we go, job done.' He looked down the yard and she could see the whiteness of his breath in the air as he spoke, but could no longer hear what he was saying. 'It's worse than I thought. It's going to snow overnight, I reckon.'

She watched his back as he walked away; as soon as he was gone she would slip out of the door and the pain, it must go. This could not be one of the nights when it remained, stabbing upwards into her belly. She had to put her plan into action, had looked at the rota before she had left her last shift to see where she would be placed.

'What are you looking at that for?' Ida had asked her. 'It's all the bloody same. There's no difference between one mop bucket and another or one floor and the next. Dirt is dirt.'

How could she explain? She had found the bins where the pigswill was kept, behind the school of nursing, and from there she could see where Biddy parked the pram under the bicycle shed on the days it didn't rain and bounced it up the steps on the days it did. She wanted to be early, to see if he had left yet, or was he still there. Would she catch sight of him on his way home? Or was he safely indoors, someone who was not his mother kissing the cheeks of her son? The rota had shown her that she and Ida were to clean the mortuary, wash the classroom floor and the stairs in the school of nursing. If he wasn't there, she would go to the home, she would find him. Just one more night without him, that was all it would be. In the school, she might be able to touch something that was his. To smell him. The thought of inhaling the air that her son had breathed, just to feel a blanket he had laid on, delighted her.

Her concentration faltered and she forgot to count; the pain knew and, with a vengeance, it rose and stabbed like a hot knife upwards. It felt, this time, as though it ripped through her heart. She tried to regain control, but it was too late, her thoughts had wandered to her baby and she was lost.

'Hey, just imagine,' Malcolm said, 'we can build a snowman for Christmas if it does snow. Now, let me make that tea before you leave and no arguments.'

'I need to sit down,' said Eva.

'Bleeding hell, you don't look good at all,' Malcolm exclaimed as he swung around and saw her clutch at the back of the chair. He pulled the chair out for her and, taking her arm, helped her to sit. He almost recoiled at the stick-thin feel of her arms. She hid her thinness well with her bulky cardigan and coat. 'Eva, what shall I do?' he asked her, his voice laced with panic. She snatched her hands away as both flew to her abdomen and she shook her head.

'Nothing,' she gasped. 'It will pass.'

'I don't like the look of you,' he said. 'Shall I get some Disprin?'

She didn't answer, but two minutes later he was back at her side with the two white tablets fizzing in a glass of water in one hand and a glass of whisky in the other. 'Here, swallow this. It's disgusting, so hold your nose.'

The edge of the pain had already calmed and she panted from the effort of trying to control it. It had been just like the labour pains that had delivered her baby boy, Elijah, only this was a pain without any joy. There was nothing at the end of it, just exhaustion and weakness. If there had been any chance of her being pregnant, she would have sworn she was in labour.

Malcolm lifted her head and held the glass to her lips, 'Here, get this down you. Your cheeks look very red and flushed. I think you might have a touch of gastric flu. We saw a lot of that during the war.'

Eva guzzled down the Disprin. Malcolm had not lied, it had tasted foul. He placed the empty glass on the table, tipped a small amount of the whisky into it, swilled it around and handed it back to her.

'Just to make sure you get every bit,' he said.

The whisky had become cloudy and she saw the white particles swilling around. She dreaded the taste, but there was none, just the strength of the whisky and the pleasant burn as it went down. She coughed and spluttered on the last drops.

'There you go. Five minutes and that will work its magic.'

'I'm sorry to be such a nuisance,' she said and Malcolm's eyes softened at the tone of her voice.

'You aren't a nuisance. It's nice to have someone to look after.' Malcolm blushed, felt he had said too much, a glance full of shyness met her own, full of relief.

'That's kind of you,' she said. 'I like being here. I have been very lucky to have found someone as nice as you, after everything.' The whisky was making her feel light-headed and, without knowing it, loosened her tongue.

Malcolm knelt down at the side of her chair. 'What do you mean "after everything"?' He took one of her hands in his own, an unfamiliar gesture, but one that felt right. She looked down at her hand, at both of their hands, as though seeing her own for the first time. 'If you need looking after, Eva, I can do that. No obligation, nothing in return. Why don't you share your secret with me and let me help you?'

Eva looked into his eyes and his kindness flooded out and weakened her. She wanted more than anything to fall onto his shoulder, to sob in the arms of this caring man. Jacob wasn't coming back. The yellowing letters she had written to him, unopened and perched under the lamp told her that.

'Tell you what. Let me go and get the tea. You don't move and I'll be back in five minutes. I'll bring you a bit of the pudding Biddy made for me too and then we can talk. Eva, I feel as though you are carrying the weight of the world upon your shoulders – and you know what they say, don't you? A problem shared is a problem halved.' Malcolm used the arm of the chair to push him-self up and the only sound in the room was the clock ticking and his knees cracking. 'Here, I'll put a match to this before I go.'

He threw the match onto the paper, watched it catch, pushed it with the poker and then turned to her and said, 'Now, don't you move until I get back, that's an order.'

He smiled down at her and, for just those few moments, she let herself believe that all was well. That she could sit in that chair in front of the warm fire feeling no pain for forever and a day, that Malcolm would return and sit with her. He would put the radio on and in complete security and companionship they would pass the night, locked away from the world, together.

She heard the kitchen door shut. He wanted her to tell him what was wrong, to share her burden. She remembered the library, the *Echo*, the headlines. POLICE SEARCH FOR MOTHER OF ABANDONED BABY FOR QUESTIONING. She had read how her son had nearly died. That no one had come for days. That he was dehydrated and on the point of death when he was found. She was an accessory to a very serious crime, attempted infanticide...

No, she would have to go through with her plan. She could hear the sound of Malcolm whistling in the kitchen, accompanied by the low whistle from the kettle. Eva pushed herself up from the chair, maintained her balance, took a deep breath, the pain had almost gone, and tiptoed out towards the front door. Picking up her bag and taking one last look at Malcolm's comfortable lounge, she closed the door with such care Malcolm couldn't possibly have heard.

★

The Disprin and the whisky had barely done their work as Eva almost ran up the road. She wanted to speak more to Ida, who she increasingly felt she could confide in. Ida had strong opinions about Emily Horton and the nurses' home and she had learnt from Ida that the housekeeper's name was Mrs Duffy. That had been useful information. And the young girl who worked in the home was her granddaughter, Gracie. Tonight, maybe she would confide in Ida. Give her the case note sheets she had taken from the clinic. Her son was not being cared for as he should, he was losing weight. Ida was nosey, but whoever they had told her to work with would have asked her a thousand questions – and Ida talked and passed her opinion much more than she asked questions.

Ida was already in the changing room when Eva arrived, smoking a cigarette and standing alone while the other women were gathered in groups, chatting and smoking.

'Hello love,' shouted one. 'How you enjoying the work, queen?'

She smiled as she fastened her apron. 'It is fine, thank you,' she said.

'Oh, get that accent! Where's it from, love?' They were all looking at her, she could not avoid answering.

'Poland,' she whispered.

The changing room fell silent. Her dark hair and eyes, the Star of David she wore around her neck… they knew.

One of the cleaners asked, in a gentle way, 'Have you got any family left, love?'

They had all seen the shocking footage of the Jewish concentration camps as they had been liberated. All knew that others had suffered an even worse war that those who lived through the May Blitz. Eva shook her head.

'Ah, God love her,' said the woman, 'you look after her, Ida, do you hear?'

Ida stubbed her cigarette out in the red fire bucket that hung from the wall. 'Why wouldn't I?' she asked, mildly put out. 'I don't care where she's from as long as she can work as hard as everyone else and doesn't leave it all to me. We get along just fine, don't we, love?'

The other women tutted and shook their heads, some threw her pitying looks.

'We get along just fine,' said Eva and Ida felt a rush of warmth towards her.

Ida wasn't a popular figure amongst the night cleaners. They thought her too high and mighty. Ida never lent and never borrowed. That was an unusual position for a woman who lived on the dock streets to take. Everyone had to borrow, sometimes. Eva, though, was relieved that Ida was unpopular. It minimised the number of inescapable personal questions she could have been faced with. And, in answer to her wildest dreams, it appeared to Eva that Ida hadn't taken against her as she appeared to have done with some of the others. Ida was on her side.

The night supervisor walked into the room. 'Will you

lot pipe down? Here, I've your allocations. Ida, you and – what's your name, love, you—?' The supervisor looked over and pointed her pencil at Eva.

'Eva, my name is Eva,' she whispered.

'Sorry, love, that's right. You two are back in the mortuary tonight and then over on the stairs, toilets and kitchens in the nursing school. Don't touch the sisters' sitting room – you know how precious Biddy is about that. That's her domain.'

Ida snorted. 'She's welcome to it,' she said. 'I won't be doing her job for her, she never does mine.'

'Oh, do leave it out,' one of the women shouted over. 'Do you ever stop moaning, Ida? It's like a wet Wednesday whatever night of the week it is when you are on.'

Ida didn't respond; instead, she turned to Eva. 'Come on,' she said. 'Follow me. Let's get cracking while this lot skive and cackle.'

Eva turned on her heel to follow Ida. She felt the twinge return in the deep low base of her abdomen, but she knew she was safe. This was the dull pain which stayed for hours, subsided and then disappeared before it returned with force. With a bit of luck she would be back at the Seaman's Stop and in her bed before it came again.

Doreen slipped into the switchboard and grinned at Madge who was on the phone and indicated towards the kettle. Madge nodded her head as she spoke into her headpiece and then, plugging in one wire, removing the next, took off her headset and turned towards Doreen.

'I'm gasping,' she said. 'It's been mad today. How are you, love?'

Doreen was quiet, thinking. 'Do you know what, Madge? I'm a bit fed up if I'm honest.'

'Why, love, what's the matter?'

'I think I found a man I might like – and some bloody woman had just, and I mean just – got her claws into him.'

Madge's eyes widened. 'Who is the fella and more importantly, who's the woman?'

Doreen, not usually one to bare her soul, told Madge everything. About how she had seen Malcolm as though for the first time ever. About the thin woman with the foreign accent who made him smile.

'I know who she is,' said Madge. 'I put her through the other day when she called from the library – not that I was listening in, but I did hear the address and thought to meself, that's Malcolm's place. I only noticed because I thought he only took in seamen.'

Doreen looked thoroughly despondent. 'So did I. Just my luck. I thought that as he was a bit older, a man of the world, so to speak, he would be understanding, you know…' Her voice trailed off but Madge knew what she meant.

'Well, she's not married to him, she's only just arrived. So don't lose hope, love. And tell you what, I'll keep an eye out here, eh? See if I hear anything.' Madge glanced at

Doreen as she sipped her tea. Poor Doreen, she thought unaware that, at St Angelus, someone thought that about Doreen at least once day.

Chapter 15

'You are the best cook, Mrs Gaskell,' said Teddy Davenport as he wiped his mouth with his napkin.

Doris beamed. 'Thank you, Teddy, you are always welcome for supper, you know you are.'

'Don't tell him that, Mother,' said Oliver as he reached over and scooped up Teddy's empty plate, 'he'll be here every night. And where is Pa tonight? It was his idea that we have a family meal and that I invite Teddy and he isn't even here.'

Teddy coughed. 'I think I know the answer to that,' he said. 'I saw him heading back towards the operating theatre with the new visiting anaesthetist.'

Oliver clasped his head and groaned. 'Oh, I forgot, he told me. He said Matron wants all the lists cleared by Christmas and so the theatres are operating until midnight each night this week with extra help. It was the anaesthetist's first day and you know what's Pa's like. He barely trusts the operating staff with the surgeons and staff who have been at the hospital for years.'

Doris smiled. 'If I don't know what your father is like by now, I never will. I don't know why you are so surprised he isn't here,' she said. 'That's been your father all of his life and I only expect him when I see him. I've been disappointed far too many times.'

Oliver had leant back on the chair and now, with a bang, let it fall forward onto the floor.

'Oliver, don't. You will break the legs.' His hair was dark and floppy, his eyes bright blue like his father's and often, as Doris looked at him sitting at her table, she could transfer herself back in time, without too much effort.

Oliver grinned. 'Ma's been saying that to me every mealtime since I was in nappies, haven't you, Ma?'

'Has Dr Gaskell always spent a lot of time at the hospital, Mrs Gaskell?' asked Teddy.

Oliver answered for her. 'Has he? I'll say. Do you know, I used to get so angry when I was little and the blackout was on, that I wanted to run back to the hospital and drag him home because Ma was so scared of the bombs and then, when the war was over, he became so busy with patients, he practically lived there. I used to get so cross.'

Teddy knew the family well enough to think he could pass comment and contribute to the conversation. 'Was that until the day you became a doctor at St Angelus and realised you were spending more time on the wards than you were at home yourself?' Teddy gave Oliver a rueful grin.

'It's the curse of St Angelus,' said Doris. 'I'm sure it's

not like this in other hospitals. Your father admits it. He says the people have a way about them. They make him his family and, do you know, he truly cares for them. He isn't just their doctor.'

'They all know that,' said Teddy. 'He was telling me once he looked after Emily Horton's mother. He said the most soul destroying thing was all the effort he would put into trying to make someone better and then Hitler would take out a whole road and a few of his patients with one bomb.'

They were all silent for a moment. Mentioning the war did that. Close enough to be remembered, and far away enough to have eased the pain that came with the memories. Life had moved on.

'Anyway, never mind your father,' said Doris, as she rose from the chair and took the plates from Teddy. 'What about you two? Not a girlfriend in sight between you. What's wrong with you young men these days? Your father and I had you long before he was the age you are now, Oliver.'

The two doctors looked at each other and raised eyebrows.

'I don't seem to have a lot of luck in that department, Mrs Gaskell,' said Teddy.

'Ha!' said Oliver, about to expose Teddy and his situation with Dana, but Teddy shook his head and Oliver backtracked. 'There's no time, Ma, for me to meet anyone. I'm too busy on my new ward, learning the ropes.'

'Don't lie to me,' said Doris as she placed a hot dish filled to the brim with bread-and-butter pudding on the table. 'Do you think your father doesn't come home and tell me all about what you have been up to? I know everything.'

Oliver had the good grace to blush. 'I just haven't met anyone like you, Ma, that's the problem,' said Oliver as he placed his arm around his mother's waist, rescuing himself in his mother's eyes as he stood and hugged her.

'Oliver, you don't want anyone like me,' she said as she undid his hands and extracted them. 'I'm very old school. What you want is a young, modern woman who isn't going to be an old bore and a stick-in-the-mud. Someone who enjoys life and wants to get out and do things.'

The phone rang just as Oliver was about to reply. 'That will be Pa, with a very good excuse,' said Oliver as he sat back in the chair.

'I can see it from the other side tonight,' said Teddy. 'I mean, your mother's side. I had no idea how awful it must be to be a doctor's wife.'

They both fell quiet as Doris spoke on the phone. 'I do have some red in the sewing box, funnily enough. It's left over from a skirt I made a few years ago. No, don't worry, I will bring it with me. Is there anything else you need?' There was a long silence before she said, 'It's no trouble, I am very happy to do it. I'm really touched that you've asked me. I'm not sure I will be as much of an expert as you at sewing, though. I'll see you tomorrow evening, then. Yes, I have a pen, which number is it?'

A few minutes later she walked into the room and Oliver thought it was very odd that she didn't relay the phone conversation to them.

'Was that Pa?' he asked and Doris answered simply, 'No. It was for me. Sometimes phone calls are, you know.' She smiled at the confused look on her son's face. That statement, in his experience, was patently untrue. He had hardly ever heard the phone ring for his mother. 'Now, back to you two and the girlfriends that neither of you have. Do you know what I heard Sister Horton say today at the Lovely Lane home?'

Oliver looked shocked. 'Ma, what do you mean, the Lovely Lane home? Even *I've* never been in there.'

Teddy grinned. 'Yes, and he's tried often enough, Mrs Gaskell.'

Oliver leant forward and kicked Teddy under the table. 'Ma, I didn't even know you knew where it was. That's not like you. What were you doing in the nurses' home?'

Doris grinned. 'I know it's not like me – the old me. The me that was here only last week. Anyway, Sister Horton was there with little Louis and she said that women today shouldn't have to give up their careers to have a baby. Can you imagine that? That's the kind of woman you need. Anyway, there must be someone around for you. Teddy, don't you know any nice young women who would make a marvellous daughter-in-law and give me grandchildren?'

'You don't want to ask me,' said Teddy, as he eyed up the huge portion of bread-and-butter pudding being heaped into a dish and hoped it was for him. 'I'm a disaster area when it comes to romance.'

Doris handed him a plate. 'Is it Dana?' she asked, and there was a gentleness to her tone that made him look up and as their eyes met, without any warning whatsoever, his own filled with tears. He blinked and dashed them away before Oliver could see.

'It is, but I'm afraid it's a lost cause and I will have to accept that I have lost the best wife a man could ever have had – and I deserve to.' He suddenly felt so sad that even the hot custard pouring over the large portion of bread-and butter-pudding made no difference at all.

'Dana, she's the Irish nurse with the red hair, isn't she? Friends with Pammy Tanner?'

Oliver's mouth almost fell open. He had no idea his mother even knew the Tanners. Teddy also looked surprised.

'Oh, I only know *of* her,' said Doris as she wafted the air with her hand. 'It's just that I will be meeting her tomorrow night.'

For almost a full minute there was silence until Oliver finally spoke. 'Tomorrow night? Ma, you don't go out at night.'

'I do now,' said Doris. Doris placed the jug on a cork

mat and sat back down in her chair, almost erupting into laughter at the sight of her son's face. She hadn't taken a single pill all day, had dared herself to skip the lunchtime pill altogether and it felt as though a fog were lifting – and yet a fog, a dark and heavy fog that disabled her every emotion, had been the reason she took the pills in the first place. 'Close your mouth, Oliver. Yes, I will see her. I'm off to the Tanners' house to help Mavis make the dresses for your brother's party, Teddy. That was her on the phone just then, asking if I had any red thread to save her a trip to St John's market in the morning. I assume Dana will be there because, funnily enough, I'm the one sewing Dana's dress.'

She looked at Teddy who shovelled an entire spoonful of pudding into his mouth. Oliver glanced at Teddy and a thought struck him.

'Ma, do you think there is anything you can seriously do for Teddy?' he asked. 'He's obviously lovesick for Dana. Surely a man can be forgiven a mistake, can't he?'

Doris served herself a portion of pudding a quarter of the size she had served the boys. 'Well, from what your father tells me, it was a little more than an indiscretion.'

Teddy blushed, his spoon poised over the bowl. Doris felt her heart go out to him. His mistake, as Oliver called it, had probably been terminal. She doubted there was anything anyone could do. The subject had come up during the cake-making when she had offered to help Mavis with the dresses.

'Dana is very strong,' Mavis had said. 'She was broken, but whatever is in the water in Ireland, she came back here and you wouldn't think anything had happened. Oh, you wouldn't want to cross Dana in a hurry.'

Mavis had left Doris in no doubt that Dana would be less than receptive to an intervention on Teddy's behalf and yet her heart went out to him.

Teddy looked up from his bowl. 'I went mad after the accident,' he said.

Doris leant over and patted his hand. 'I know,' she said. 'My husband said that trauma can do that to people, that he's seen it before and he thinks it's all credit to you that you didn't just give up under strain and that you are still practising as a doctor. Most would have just thrown in the towel. You had a mountain to climb to recover. I'm not sure I would like to be bed bound like you were, or suffer from the pain you did, for that amount of time.'

Oliver, who hadn't stopped eating, scraped his bowl with his spoon. 'Oh, I don't know,' he said as he picked up his napkin and wiped his mouth, 'he's a year behind me now because he got put back, and that gives me no end of authority over him. How long until the party anyway, do we all know how we are getting there?'

'With your father in the car,' said Doris. 'And let's pray it doesn't snow.' The phone rang out again. 'Heavens above, boys, it's busier than Lime Street in here!'

'They've run out of blue,' said Oliver grinning as Doris hurried back down the hallway.

A moment later they heard, 'Yes, Matron, of course. I would be delighted.'

'Matron?' mouthed Oliver to Teddy. 'She's going to need her own personal switchboard installing before long. I've never heard my mother talk so much.'

'If it carries on, she'll be getting a call from the Pope, next,' said Teddy as he finished the last morsel of pudding. They both unashamedly strained to hear what she was saying.

'Oh, I do know where the children's ward is, yes. Oliver was in there as a baby, you may remember. Yes, I met Sister Aileen at your drinks do. I'm not surprised. Yes, my husband told me. An unprecedented number of babies with bronchitis... Matron, I love babies and especially at Christmas, it will be my pleasure.'

A short time later Doris sat back down at the table and grinned. 'Well, that was nice. Apparently Sister Aileen is run off her feet on the children's ward and Mavis is busy with the WVS so Matron has asked would I help with decorating the ward on Saturday. In fact, she asked me if I would become involved with the children's ward as a visitor and general organiser. What's more, they are down in the numbers for the ward carol singers because some of the nuns are poorly, so would I help out there, too.'

Oliver frowned. His reputation as a ladies' man was safe from his mother, or so he thought, and he liked it that way. A father at the hospital who gave a wry smile was very different from a mother with an opinion.

'Really? What did you say?'

'I said I would love to, of course, and that I will be there at ten on Saturday morning and every night at visiting for the carol singing.' She grinned and clapped her hands. 'I can't wait – and Oliver, I am sure I am going to hear a lot about my son when I'm there!'

Ida leant her mop up against the classroom door in the school of nursing and took her tobacco tin out of her apron pocket. 'Come on, stop,' she said. 'You've been working too fast and you'll 'ave all the others on me back, complaining.' She struck a match and lit the cigarette. 'Want one?' she asked and proffered the tin to Eva. Ida didn't like to part with cigarettes, especially not to relative strangers, but, in her experience, many a secret was shared over a ciggie. She was disappointed when Eva shook her head.

'Come on then, with you being such a fast worker there's one benefit to being stuck over here – they have their own kettle and teapot. I've never finished the mortuary as fast as that before, you near wore the mop out.'

Eva put her mop in the bucket and pummelled it up and down before she began to squeeze it dry as if to make a point. 'I'm sorry,' she said. 'I didn't realise.'

How could she confess to Ida that she had been desperate to get over to the school of nursing as fast as she could. So far, she had been disappointed. All she had seen were chairs and desks and fake skeletons that made her feel creepy. Ida had noticed.

'Oh, don't be worrying about those,' she had said. 'I get them all, I do. Dead bodies over there in the mortuary, fake skeletons over here. Good job I'm not easily scared, isn't it? Sometimes I have to do half a job on my own in both places because Matron has trouble getting people to work over here with me. Reckon it's the skeletons puts them off but I've got used to it meself.'

Ida pulled on her cigarette and blew the smoke backwards over her shoulder. 'Honestly, I know you think I'm kidding, but that Matron, she has eyes in the back of her head. Always sat at the window in that flat of hers she is, every bleeding night. If we walk out of here too soon and back over to the main block, she'll cut the time she allows for cleaning the mortuary – or worse still, leave me on me own for good and put you somewhere else.'

Eva barely listened to Ida and looked about her nervously, as though expecting to see someone walking up the stairs. 'I didn't mean to work too quick, or to get you into trouble, I just thought you would want to get done as quickly as possible,' said Eva.

Ida frowned at her. 'What's the point in that? We can't leave any earlier than seven in the morning. They'll just give us more to do and have us helping that lazy lot over on the corridors.'

Eva was relieved that the pains hadn't come back.

Sometimes they came in unrelenting intervals and when that happened, she almost lost the will to live, wanted to throw herself in the Mersey. The past few weeks she had felt the swelling in her belly, but the pains had not come as often and tonight they seemed to have disappeared altogether.

'Look at that in there,' Ida nodded to the wooden door of Emily Horton's sitting room, 'they live the life of luxury over here. Bloody disgrace that they have so much time on their hands that they use the place as a nursery for the little lad, who by rights should have gone to the children's home. Come on, let's go in. We aren't supposed to, mind, that's an order. Can you imagine? The state of Biddy Kennedy laying the rules down to me.'

Eva walked over to the door and, placing her hands on either side of the glass window, peered through.

'Oi, watch the glass – I'll have to clean it if you mark it. You'd think that room was Buckingham Palace, you would.'

Eva didn't move but remained at the window and, as if she hadn't heard a word Ida had said, leant her hot forehead on the cool glass. She had felt the heat building; no pain, just nausea that she breathed back down and tried to force to settle. She wondered if the Disprin was wearing off. The sitting room contained a desk in front of a window with papers, neatly piled. The fireplace was covered by a guard and, at the side, stood a baby's cot. Over the rails of the cot lay a matinee coat and a blanket. Next to the cot stood a basket, full to the brim with soft toys and a brightly painted pull-along wooden train. Eva's breath shuddered in her chest and, without a word, her hand rested on the cold brass handle of the door.

'Oh, Jesus wept, we'll have to polish that as well now,' said Ida as she flicked the butt of her cigarette into the mop bucket. A sizzle filled the air. 'Come on, as you've opened the door, let's reuse the last tea leaves in their pot – they'll be none the wiser and you can sit down for a minute. I know it's not my business, but you do look peaky. Is it your time of the month? You look thinner and paler than you did the other night.'

Eva wasn't listening. She walked, as though in a trance, over to the cot. She picked up the blanket and buried her face in it as she inhaled deeply. She ignored the pain, would have walked through fire to reach that cot just to smell him. Ida went to a table against the wall with the neatly laid out tea tray. She picked up the teapot lid.

'Bleedin' hell, that Biddy Kennedy's only gone and emptied the leaves out. The mean mare.' Eva still didn't respond and appeared to be rocking back and forth. 'My, you're a funny one,' said Ida. 'Look at you, not a word of thanks. I've just said you could have a brew and you'd think I'd said I was going to sell your firstborn child. Come on, let's get the kettle on, quick. If she isn't going to leave us the used leaves, we will get some out of this caddy and Biddy Kennedy can blame herself. Tell you what, why don't you put the kettle on and I'll go to the doctors' sitting room. It's only next door and one of the greedy buggers may have left a cake or a few biscuits on the plate. They said the theatre is operating until late tonight so Biddy will have left food out for them.'

Ida returned in less than ten minutes, almost whooping for joy. 'Would you look at that, there was no bugger there so I helped meself, I did. I got us two fish paste butties and four of Biddy's scones. I'll put two of those in me bag for our Bertie in the morning – not that he deserves it, mind.'

Ida heard the noise as she unwrapped the fish paste sandwiches. It sounded like the wail of an injured animal, a sound that evoked memories from the war, from neighbours, mothers who read telegrams that told them the worst news, that their sons were lost in battle. Something was very wrong and the noise Eva was making frightened her and Ida felt a chill run down her spine. Eva was rocking on her feet, backwards and forwards, backwards and forwards.

'Eva, put that blanket down,' she said. 'What's up with you?'

Eva turned, her face pouring with tears, her eyes wide and almost animal-like and the noise came again before she screamed, placed her hands on her belly and, grabbing the back of a chair next to the cot, still clutching the blanket, lowered herself down.

'Holy Mother of God, what is wrong with you?' said

Ida, her voice filled with alarm and an unfamiliar emotion, concern. It didn't take Ida many seconds to piece it all together: the look she had given Emily Horton when she had been pushing her baby, the cot, the blanket she was holding and smelling... 'You've had a child out of wedlock, haven't you?'

Eva nodded her head but could not speak. Her tears poured and Ida did another thing she wasn't used to, she put her arms around Eva to comfort her. She didn't know much about Eva, but she did know that she was the first woman she had ever worked with who appeared to like her.

'It happens all the time around these streets,' said Ida. 'I don't know what happened, love, but if you'd like to tell me? I know it must be hard, what with Christmas coming too, but you can talk to me.'

She assumed that, through her distress, Eva had heard her, but she gave no response and Ida settled on her knees on the floor next to her and decided that, for once, she would do the right thing. She wouldn't pry. She moved to place both of her arms around Eva and rocked her but she was too late, Eva slumped in the chair and Ida just caught her in time before she slumped sideways onto the floor.

Doris wound her son's scarf around his neck as he was leaving, just as she had done when he was a boy.

'Don't worry, Ma, Pa will be home soon,' said Oliver as he hugged her on the doorstep.

'Oh, I'm not worried for me, it's him,' said Doris. 'He's getting too old to be working these sorts of hours. I'm sure the anaesthetist is well qualified; your father should trust him.'

'He does, Ma, but you know what he's like. He likes to be there when his patients wake up.'

'I know, I know, I married a saint. I'm used to it.'

As Oliver tucked his scarf inside his coat, he leant in to kiss his mother's cheek. 'See if you can have a word with Dana,' he whispered. 'Teddy is a mess without her. I've never known anyone so remorseful.'

Doris squeezed her son's hand. 'I will, but I'm afraid my sympathies lie with Dana. It all depends on how she feels about him and whether or not she's the forgiving type. I'll see what I can do.'

Oliver beamed. 'Ma, you can work miracles.' He turned and strode down the path towards Teddy, who was waiting for him under the lamppost. 'Come on, Ted,' he said as he patted his friend on the back, 'there's time for a quick one in the Admiral before we head back.'

Doris placed the washed and dried custard jug in the cabinet and closed the doors. She had watched and waved until the dark night had swallowed the young men up and had returned indoors into the warm, satisfied that they had eaten every morsel of food she had placed before them. Then, just as she did every night, she filled a glass with water, located the brown bottle and shook her blue friend out into her hand and sighed deeply. She felt happier than she had in a very long time. She had skipped the lunchtime dose completely, swallowed down the panic and counted to ten. Now, she didn't even feel any sense of panic wash over her as she contemplated slipping the tablet back in the bottle.

'Shall I?' she said to her reflection in the mirror on the wall. She thought about her week, the women she had met who had much harder lives than she did, who juggled homes, families and jobs. She felt a sense of shame and, with determination, put the blue pill back, screwed the top on the bottle and almost slammed the cabinet door.

Eva felt the hand on the back of her neck and pushed up against it in an attempt to shake it away. She had opened her eyes, but there was only darkness until the double vision gave way and she focused her eyes on the baby blanket on the floor. Ida was holding her head down between her knees.

'Oh, bleedin' hell, thank God you've come around,' she said. 'I was out of me mind and thought I'd have to try and use that phone to the switchboard.'

'No, no, please don't do that,' said Eva, panic in her

voice, bewilderment lighting her eyes. 'I don't want anyone to know.' She stood up with Ida's help and sat up on
a chair, pulling her skirt down, straightening her apron.
Ida looked at her.

'Eva, I know you have had a child, but you'd better
let me know: are you pregnant now?'

Eva shook her head. 'No, no. I'm definitely not pregnant,' she said as her eyes filled with tears.

Ida placed a scone and a cup of tea on the table in
front of her. 'Well, that's something I suppose,' she said.
'I think your problem is that you aren't eating enough.
You're very thin, so get stuck into that lot, go on.' Eva
picked up the tea and flinched as she sipped it. 'Sorry,
queen. I put four sugars in – you need it.' Ida pulled
on her cigarette and blew the smoke into the air. 'No
need to rush. We'll only do the staircase tonight, no one
will notice.'

Eva felt the heat flush into her face. There it was again.
It wasn't a lack of food that had made her faint, she knew
that. But the heat and the shivers and the pain in the base
of her belly sometimes became too much. The yellowness
in her eyes, it was new, and the pain in her side along
with the pain in her belly. Maja had told her the pain
would go with time, but it was still there. She thought
of Maja as she sipped her tea. Wondered how she was
bearing her own heartache and felt guilty for leaving her,
but there was nothing she could do. Wherever she was
in the world, she would not rest until she had found her

son. It will have to be tomorrow, she thought. I will have to find a way and move quickly, I'm running out of time.

'So, Eva,' Ida said, 'there's a reason why you are here, isn't there? If you don't tell me, I can't help you, so what is it, Eva? You can trust me.'

Chapter 16

Roland sat back in the bedroom armchair and lit his cigar. It was late evening and the heavy fringed bedside lamps and the fire he had lit in the grate made the bedroom feel warmer than it was and very cosy. He had taken a bath after dinner as he waited for Victoria to finish trying on dresses before they had an early night.

'Oh, no, why didn't I think of this?' Victoria wailed as she tugged and pulled.

Roland picked up his glass, which contained his customary two fingers of Scotch and one lump of ice, from the side table. 'Well, you are eight months pregnant, darling,' he said, with as much diplomacy and delicacy as he could muster.

'Roland, I feel like I'm about to burst. I never thought it would be possible for my body to stretch this much. My skin is so tight, it hurts – and look at these huge purple train tracks running all over my bump! Will they ever disappear?'

Roland wasn't sure what the answer to this comment

should be, thought hard and was almost relieved as Victoria turned from the mirror to face him. 'Roland, I spoke to Mrs Tanner on the phone today and she told me they were having a sewing night at her house tomorrow night for the girls' dresses. I just know she could slip an elastic panel in this frock, so can we go over in the car?'

Roland looked concerned. 'Well, I don't mind, but are you sure?'

Victoria sat on the side of the bed and promptly burst into tears. Roland, alarmed, leapt from the chair and was at her side within seconds.

'Vicky, what's wrong? Are you all right?' He took his handkerchief from his pocket and handed it to her.

'Oh, Roland, I think I just miss everyone. I felt so sad when Mrs Tanner told me they were having one of their girls' days and that they were all going to be together. It's almost Christmas and I want to be there too.' Victoria's tears were cut dead by the sound of the telephone on the bedside table ringing.

'I'll get it,' said Roland as he lifted the handset. 'Aunt Minnie, how lovely to hear from you.' He turned to Victoria and pulled a face which, despite her tears, made her smile. 'That is not good news.' He frowned and the tone of his voice told Victoria that her only female relative, her only anticipated company in the house, would not be arriving as expected. Her heart sank and it showed in her face. By the time Roland replaced the receiver, his mind was made up.

'Trust Aunt Minnie to be flat on her back with a cold,' he said. 'I'm amazed the gin gave the cold a look in, though. Aunt Minnie thinks she might be able to travel on the day of the party, but certainly not before. She said the doctor's orders are to stay indoors and to drink lots of hot toddies for the rest of the week.

'So, my princess, if a trip to Liverpool is what you want us to do, it shall happen. I shall take you to the sewing circle of gaggling women over in Mrs Tanner's house in the dock streets in Liverpool. And I can't think of a better place to be, if that is where you would rather spend your time than with your husband.'

Victoria's face fell and he immediately placed his arm around her shoulder. 'I'm only joking! Hey, where's my Victoria gone?'

Victoria dabbed at her eyes. 'I don't know. I feel as though I want to burst into tears every few minutes. I'm really looking forward to the party, to everyone being here, but I'm just feeling a bit lonely right now. What about you? If you drive me over, what will you do?'

Roland pulled up the candlewick cover and placed it around his wife's shoulders. The fire may have been lit, but it was an old house and the high ceilings meant that keeping warm was a constant effort. 'Don't you worry about me. I will visit the doctors' residence and then drag my brother out to the Grapes for a pint and a bit of lunch. I'm looking forward to catching up with him. I spoke to Oliver on the phone when I was in work today,' Victoria looked puzzled, 'I speak to him once a week to see how my little brother is doing, and he said that Teddy was still a miserable toad. I reckon there's a competition for that title now in our family.' He pushed her hair behind her ear and kissed her gently on the temple.

Victoria smiled weakly through her tears. 'I'm pathetic, aren't I?'

Roland pulled her to him. 'No, darling, you are pregnant, not pathetic. There is a slight difference. And I'll tell you what, tomorrow is Saturday so no office and we can leave straight after breakfast and take a leisurely drive over. We'll be there for eleven, stay for supper – I'm sure someone will feed us – and be back home by bedtime. What do you think?'

Victoria lay her hand on top of his. 'I'm missing everyone so much. I know that when the baby arrives I'll be too busy to be missing anyone or anything, but right now I feel as though I need my friends around me.'

Roland placed his arms around his wife's shoulders. 'I know, Vic, and honestly, don't worry, you will be fine. Aunt Minnie will be recovered soon enough and be here for Christmas, so we'll have the party just as planned. It will all be just absolutely fine.'

Mrs Duffy had pushed the night-time drinks trolley along the corridor from the kitchen to the television room where the nurses had gathered to watch the news.

Her bag was ready by the front door. She would serve the drinks and one of the nurses would clear them away when she went to catch her bus home. They didn't know that she knew that Nurse Beth stood and watched her from behind the curtains every night until she was happy that Mrs Duffy was safely on the bus home.

'Drinks, everyone,' she said as she dragged the trolley through the door. Pammy was lying on the floor in front of the fire reading a magazine and most of the probationers were sitting with their heads in their notes and testing each other ready for the following morning's exam. It was coming to the end of the probationers' first twelve-week session in the school and the following week would see many of them on the wards for the first time.

'Come along, nurses, time to stop that. I've done Horlicks and hot chocolate tonight.' She pushed the trolley against the wall.

'Here, let me do that,' said Dana. 'I'll serve and you go and get the bus.'

Beth came into the room in her dressing gown, her hair wrapped in a towel. 'Oh, just in time,' she said as the phone rang in the laundry room next door. 'Don't worry, Mrs Duffy, I'll get it.'

The television was on low in the background and the news began as Mrs Duffy and Dana began to ask the probationer nurses what they would like to drink.

'Oh, would you look at that,' said Mrs Duffy. 'He's just said that snow is expected.'

'When?' asked Dana as they all fell silent and watched the screen.

'Tomorrow. Well, no point in thinking it will be a white Christmas; it will all be gone in days and all we will have left is the sludge.'

Dana picked up the Horlicks jug and using the extra-long spoon, stirred the white paste from the bottom round and round until golden fragments of husks floated to the surface. It reminded her of home, of fields of oats and wheat and she lifted the jug to breathe in the steam. 'Oh, I don't know,' she said as she began to pour the Horlicks into a cup, 'it may snow for more than one day.' And then her face dropped. 'Oh, I hope not! Poor Victoria doesn't want it to snow before the party.'

Two minutes later, Beth returned. 'Well, you will never guess what,' she announced as she walked back into the room. 'Victoria is coming over tomorrow. It's Saturday and so Roland is going to drop her here and then she's coming to Pammy's house with the rest of us who are off so I'm going to call in on my split shift.'

Mrs Duffy tutted and shook her head. 'Well, let's hope that weather man was wrong – because if it does snow, Victoria won't be going anywhere.'

Emily and Dessie sat in Matron's sitting room, with Dr Gaskell in the chair next to the fire with Louis on his knee. Louis was biting down hard on the key to

Dr Gaskell's car and the atmosphere in the room was heavy, the set of Matron's jaw tight.

'I know her only too well, Emily, and this is no easy task. She is hardly likely to take any notice of me because she's the sort of person who survives by considering herself to be superior to everyone she meets, even me. Oh, why did you not tell me?' she asked.

Emily stared at the handkerchief that she was winding round and round in her hand. Dessie, even though they were in Matron's office, slipped his arm around her shoulders. They were sitting next to each other on the sofa, Matron on the chair opposite to Dr Gaskell.

'You are going to have to see Miss Devonshire, Matron,' said Dr Gaskell. 'You are going to have to tell her that the hospital needed Emily. That we are slap bang in the fifties, with so much change happening, new nurses arriving from Ireland any day now who will all need to be trained. It's all changed, hasn't it, young man?' He was now speaking to Louis, who looked up at him, grinning, and tried to insert the car key into the doctor's own mouth. 'Not now, I'll eat the keys later,' he said kindly as he gently moved his hand away.

'I let you down,' Emily half-spoke the words, half-whispered. They were words she had hoped she would never have to say to the woman she had grown to regard as a mother, the person she respected most in all the world. 'You deserved better from me and so did Dessie. I've let you both down.' Her tears ran afresh.

'You could never let either of us down. You have been the best mother any child could ever have wanted. And the best nurse tutor any hospital could have wanted or needed. Emily, I am not cross about you not telling me, although I really wish you had. I could probably have argued your case the day you took him home. Remember, the Strawberry Fields baby unit was full at the time and we had all the cards in our hands. However, that was then. Now we have to find a way out – and there is one aspect in all of this I am the most worried about—' She fell silent as Elsie opened the door that connected Matron's apartment to the small kitchen at the rear.

'Do you need me for anything else, Matron?' asked Elsie.

Matron looked startled. 'Elsie, I thought you had gone half an hour ago. Go home, it's getting late.'

'I will. Do you need any help with the little fella, Emily? Want me to take him to ours and you collect him on your way home?'

As if he knew what Elsie had said, Louis pulled himself up onto his feet and began gabbling excitedly. 'I think he agrees with me,' said Elsie as she walked over and put out her arms and picked him up. Everyone in the room laughed. 'I'll get him ready,' said Elsie.

A few minutes later, as she put Louis' coat on in the kitchen, she heard Matron say, 'It's the letter of complaint that is the problem. Whoever has sent this has been watching you very carefully. I am happy to say that he was here, in my rooms in the hospital, being looked after by an army of doting women, but that does not alter the fact that he was being pushed out in his pram, late at night. I can add context and meaning, but I cannot alter the facts. This letter stating that he is being brought up by a variety of people twists the meaning, but not the evidence. I'm afraid it is a dangerous complaint because it is largely based on truth.'

Elsie listened to every word. 'Well, I never,' she said to Louis as she carried him to the pram that was parked at the bottom of the steps leading to Matron's apartment, 'who would ever make a complaint about your mammy, young man?'

As she strode out to the back gates that led to the dock streets, she was entirely unaware that she was being watched. Ida and Eva were standing at the classroom window, Ida leaning on her mop handle and smoking, watching as she went.

'See that?' Ida said. 'That poor little beggar doesn't even sleep in his own house half of the time. She's probably taking him home to hers so those two can go gallivanting about. You wouldn't credit it, would you? I hope someone has seen the letter I've sent.'

'What letter?' Eva had her face placed against the glass, her eyes fixed on her son, trying to catch a glimpse over the canopy that covered most of him. All she could see was a little hand, grasping the top as he used the canopy to try pull himself up.

'I've written a stinker to the children's services. About just that!' She jabbed her finger, towards Elsie. 'He's being dragged up. That kid deserves better.'

Eva turned to face Ida. 'What did you say,' she asked, 'in the letter?'

Ida pulled hard on her cigarette and blew her smoke into the air. 'I said that they should be doing more to find his real mother. That he wasn't being brought up proper. That his real mother might have been sick, or the baby might have been kidnapped. Seems to me the police around here haven't got a clue.'

'And – and do you really think that – that he should be with his real mother?'

Ida furrowed her brow. 'I do, Eva love. All babies should be with their real mother, of course they should. What mother would want a child raised by the likes of Biddy Kennedy and Elsie and the entire army of staff in a hospital? Not many, I can tell you. That's not an upbringing – it's an extension of being a patient and not right at all.'

Eva reached into her apron pocket and, pulling out the green weighing slip, handed it to Ida.

'What's that?' Ida asked.

Eva took out another page, from the hospital notes and waited for Ida to take it from her hand. 'It's his clinic notes,' whispered Eva. 'He's not being looked after properly by anyone. He's losing weight and they are lying about him seeing the doctor. She doesn't even take him to the baby clinic! She pretends to, but I was watching and she didn't. They have made it all up.'

Ida looked at the notes and gasped. 'Eva, love, what are you doing with these notes? Why were you watching?' Ida felt her mouth go dry; something was very wrong and she suspected she was about to find out what. She studied Eva's face, the sallow skin, the brown eyes, the whites of her eyes tinged with yellow, her dark hair – and it was as if she had received a shock as she made the connection. But before she could voice the suspicions hovering around the edge of her thoughts, Eva put her out of her misery. 'Ida, he's my baby.'

Eva had played this moment over in her mind on the ship over so many times. She had practised the words, wondered how she would feel, only in her own rehearsals she had been talking to a policeman. She had thought she would cry, shake, be unable to speak, but there were none of the emotions she had thought would trip her up and rob her of the words she required to explain herself. She felt calm, in control. And she knew that here she had someone she thought may help her, who could be on her side.

'I am the mother who left him,' she said, 'only I didn't leave him. Ida, I am Jewish, from Poland. We fled before the war and hid and we were fleeing again from the Stalinist agents after the war. They caught up with us and my guardian, Benjamin, he wouldn't let me stay. The woman, his contact, she was at the customs hall to meet us and she gave me a tablet. I thought it was for the pain and I took it – but it wasn't for the pain, it drugged me. She told Benjamin that she would call the police, that someone would go and find my baby right away.' She began to cry.

Ida blinked, rapidly. 'Oh, Holy Mary Mother of God, I can see the resemblance! No one in their right mind would doubt that you are his real mother. He looks like you. But are you sure that's what happened? It all sounds pretty bloody fantastical to me?'

Eva nodded as she took her handkerchief out of her pocket. It occurred to Ida that even if she called the police there and then, Eva wouldn't move a muscle to resist. She was weak and done with running, that much was obvious. Ida needed time to think and the half-mopped floor would not wait.

'Eva,' she said, 'we are both off tomorrow night. After your sleep, come to my house – I'll write the address down – and we will decide what to do. Bertie will be at the pub so it will only be us. If you're his mother, you should have your baby. And I'll get the priest to help us – he'll know what to do. Hah, that'll teach him to pull a face at me in the confessional like he did when I told him I had written my letter, I could feel it, so I could. But here, have you got anywhere to live?'

'Only the Seaman's Stop,' said Eva, and she thought of Malcolm, of how Melly was leaving him, of how she could take her place. If she could get her baby back, she didn't think Malcolm would throw her out. She could feel a warmth in Malcolm and maybe it could be more... no, she *knew* it could. Since she'd seen the letters piled up under the lamp, she'd known Jacob had no intention of returning, had probably already forgotten her. So unlike Malcolm, who had made her feel welcome, looked at her with a mixture of pity and respect in his eyes. He made her feel safe, cared for, secure. She dared to hope that there might be a future there.

'I'll come,' she whispered. 'I will.'

Ida's eyes were bright, her face alight. 'Good. Right, now let's clean this place or we'll both be sacked. And don't you worry – we'll get you your baby back. And now I know what the hell is wrong with you with all your fainting and malarkey... it's distress at being separated from your own son.'

Ida was turning the mop in the bucket, wringing out the dirty water. Eva picked up her own and began mopping under a desk. Is that all the pains were? That she was distressed at being separated from her baby? In her heart, she thought not. The pains had begun a week after his birth, which she remembered vividly. Maja, trying not to panic, Louis coming quickly. Too quickly. The tears that had been left to heal without stitches and the pain – the pain which had just never gone away. If it hadn't been for the pain, she would never have taken the pill in the customs hall. She would have run, but at the wrong time, the worst time, she had been desperate to stop the pain and, as a result, lost her son. She lifted her head from her mopping and looked out of the window to see Emily and Dessie hurrying up the back path, Dessie with his arm around Emily and for the first time, she felt hopeful. Ida would help her. Soon, she would have her son back.

'I'm just popping into the sitting room,' said Ida. 'I'll be back in a minute.'

The phone book sat on Emily's desk next to her phone. Ida knew the name of the woman from children's services, they had given that out on the phone, but would not give her a home address. 'There can't be many Devonshires around this part of Liverpool,' she said to herself, and she was right, there was just one. She took a pencil out of the pot on Emily's desk, and a piece of paper from a pad and scribbled down the phone number and address.

'Right, you pop to Elsie's and I'll go to the pub and bring back a pint in my pot and a gin and orange squash for you. I think we have something to celebrate tonight.' He cupped his wife's face in his hands and he kissed her.

'Dessie, not in public,' said Emily as she pulled away.

Her husband grinned. 'I don't know how you do it, Emily, but you just did make everything right, didn't you?'

'I hope so. The fact that Dr Gaskell and Matron are going to see her together has to be a good sign, doesn't it. It's a big thing, them offering to do that. She won't say no to them and she will believe them.' Emily gave a big sigh and felt the weight fall from her shoulders. 'No one says no to Dr Gaskell. He knew my mam and my dad, you know.'

'I know he did,' said Dessie as he pulled her into him. 'That's why Dr Gaskell will make this work for you. And like the rest of us, he loves Louis too.'

Emily pushed Dessie away. 'Yes, and you are keeping him away from me with all this chatter. Go on, Mr Big Talk. Go and get us a drink and I'll be home with him in ten minutes. I promised Elsie I would let her know what happened. Biddy gave him mashed potato with gravy for lunch and you should have seen how fast it went down – he loved it. There's some in the pram for him, with mashed carrots. Is egg and chips okay for you?'

Dessie roared with laughter. 'It is. I know my place. Best steak gravy for our baby boy, egg and chips for me.'

Emily turned in through Elsie's back gate. She had never felt as relaxed as she did right now because she was free from the lie she had told Matron all those months ago. As she lifted the latch to Elsie's kitchen, her son, sitting on Elsie's lap, babbled out to her and put out his arms.

'Oh, it's you. That's good timing, because I need to stir up a bit of chocolate to put on a cake to take to Mavis's and there's no way I could do that with this wriggler around!'

Emily was stirring a bowl of cake mix, looked up and smiled.

'I couldn't help overhearing,' she said. 'Is it all sorted? Will you be able to stay at the hospital?'

Emily nodded. 'I think so. I'm sure, I mean. Matron and Dr Gaskell are going to see the lady from children's services and tell them what a happy little boy he is, aren't you?' She kissed her son on the temple and hugged him into her.

Elsie said, 'Emily, I heard about the complaint – if I find out who that was, I'll skin them alive. How dare they! God knows, we all love this lad to bits.'

'Do you know what, Elsie, I don't care. I have every faith in the plan Matron and Dr Gaskell have put together. He said he would go further if he had to, that he and his wife loved this little one. Matron also said that as I had been working and doing such a good job so far, there was no reason for me to stop, and I'm delighted about that, not least because I love singing the carols around the wards at Christmas time. It's funny what you realise you will miss when you are faced with it.'

'Don't you think it's funny how Mrs Gaskell has suddenly come onto the scene?' said Elsie, looking directly at Emily.

'No, not at all,' said Emily. 'I do think it's a good thing, though. She's a nice lady. A little quiet, but I expect you will bring her out of her shell, Elsie, you and Biddy together.'

'I'll try my best,' said Elsie, aware that she had failed in her quest for information. She suspected that Emily knew a lot more about the Doris Gaskell situation than she was letting on, but she wouldn't push her any further. In Elsie's book, everything happened for a reason and she was sure they would discover the reason for Mrs Gaskell's appearance into their lives soon enough.

Later that night, as they lay in bed, Emily in the crook of Dessie's arm, they were both silent, listening for the soft breathing of their son coming from the next room.

'How do you feel?' asked Dessie. 'You seemed happier tonight than you have for a long time.'

'I was. I am. I hadn't realised that a lie weighed so much. It'd pulled me down, to be honest, made me panicky, horrible. I'll never tell a lie again, I promise.' She reached up and kissed her husband gently on the lips.

'Did tonight's gin and orange do the trick?' He had turned onto his side and spoke into her ear as his lips found her neck and his hands her breasts.

Emily felt an immediate response along with a light-headedness she was unused to, brought on by the extra-large gin. 'Oh, I think it did,' she laughed as her own hands wandered down towards his belly and below. Dessie groaned with pleasure as he gently pushed Emily's legs apart and then they both stopped dead as a little voice cried out from the next room, 'Ma, Ma, Mama, Ma,' for the very first time.

Chapter 17

Dana packed her sewing box into her bag just as Beth and Pammy walked into her room. She was off for the day and so was Pammy who was on clinics and enjoying not having to work weekends in the weeks leading to Christmas.

'Mrs Tanner has asked for us all to take our sewing boxes with us,' said Dana and Beth held up a carpet bag for inspection.

'I've got mine to take to the wards. I'll see you at one thirty.'

'Aren't you going to go down for breakfast? You don't want to be late,' said Dana, with a wink to Beth who tucked her cape under her legs and sat on the edge of the unmade bed, her starched linen cap in her hand, ready to clip into place before she left.

'I've already been down, thank you very much, and I've come to tell you, Mrs Duffy is making you poached eggs because she's in a good mood.'

Dana smiled. 'The Christmas trees are coming this

morning, that's why she's happy. It's all go, sewing day today, finish off tomorrow, trees decorating, rehearsal for the carol concert in the main hall, decorating the children's ward, Victoria's party next week and then, wham, Christmas is upon us.'

Dana picked up a letter opener off her desk and began to tease the edges of an envelope as a tentative knock came on the door and then the face of Gracie peered around the corner.

'Oh, sorry,' she said. 'I thought you were on your way down, I was coming to give the room a clean.'

'Gracie, come in. You don't have to say you're sorry,' said Dana.

Pammy suddenly exclaimed, 'Gracie, I've just remembered something! You can sew, can't you?'

Gracie nodded. 'Me and Mam make all our lads pants for school and the dresses. Mam wants me to try the factories as a seamstress or a pattern cutter, but they won't take you on until you're sixteen.'

Pammy threw her arms around Gracie, making her smile. 'God, I love you,' she said. 'You don't fancy coming to our house when you finish today, do you? To give a hand with the seams? We've got four dresses to knock out and now Victoria wants a panel put in. Between all of us, it's doable, but I'm no way as skilled with a needle as you and me mam. There'll be a good spread.'

Dana laughed. 'Aye, and the craic is always good too. You'll enjoy it, Gracie. I know I always do.'

Gracie wanted to tell them to stop. They didn't have to persuade or entice her. Just to be a part of their day, to be invited out, even if it was just because she could sew, made her feel included and she felt a warmth flow through her.

'I'll just have to go home first and let Mam know where I am. What time?' Gracie asked.

'Oh, you are a love,' said Pammy, who squeezed her tight again. 'We are off after breakfast, but look, if you need to do anything to help at home first, just come when you can. Mam is making a pan of scouse for us all for our dinners. Honest to God, she makes it on a Saturday in a ship-sized pan, if you know what I mean. Tell your mam to send your kids down to ours and we'll feed them – then she won't need to cook today and she'll be able to spare you.'

Gracie grinned. 'Right, I will.'

'And I'm off. I can't be late because Antrobus is on earlies – you going down to breakfast?' said Beth.

'Yes, I'm coming,' said Pammy.

Dana was scanning her letter. 'I'll be down in a moment,' she said and the two nurses left without a backward glance.

'Do you want me to leave?' asked Gracie.

Dana looked up, distracted. 'No, I'll only be a minute,' she said as she sat on the edge of the bed.

Gracie, who knew when to be quiet, began to polish the desk and averted her gaze, but not before she saw the tears spring to Dana's eyes as she read her letter.

Dear Dana,

I am beside myself with grief. For the man I was, the couple we were and for all that I have lost. I don't blame you for not wanting me back. I wouldn't blame you for wanting me dead. All I want is for you to know that I think of you every waking moment of my day. That if I could turn the clock back, I would. That I know I have no excuse but I am compelled to let you know, for all of my life, I will never be able to forgive myself for what I did to you. I will live with that guilt – and hopefully you will go on to meet someone who will treat you like the angel you are, love you as you deserve to be loved and respect you in a way I catastrophically failed to do. I will love you to the end of my days, my heart scarred with the footsteps you left, to remind me of what I had and then lost.

I will love you forever,
Yours, the biggest fool that ever lived,
Teddy.

A pain burnt in Dana's heart and her eyes stung. She felt a familiar surge of anger rise and almost consume her. How right he was in all that he had written – he *had* failed to respect her or love her. He had cheated on her, treated her abominably. There was no way back from that. It was over, forever, and all he had done by writing to her was to try to weaken her resolve, to reopen the pain and the hurt. How dare he! She saw a flicker in the corner of her eye – a handkerchief that Gracie held out towards her.

'Thank you,' she said and half smiled as she dabbed at her eyes. 'Sorry, I'm a bit of a fool.'

'No you aren't,' said Gracie in a very matter-of-fact manner. 'My mam cries all the time and she's no fool. Best woman in the world, my mam. It's men who are the fools. You should meet my da. He's the biggest of the lot.' Dana looked into the earnest face of the fifteen-year-old who could clean, sew, help run the nurses' home and take a view of the world that in Dana's eyes, appeared to be about right.

'I'd better go for breakfast,' said Dana as she patted Gracie on the hand. 'Otherwise Scamp will be licking his lips. See you later at the Tanners'.'

Gracie grinned. 'I can't wait,' she said.

The school of nursing was closed at weekends and that was one of the reasons Biddy loved her job so much. No shifts, no weekends and a pattern that never altered, a bit like her life.

'I'm getting me Christmas shopping done today,' she said to Elsie. 'I'm going into town, to look for some ideas for our baby Louis. He has that much stuff it's hard to know what to get for him. I've got him for the day and then I'm going to take him to the grotto in Lewis's.'

'He's too young for Father Christmas,' said Elsie. 'He won't have clue what's going on.'

'I wish I knew what was going on,' said Biddy. 'Emily and Dessie are happy, though, that's all that matters. She wanted to come with me but I said to her, when are you going to mark those exam papers, then? Christmas Day, eh? Those nurses are expecting their results before then.'

Elsie was kneeling on a mat on the street, cleaning her front step and Biddy was on her way to Emily's house to collect Louis.

'There's a lot going on, isn't there?' said Elsie as she leant back on her heels, the back of her headscarf lifting in the cold breeze. 'Where is that snow they said was coming, that's what I would like to know? I don't like to go out in the snow, you know that.'

Biddy held the strap of her handbag before her and looked up at the heavy grey sky. 'You can't trust the weather men on the telly,' she said. 'The man after the news on the radio is more accurate. He says no snow and I believe him.'

Elsie, sprightly for a woman of her age, sprang to her feet and picked up her bucket. 'I'd better crack on, I don't want to miss the bus. Are you at Mavis's tonight?'

'I am,' said Biddy, 'although my fingers are that cold, I'm not sure I'll be that much use at sewing.'

Elsie closed the door and as Biddy made her way towards Emily's house, she decided that after she had collected Louis, she would call into Malcolm's. She would let Louis have his morning sleep, give him a bottle, and then carry on into town. Malcolm had been out of sorts since Melly had told him she was leaving and she would let him know he was not to worry, that she would help him find the right person to help out. He couldn't worry before Christmas.

As she reached Malcolm's door, Louis was fast asleep in the pram. It had been a struggle to prise him out of Emily's arms.

'I'm sure I can mark the papers while he is in the room,' she had said.

'No, you can't, Emily,' Biddy had said firmly. 'I'm taking him with me. If we are out of your way, you can get them all finished today.'

'He may not be of royal blood but he may as well be a prince,' said Emily, 'he's that much fought over.' She smothered her son in kisses as he flung himself forwards and collapsed into a rapture of helpless giggles. 'He called me mam, last night,' Emily said to Biddy, her voice full of pride.

'Well, that's as it should be, because you are – and the best one I've ever known too. Was everything all right, with Matron?' Biddy looked worried. Matron was a stickler for the rules and it could easily be that she had chosen not to support Emily for not having done the right thing.

The smile had fallen from Emily's face. 'Matron was fine. She and Dr Gaskell are going to see the old bat,

Miss Devonshire, today and Dr Gaskell suggested he take Dr William with him.'

'Really,' said Biddy, 'why?'

'Well, he's Louis' own doctor – he saw him when he had a cold and then an ear infection and he knows how much I panicked. As he said himself, it was quite a remarkable and pathetic performance from me, considering that I am a trained nurse. I was a wreck on both occasions if you remember.'

Biddy fastened Louis' harness to the side of the pram and puffed up the pillow behind him to make sure he was comfortable. Louis stuck his thumb in his mouth, sucked hard and looked up at Biddy as if waiting for something. She rubbed the top of his head with her hand and gave him a smile filled with such affection, he removed his thumb and beamed up at her.

'You old heartbreaker you,' she said. 'And yes, Emily, I remember it well; no one can ever doubt how much you love this one. If you ask me, it's the letter of complaint that is the big hurdle to get over. Someone out there has it in for you, Emily, and it's not nice to know, but God himself knows that you and Dessie have been the best and that's all they need to know – but with Matron on your side, all will be well. She's not God, but she runs a close second.'

Now Biddy flicked the brake on the pram and knocked on Malcolm's door. She didn't have to wait long for him to answer.

'Oh, you've got the little lad with you,' he said as he peered in the pram.

'I have and I'm just going to leave him out here to finish his sleep before I give him his bottle and carry on into town and I thought, what better place to call than here for a nice cuppa before I go.'

'Will he be all right out here?' asked Malcolm as he looked down the street. 'Not too cold, is it?'

There were two prams containing sleeping babies within view and Biddy smiled. 'Malcolm, babies sleep best outside in the pram in all weathers.'

'I'm sure you're right,' said Malcolm. 'Come on in, Melly's doing the rooms.' Malcolm walked into the kitchen, drawn by the pied piper effect of the whistling, steaming kettle as Biddy hovered in the hall.

'She's already mopped in there, I'm not going in in my outdoor shoes.'

'Don't worry, I'll bring a tray through,' said Malcolm and as he pottered about, placing cups on saucers and pouring milk into a jug, Biddy picked up the envelopes on the hall table.

'Malcolm, have you ever thought that these letters might be important? I mean, he obviously isn't coming back, is he? Why don't you open them, see who it is who is writing and put the poor girl out of her misery?'

Malcolm walked out of the kitchen and into the parlour. 'The thought has crossed my mind, but you know, the last one came from America and that put me off.

I've spoken to some of the sailors and they all tell me they haven't seen sight nor sound of him since Jacko gave him the first one in Rotterdam. Told me he was last heard of en route to the West Indies.'

'Aye, well, we know what happens there, don't we?' said Biddy disapprovingly as she took the tea Malcolm gave her. 'And half of them never come back.'

Eva walked slowly up the street. She had worked out herself that the pains were worse the quicker she walked and that if she took her time, she could breathe through them, hold them at bay for a little longer. The heat and the light-headedness was harder to deal with, but she had been to the chemist and bought the Disprin, minus the whisky, that Malcolm had given her, and for a short time that helped. Then, as she got nearer to Malcolm's door, she saw the pram and stopped dead in her tracks. Her heart beat so fast she could feel it hammering against her ribs and breathing became difficult. Her hands were in her coat pocket and between her fingers, she felt the slip of paper that Ida had written her address on.

'Come round to my house after you've had a sleep and we'll decide what we are going to do,' she'd said. 'If he's your baby, you should have him and as far as I'm concerned, there's no law in the land that would separate a mother from her child. We will find a way, Eva.

All the problems of the world have been solved around a kitchen table.'

Eva doubted that was true, but Ida was offering hope and that invitation, after so long with none, was irresistible.

At first, her legs would not move; she placed her hand on the brick wall of the Silvestrian pub next to her, to steady herself, and looked around. Everyone lived in the back of their houses and used the back entries and the street was empty. She took one tentative step and then another, and within minutes her hands were on the chrome handle.

'Elijah,' she gasped his name, and looked into the pram.

His head was turned to one side, his arms splayed up and around him. A faint smile played on the corner of his lips – he was dreaming. Eva could no longer see as the tears filled her eyes and she lost all sense of reason as, with one last blurred glance up and down the street, she bent down, silently dropped the brake and, placing both hands on the pram handles, walked as swiftly as she could down the street.

Biddy heard a noise outside, looked up at the net curtains on the front room window, and saw a woman with a bowed head passing by, pushing a pram.

'Well, if you ask my opinion, I think you should open the letters,' she said. 'You just never know, Malcolm. You could put some poor girl out of her misery.'

Malcolm rose. 'Do you know what? I'm sick of looking at them,' he said. 'And, truth be told, it's been at least three months since the last one; do you really think we should, Biddy?'

'Aye, go on,' said Biddy. 'It can't do any harm and the best thing that can happen is if there's an address you can return the letters to. Let some poor girl move on with her life, eh?'

Melly tutted as she wiped the condensation from the bedroom window with a cloth. It was cold outside and the warmth from the paraffin heater and the sleeping bodies had long gone, leaving the wet windows and black encroaching crusts of mould for Melly to clean away.

'God, there has to be more to life than this,' she said as she wrung the cloth out into her bucket. As she bent to clean the lower panes, she saw Eva walking away, pushing the pram. She must have offered to take the baby for a walk, to give Biddy a break, she mused and then, thought nothing more of it as she turned to make the bunks.

Chapter 18

Dr Gaskell had been on the phone in his hallway for almost fifteen minutes and as Doris finished her jobs in the kitchen, she kept glancing towards the cupboard. The pills were whispering her name, enticing her over. She dried her hands on a tea towel. And considered removing the bottle and tipping the contents down the sink. I don't need you, she thought, not one little bit. No, it wasn't easy, but she had become very well aware that keeping busy was the key to her future success. She never wanted to spend another morning sitting in the fireside chair in a haze, waiting for the hours to pass.

She moved towards the cabinet, heard the receiver ding in the hallway and her husband's footsteps as he walked slowly back into the kitchen. She could tell instantly, by his slow and weighty tread, something was wrong. She removed her hand from the cabinet handle and turned to face him with a bright smile.

'Who was that? It's a Saturday. Something wrong at the hospital or has your golf partner cried off?' she asked, knowing that both events could be treated with equal dismay. He looked distracted as he rubbed his chin and almost fell over a large bag in the hallway.

'Doris,' he shouted, 'what on earth is all this?'

'Oh, I'm sorry, it's my sewing stuff. I'll be off in a minute. Not that you would have a clue what I'm up to, seeing as how you didn't get home until gone eleven and missed out on supper with your own son and Teddy.'

Dr Gaskell slapped his hand to his forehead.

'Don't bother with an excuse,' she said. 'I've heard them all before. And why is it my sewing bag is a problem? You have just swerved to miss your own golf bag.' She bent down and lifted her bag from the rug onto the chair.

Dr Gaskell smiled at his wife who had recently morphed into a new woman, one he didn't know; and it dawned on him that he found this new woman, who was answering him back, quite exciting.

'Well, Mrs Know-it-all, I can guarantee, you won't have heard this one.'

Doris raised her eyebrows. 'Try me,' she said. 'Only don't take long – I don't want to be late at Mavis's house.'

'Mrs Tanner's?' He looked even more surprised. 'From the WVS? Nurse Tanner's mother?'

'Yes, the very same Mrs Tanner. The nurses need dresses running up for Nurse Davenport's party and I said I would help – although there is no way I am going to ask about the provenance of the fabric. When I remarked on it sounding like such beautiful silk fabric, one you would struggle to find as good in George Henry Lee's, I heard the words "fell off the back of a ship" and I changed the subject, quick.'

Now her husband did laugh out loud. 'Well, they do live on the dock streets and by those very docks, they thrive or fail,' he said. 'Look, Doris, I'm sorry about last night, there has been a bit of a catastrophe at the hospital and that was Dr William I was on the phone to. A letter of complaint has been sent into children's services about the way Emily and Dessie have been raising Louis and, well, one of the conditions of the pre-adoption fostering, was that Emily gave up work.'

'But she hasn't,' she said. 'She was telling me at Matron's drinks that her nurses were sitting exams that week.'

'That's right, she hasn't, and children's services are being very difficult about it. She was also less than honest with Matron, but Matron understands why and, to be frank, that is the least of their worries, or should I say, our worries.'

Doris picked up the teapot to empty it down the sink. 'Do you want another cup, there's one left in here?'

He shook his head and said, 'Doris, I think that they may be about to lose Louis.'

'About to lose him? That's not possible!' The smile Louis had given her, the moments of bonding while she had fed him had lit a torch in her heart.

'I'm afraid it is true. Matron has telephoned the new woman who runs children's services – and you know as well as I do that Matron can work miracles. It would appear, however, not to be the case this time. This nightmare of a woman apparently received a second letter of complaint, just before Matron telephoned her, pushed through her own letter box this morning, with pages from Louis' hospital notes, showing that he is failing to attend appointments and has lost a considerable amount of weight.'

Doris was shocked. 'I fed him myself,' she said. 'He was a bouncing healthy weight. Considering what he was like a few months ago, it is quite remarkable. Does this mean that it's someone from the hospital making the complaints?'

'It looks that way. I had him on my knee last night,' said Dr Gaskell as he slipped his hands into his trouser pockets and began to pace the floor. 'Emily came to see Matron and I, to confess what she had done – even Dessie didn't know that she had carried on working without permission – and to be honest, without these letters of complaint, it would have been an easier battle to fight. As it is, Miss Devonshire has just told me she won't see Dr William or I and would we do her the courtesy of driving around to Emily and Dessie's house, as we are so concerned, to let them both know – and there were no ifs or buts – that she will be collecting Louis later today, to take him to Strawberry Fields children's home just as soon as they confirm that they have a cot available.'

Dana and Pammy were the first to arrive at Mavis's house where a line of children were standing at the kitchen door, having gloves, hats and scarves inspected by the lady of the house.

'Now,' she said, 'off, the lot of you – and if one of you comes back with a scarf missing, you'll feel the back of my slipper across your backside, do you hear.'

There was a chorus of 'Yes, Mam', then the children all shouted 'Pammy!' and jumped up to kiss their older sister, before running out into the entry, pushing and shoving, squealing and shouting as they did so.

'If they had to knit the scarves themselves, they wouldn't lose them, I can tell you,' said Mavis. 'Our Lorraine is at the college and God, I do miss her looking after them. Go on, into the front room, you two, I've got everything laid out. I'm just going to put a flame under this pan and then I can leave it to simmer all morning and I haven't got to worry about the food then. The crew from the *Queen Elizabeth* could walk in through our door unannounced and there'd be enough. Mind you, sometimes I think our Stan could eat enough for ten men and look at the size of him – Skinny Stanny I call him. I'll drop the spuds in at twelve and bingo, we're onto a winner, eh, Dana?'

Dana laughed. She didn't think she had ever met anyone in her life as full of life as Mavis Tanner.

'I just hope Mrs Gaskell doesn't turn her nose up at it. I mean, I said to our Stan, I have no idea what the likes of the lah-di-dahs eat. I never see anyone down our shops without curlers in – and even when I popped around to their house, which is lovely, by the way – there she was, she doesn't even wear a housecoat.'

'Is she definitely coming?' asked Pammy.

'She is, and with Beth and Victoria, Madge, Doreen, Gracie, Biddy, and Elsie that's a army. Easy-peasy, eh, girls? We'll have those dresses knocked out in no time.'

Dana walked into the lounge and saw two bolts of fabric leant up against the wall. One was an emerald green satin and the other a black shot silk, while a wad of cream organza sat on the table with a navy-blue silk next to it. The girls gave a sharp intake of breath.

'Where did this come from?' gasped Dana.

Pammy looked at her and grinned. 'My mam's done well.' The blow of a ship's horn filled the room. 'See that ship down on the docks? Me da will have met one of the sailors down the pub. That's how. We might be poor down on the dock streets, but we rarely go without. Right, me mam's got everyone's measurements written down somewhere, so let's get everything ready while we wait for the others.'

*

Doris Gaskell lowered herself into the chair; she felt shocked to her core. She had seen with her own eyes the bond between Emily and Louis, could not believe that the child was about to be taken off her.

'It's a disaster, it is a complete catastrophe,' she said as she looked up to her husband.

'I told you it was,' he said as he pulled out the chair next to her. He placed his elbows on the table. 'There was no reasoning with Miss Devonshire, I'm afraid, she would hear none of it. I tried my best.'

Doris looked straight at him. 'Miss Devonshire, you say. As in Dukie?'

'Who?' her husband asked.

'Dukie, she worked down at the shipping office with me, very well-to-do. Her fiancé died in the war and left her in difficult circumstances.' She pushed the chair back and rose to her feet. 'Are you still going to see her with Dr William?'

'No,' her husband said, looking mildly confused. 'There's no point. I've just asked Dr William to come here so that we can both go and tell Emily and Dessie that the baby is being taken off them. I've told many people many things, and many of them have been the worst news, and God himself knows I've never been one of those doctors who could just shrug it off, but this... this is different. I know and work with Emily and Dessie. This will break her heart and hasn't she been through enough losing her entire family in the Blitz?'

'No, you are not going to Emily and Dessie's house. You are both taking me to Miss Devonshire's house and she can hear from me before you both do anything. Right, where's my hat?'

Chapter 19

Biddy fetched the letters and placed them in front of Malcolm. He peered at them as though Biddy had placed a nest of cockroaches on his dining table.

'I can't open them, I feel guilty,' he said. 'I mean, isn't it illegal to open someone else's mail?'

'Malcolm, you've said yourself, he isn't coming back. It's up to you, but I would find out who is sending them and then put them all into one envelope and return to sender. Hurry up, because I'll have to go and check on the baby in a minute.'

Malcolm opened the first letter and began to read it out loud; only when he got to the bottom did the colour leave his face.

Dear Jacob,
I am going to push this letter through the door of your lodgings and I don't have long to write it. I am in desperate trouble. I think I am having your baby and

I haven't heard anything from you for weeks. You said you would be back within three months and there has been no sign of your ship. I have told Maja and I thought she would be angry, but she was so kind. However, she doesn't want me to tell Benjamin. He is always worried and suspicious. Always looking over his shoulder for the Gestapo. Sometimes I think he is going mad and others, that maybe he knows something he just won't tell us for fear of scaring us.

Maja said it would be better to wait until you come home and then you and I can tell him together. Maja has told Ben that she wanted me to give up work at the café and to be at home with her because her bones are aching and he agreed. He always let me keep the money from the café and I have it saved.

Ben is always receiving news from Poland. He says that a net like a spider's web has been thrown across the world and that everyone who fled Poland in the war will be found and have to pay Poland back. Ben has a contact from home that he meets every week, a woman. She has been to the house to talk to both Maja and I and I will not tell her my predicament. Maja says she was a spy during the war and now she works against the new regime.

Please, Jacob. The second you come ashore and read this letter, run to the house. Come to me. I can only do this with you at my side. I believed you when you said you loved me and you know I love you – how could I

*not? Our love has given us more than we thought before
we could marry. Come safely home, my love, and then,
run to me.*

Your Eva

Malcolm looked up at Biddy, his hand trembling, and
the paper crackled as it slipped from his fingers onto
the table. 'Biddy, these letters – they've been written by
Eva.'

'What, your Eva, the girl who is staying here?'

'Yes, it has to be the same one. How many Evas do
you know in Liverpool? It all fits into place now, the way
she looked at those letters on the stand, the night she
arrived.'

'The poor girl! Well, there's no baby in tow so I wonder
what happened.'

'That's none of our business,' said Malcolm. 'Now I
feel really terrible; she's going to come back this morning
and see those letters have gone. What am I going to say?'
Malcolm had felt his heart slide down into his boots and
he realised, with a shock of surprise, that his feelings for
Eva were strong.

'In for a penny, in for a pound I say,' said Biddy. 'Look,
why don't you open the next one? You can't put them
back with one missing.'

'I can't,' said Malcolm. 'I don't want to upset her.'

'Flamin' hell, Malcolm, you'll upset me if you don't.
Look, take my advice; best thing to do is to tell her he's

not coming back so you put the letters on the fire. That way, she can move on – and if you don't mind my saying, so can you.'

Malcolm removed his glasses. 'What do you mean, Biddy?'

Biddy dragged her chair across the rug and positioned it next to his. 'Malcolm, it's as plain as the nose on your face that you like her, don't you?'

Malcolm thought, his face flushed, and a light sprang into his eyes as he turned to Biddy. 'I do.'

'Well, lad, take my advice – you know I'm never wrong. Let's get those letters read and burnt, then you will know what you are dealing with.' Malcolm stared down at the pile. 'Oh, for goodness' sake, give them here.' And Biddy snatched the pile and opened the next letter.

Dear Jacob,

I feel as though I am at my wit's end. You haven't replied to my letter and you must surely have read it by now. My heart is breaking and I am so confused. I think that maybe you have it but have no way to post a letter back to me? Maja said that the tramp ship sailors had the best money, but the worst lives. She said they were the ships that took the cargos to the places others wouldn't. Jacob, you never told me that. Maja made it sound dangerous and I think you were just being brave and that when you told me you didn't know where you were sailing to after Portugal, you didn't tell me the truth to spare me the worry.

Maja told Ben about the baby, she had to. Our child refuses to be hidden and it is very obvious to anyone who would see me that I am pregnant. Ben lost his temper and has ordered Maja to make sure I stay indoors. He is not a bad man, he never shouts, but lately, he has been restless and anxious. Maja says it is because he received a letter from one of his friends who was in the orchestra with him in Warsaw and who escaped to London. Ben collects his post from a post box number in town, he doesn't even have the mail delivered here and he has been like a caged lion since that day. He insists we eat in the back of the house and now I am not even allowed out in the street until after the baby is born.

Ben has brought the car into the garage and he walks into town with his hat down and travels on the bus from Menlove Avenue, not from the bottom of our own road. Maja says he writes down all the details of every car he sees parked outside and checks the list each morning when he is on the bus. We have a story, that we have been living in London since before the war and came to Liverpool for Ben's job. No one in the Avenue knows what he does. They think he is a music teacher and we have never spoken to our neighbours. When they knock on the door, he won't allow us to open it.

Oh Jacob, I remembered the last conversation we had so well, when we sat on the bench looking out over the dock. Do you remember? There were so many stars shining on the black water. Your ship was the only one docked in the Princess dock that night and it creaked and groaned. I laughed and said it sounded like a moaning old man was watching us. The dock was empty apart from the two of us and I remember your words, you said that you would make one more journey on the tramp ship and then, when you came back, we would take the train to London and then onto Poland, together. You said you would take me back and with the money you had earned and I had saved, we had enough to make our own home. I remember your eyes, Jacob. You had the kindest eyes and then you kissed me for that last time and I thought I had fainted and gone to heaven. I feel closer to you, as though we have just spoken, and our baby is calmer because I know that the moment you can, you will come looking for me, for us.

Your loving Eva.

Melly walked into the room, clanking a mop and bucket at her side. 'I haven't mopped in here, yet,' she said as she folded her arms and glared at Biddy. She had never liked Biddy, liked Eva even less. 'Are those the letters off the rack?' She didn't wait for a reply. 'Thank God, I thought you were never going to get rid of them. I was going to chuck them myself if they hadn't gone by Christmas.'

Biddy wasn't listening, she was reading the next letter as fast as she could.

'Malcolm, I've put the meat from the butcher under a towel next to the sink, he just dropped it off,' Melly said. 'We need to check the weight – it was short weight last week.' But Malcolm wasn't listening. His eyes were fixed on Biddy and he was listening intently to her every word.

Dear Jacob,

Still no word and my time must be near. I feel in my heart that you are thinking of me, of us. I know you cannot have had the letters, or you would have replied. Every day Maja asks me the same questions: are you sure he said he was coming back? Are you sure he talked about marrying? She doesn't mean to upset me or to hurt me but now I no longer answer her questions, I make myself busy and in doing so, make my point.

Ben says that most Polish women have their babies at home and that I will too. He says that Maja knows what to do.

But Ben sounds more confident than Maja; I don't think she has any idea at all. She seems very nervous when I mention it. She has no children of her own so how can she possibly know what to do? Because Ben doesn't want me to be seen out in the Avenue, Maja walked down to the footpath and checked the way was clear before we left today and she said we would have to stay out until it was dark before we could come back home. I was so tired. We went to a café in town and

Maja kept saying all the time, 'Don't make eye contact with anyone, Ben would be so cross.'

I think something is very wrong. I am sure that Benjamin is imagining all of this and that when our baby is born, somehow, I have to get away. This environment is no good for either me or the baby and I cannot hide our son or daughter away. I love Maja and Ben so much, but it is all getting so much worse. He brings letters back from the group he visits on Mondays and shows them to Maja, but not to me. He and Maja read them when I wash up after supper and he is making Maja as mad as he is.

If you haven't returned before I run away, I will make sure to leave the address to let you know where I am at the Seaman's Stop. Our baby is oblivious to all of this is and keeps kicking me to let me know he or she is there. I wish you could see, my kochanie. When I am in bed at night, I whisper to our child and I say that if it is a boy, I will name him after my father and you, Elijah Jacob, and if it is a girl, after my mother, Ella. I wish I knew where it was your mother lived; I would run to her and tell her I was carrying your child and we needed somewhere to wait for you. This is all so hard to bear. Sail safely home and run to us,

Your loving Eva.

Melly leant on her mop. 'Silly cow. The docks are paved with broken hearts...'

The next letter was the last and much thicker than the others. Biddy felt a strong sense of foreboding and as she hesitated. She glanced towards the window; no sound from Louis. He must still be asleep. She would read this last letter and then she would bring him in, he had slept for long enough.

'Come on then, let's weigh the meat,' said Malcolm. 'How short was it last week?'

'Four ounces I'm guessing,' said Melly. 'I'm not saying he does it deliberate, mind, I mean he drinks in the Silly and I see him every night, it could be that lad of his, but it's worth checking.'

Their voices began to fade as they moved towards the kitchen. Malcolm glanced back. He wanted to know what the letter contained, but he also dreaded knowing, so he was happy for Biddy to read it alone...

Biddy slipped the final and longest letter out of its envelope. This letter was in an air mail envelope and had a postage mark from New York.

Dear Jacob,
I have given birth to our little boy, Elijah Jacob. We did not get to the hospital because Ben wouldn't let us, even though Maja pleaded with him. Elijah Jacob made an undignified entrance here on the bathroom floor, one week ago. We are not allowed out. I cried when Benjamin said that. I can bear anything, but not our baby being denied fresh air and sunshine.

I heard Maja and Benjamin arguing; she said he was going mad and the next day the Polish woman came to the house in a van and brought a pram which Benjamin put in the garage. Maja had made him tell her and to ask for her help. He has said that when the baby is ready for fresh air, he can go in the garage in the pram and that I may leave the doors open because they face the kitchen window, but only when he is asleep. He must not be allowed to cry and attract attention.

Elijah and I have been upstairs since he was born and Maja has been looking after us. I was sick and had a temperature and Maja and I thought we might have to call a doctor. Ben said that if I didn't get better, the Polish woman would bring a doctor, but first, she came to see me. Maja said she wasn't allowed to know the Polish woman's name, but she had come to Liverpool from London.

As soon as the woman left, Maja came upstairs with herb tea for me. 'I think something has happened in Liverpool,' she said. 'The woman said that the agents are here. She said they had only been in London until now, looking for those who came from Poland but now they were in Liverpool and Manchester and that they were brutes. She said that she was there to help the families who wanted to leave Liverpool now and take the ship to New York where there was more protection for Polish Jews. That they had set up a network for people to be received and helped when they got there.

Maja said we won't have to go, that Ben will never leave the orchestra behind. I hope Maja is right. I want to be here when you return. Even if we have to live as prisoners, hidden away, we will wait.

Your son, he has no hair yet. He does have your brown eyes and if I tell you that he is the most beautiful baby I have ever laid eyes on, I am not telling you the truth, because he is more than that. I cannot tear my eyes away from him. But I don't think I have enough milk for Elijah and he is too thin. Ben will only let Maja go out if she is with him and we aren't even allowed the lights on when it is dark, we sit in the back of the house in candlelight. Our precious son has woken from his sleep, I will continue tomorrow.

Jacob, I pray every day to God that you will soon return. I have faith in you. I know you are coming. I cannot think otherwise because if you don't, I fear something very bad is going to happen.

Dear Jacob,
I have little time to write. It is the last time Maja will leave the house before Benjamin returns and so I must be quick. The enforcement agents from Poland have found Ben and we have to leave tonight. He has told me that I cannot take Elijah, that I have to leave him at the gate to the children's home, Strawberry Fields. The community we are being taken to join in New York has not been told that I am an unmarried mother and

it may jeopardise their welcome to us if they know. Benjamin thinks people will be suspicious of him and wonder who the father is. I will not do this. By the time tonight arrives, I will have found some way for us to escape.

Ben has told the woman that I am his niece but he says people have evil minds and he says that you are not coming back to us. He does not know or understand you, my love. I know you are thinking about me right now, as I am thinking about you.

The woman brought some tablets for me. I have been sick since Elijah's birth. I wake in the night, hot and covered in perspiration and always shivering. I have had headaches that make it hard for me to move and I cannot lift my head up without effort and the pains in my belly make me feel so sick.

The woman has told Ben she already has a place for him with an orchestra in New York. I cannot go and leave Elijah behind. He is not well. He is too thin and pale but his eyes smile. I tell him about you every day. About how his daddy is working hard to save up money so that we can all return to live in Poland. Hurry. I feel as though something terrible is about to happen. There is a banging on the door, I have to go. Maja is taking this letter for me. Hurry, please.

'No need to open the rest of the letters. I think we know enough now,' said Biddy.

Malcolm and Melly walked back in as Biddy was folding the letter.

She felt sick to her stomach; the penny had dropped. Elijah was Louis. Eva was Louis' real mother. God, what was the right thing to do? She had to go to the police, there was no option, but Emily, Dessie? She rose to her feet and felt giddy herself.

'Shouldn't you be going now?' said Melly. 'Isn't it time that Eva brought the baby back?' Melly lit a cigarette as Biddy put her hand on the back of the chair to steady herself. She felt as though someone was tugging at the edges of the rug she was stood on.

'Bring what baby back?'

'Your baby, little Louis. I saw her take him fifteen minutes ago.'

'What do you mean, took him? Are you sure?' Her words ended on a shrill note and Melly looked more scared than cocky.

'Am I sure? Of course I'm sure. I thought you must have known.'

Biddy ran to the front door and flung it open. And then, in something that sounded between a shout and a scream, she yelled, 'Malcolm, call the police.'

Chapter 20

Ida wasn't used to anyone knocking on the front door, other than the rent man, and he came on Thursdays. 'Who the hell is this?' she said to the dog. 'Just as I'm about to go for my sleep.'

The knock came again, loud and impatient. 'Hang on, hang on, I'm coming,' she shouted, hurrying down the hallway. She flung open the door to see Eva standing there with the pram.

'I've got him,' she said. 'Can we come in?'

'Holy Mother of God,' said Ida. 'How the hell did you do that? Quick, go and push him down the back entry and in through the gate and leave the pram in the yard, I'll meet you at the back door.' She looked up to the sky and felt the first flakes of snow melt on her skin. 'Well, that's an omen if ever I saw one,' she said as she closed the front door and hurried to the yard.

*

Roland and Victoria were halfway to Liverpool when the pains began. 'Gosh, the Braxton Hicks are strong today,' she said. 'I think it was the bumpy road out of the village that did it. I can't say I'm actually looking forward to labour itself if the practice pains are this bad.'

Roland looked concerned. 'Do you want me to turn back?' he asked.

'Don't be a silly billy,' said Victoria. 'I was so excited about today, I could hardly sleep last night. Did you call Teddy?'

Roland grinned. 'I did indeed. He and Oliver and I are going to watch the football, so don't you worry about me. This is the best idea you have had this week! You sew and we go off to the match.' He grinned as he kept his eyes forward on the road.

Victoria would have answered if she could, but the Braxton Hicks were making her short of breath, so she couldn't. Instead, she grabbed the side of her seat and panted, waiting for it to pass.

Eva sat on the sofa in Ida's kitchen with her son on her knee. He didn't smile, but he did put his hand on her cheek, a look of confusion and bewilderment on his face.

'He knows it's me,' said Eva as she looked at Ida who was digging around in the back of a cupboard.

'We've got a spare bottle here. We've got more than

enough grandchildren. I always keep one in, just in case. I'll warm up some milk.'

'Ida, what do I do now?' said Eva. 'He was outside the house, so I hope Malcolm doesn't get the blame for me taking him. I don't know what he was doing there. Do you think Malcolm knew and got him for me?'

'I doubt it, love,' said Ida, placing her hand on Eva's brow. 'Are you hot, Eva?' she asked, with a kindliness Ida was unused to.

'I've been hot since he was born, it comes and goes. I've never been right since he was born.'

Ida poured the milk into a pan, as she spoke. 'Where did you have him?'

'On the bathroom floor, with Maja. She had never done anything like that before, but she did her best. Her and Ben, they never had children.'

'Where is Maja now?' Ida switched on the gas and checked under the pan to see that it was lit.

'Ben died of a heart attack on the boat on the way to America. I actually thought about throwing myself overboard on that day. I felt as though I was in a living hell.'

'Jesus wept,' said Ida. She was a woman who found pity a difficult emotion to muster, but faced with Eva in her kitchen, she managed. 'Where is Maja now then?' she asked.

'Maja is safe. She is living with a lady we met as soon as we arrived in New York. She and Maja knew each other's families and now Maja is staying with her. No one will come after her now.'

Louis' bottom lip wobbled and he became an eruption of tears and fretful emotion in no time at all. Eva looked scared, but not as scared as Louis.

'Don't worry,' said Ida with a tenderness she was unused to. 'He's just hungry. How did you get back here? It must have been expensive.'

Eva stood and bounced Louis on her hip, but it didn't work and the volume of his outpouring rose. 'Maja gave me some of the money out of the violin case that Ben had stored, to come back and get Elijah. She is waiting for me to go back and look after her; life is hard for her with Ben gone.'

'Elijah? A violin case?' Ida sounded incredulous. 'Eva, you are making no sense to me whatsoever. Look, what I think we do is give the baby a bottle and I'll go and see if we have any old nappies in our airing cupboard. Then we can take him in his pram to the house of the lady who runs children's services. She doesn't live far – I've already been to her house once today.' Ida winked at Eva and gave her a knowing smile.

Eva barely noticed as she cradled her son into her. She was pressing her son against the pain that was creeping into her belly, using the warmth of him to hold it down. She focused her mind on her son on her lap, on the smell of him, the softness of the skin on his hands, the wispiness of the dark hair she was kissing over and over again. But it wasn't working; the pain refused to abate, it was draining her, the pain, rising sharper and faster than before and this time her mind was failing her. She breathed in deeply, *not now, not now,* she thought, but she knew she was lost. With the relentless speed with which the pain was rising, she would not be able to stand. Her peripheral vision began to blur, her son in her arms felt too heavy.

'Ida,' she whispered, but Ida wasn't listening. She was rinsing out a bottle under the tap.

'I put the green sheet in an envelope and wrote to her that the baby wasn't being looked after properly. She doesn't need to know that was me, though, so don't say anything when we get there. Let's just get him ready and go – you can explain everything to her. He's your flesh and blood, and you will be keeping him.' She lifted the net curtain up on the window above the sink. 'God Almighty, would you look at that. It's snowing, we had better get a wiggle on.' As Ida poured the milk from the pan into the bottle, the sound of a police car's siren ringing out its urgency filled the room.

Emily had made a good start on the exams. The post-operative care of an appendicectomy was written across the top of the paper before her. She smiled; the scores had been good, her second term nurses had been paying attention. The back door opened and startled her as

Dessie walked in and banged his boots on the coconut hair mat.

'Oh hello, I thought you had an oxygen delivery to meet?'

'I did,' said Dessie, 'but it arrived early because they were expecting the snow and the night porter checked off most of it.'

Emily sat back on the chair and watched as her husband removed his brown coat and, without a word, walked over, took her hands in his and lifted her to her feet.

'What?' she asked.

'Well, I was thinking, if Biddy has taken Louis out for most of the day, and I'm home early, we can finish off what we started last night.'

Emily giggled and they both ran up the stairs to the sound of a police car's siren passing down the road. Dessie stopped in his tracks.

'What's up?' asked Emily.

'Nothing, it's a police car, not an ambulance; just making sure it wasn't turning in through the hospital gates but it hasn't, it's carried on to the docks. Now, move!' He clapped his hands behind Emily and made her squeal as she ran into the bedroom before him.

Matron heard the siren too and turned the chair from her desk to the window and watched the progress of the police car as it passed by the gates of the hospital. She bent and stroked Blackie's head. 'Not for us, thank goodness Blackie. We need a quiet day. Look at that snow.'

Down in the yard, she saw Jake hauling Christmas trees onto a trailer he had attached to the back of his van. Matron felt a thrill of excitement run through her. She had no one of her own. The hospital, the patients and its staff, they were her family. She rose and walking over to the stationery cupboard, wheeled out a horse on wooden runners and castors.

'We had better get this wrapped up and put next to the tree, Blackie, ready for Louis to open.' She stroked the mane of the horse and sighed. She knew nothing of the second complaint or the edict issued by Miss Devonshire that she would be taking Louis to Strawberry Fields. As far as she was concerned, Dr Gaskell and Dr William would have worked their charm and magic and all would be well. She glanced at the phone on her desk, willing Dr Gaskell to call with some good news.

Elsie arrived at Mavis's just as Roland pulled up outside and sprang out to open the door for Victoria.

'Well, would you look at you,' said Elsie. 'You look a bit flushed – are you all right?'

'She insisted on having the heater on,' said Roland. 'I'm off to the match so will you look after her for me, Elsie?'

'Of course I will, Roland, off you go. We'll see you later.'

Victoria stood and waved off her husband, who stopped at the end of the road to let the police car past.

'Flippin' heck, that was going fast,' said Elsie as they walked in through the back door. 'Hope it's not for the hospital. Be careful with the snow, Victoria. It's not sticking but it will be slippy.'

'I'm only having a baby, Elsie. I just said to Roland, even the Queen does that without too much fuss.'

'Yes, well, to your Roland you are his princess and he's worried about you.'

'Honestly, we've got three weeks to go. You would think the baby was coming any day the way he behaves.'

Elsie smiled and kept her thoughts to herself. She wasn't sure that Victoria even had three *days* and she had no idea why they were all there to sew the dresses because any idea of a party was pie in the sky. She wondered if she should tell Victoria and decided against. 'Here we are, here's Victoria, everyone,' she said as she walked in through the door.

The kitchen at Mavis's house was a hive of activity within minutes. 'Will you check my waist, Mam?' said Pammy. 'I'm sure I've put weight on.'

'It had better be only weight, my girl,' said Mavis.

'Mam!' said Pammy, affronted. 'Of course it is – what a thing to say!'

At that moment, everyone turned to Victoria and Pammy slammed her hand across her mouth. 'Oh Vic, I'm so sorry, I didn't mean...'

Victoria waved her apology away. 'Pammy, it's fine. *I'm* fine. I'm a married woman, and honestly, I'd be cross with you too if it wasn't just a bit of weight.'

Everyone laughed, crisis averted. Madge was at the sink, her preferred place where sewing was concerned. Elsie placed a cup and saucer in the bowl and both women faced the window.

'Does she know that baby is coming early and about to drop any minute?' said Madge.

'She does not,' said Elsie as she rinsed the cup.

'Are you going to tell her? She's never going to be having a party.'

'I know that,' said Elsie, 'but there won't be a bit of use in anyone telling her. I remember when I began stripping the wallpaper in the kitchen. Everyone told me I'd be having the baby in the middle of it and I wouldn't listen to a word anyone said. I still carried on. I almost had my baby on the pasting table. What will be will be and the frocks will always come in useful – and let's face it, they won't have cost anything.'

Both women turned and looked at Victoria, her arms held up in the air while Mavis cut a piece of wide elastic next to her.

'Mavis won't be telling her either,' said Elsie as she left Madge to dry the cups.

Gracie was cutting out a piece of cloth according to Mavis's instructions.

'Can you hold the end for me please, Doreen?'

'I've never seen such a beautiful bolt,' said Doreen as Madge shouted, 'Right, count me out of the sewing for now, I'll make the butties. I'm always happier in the kitchen, anyway and you know me, Mavis, I'm good at zips and buttons but I can't sew a straight seam to save my life.'

'I'll do your seams,' said Doreen, 'you make nice butties. Can I have my egg with salad cream? Did anyone bring any Battenberg?'

Gracie looked uncomfortable. 'I'm sorry, I didn't know to bring anything and I haven't been home.'

Only Gracie knew that even if she had been home, there would have been nothing to bring with her. Her money had to spread far and wide at home and, with Christmas coming, every penny was accounted for.

'Oh, Gracie, love,' Mavis said, 'you weren't expected to bring anything, for goodness' sake and I'll tell you what, if your mam doesn't mind, there will be loads of leftovers – do you think your kids would fancy them for tomorrow?'

Gracie's eyes lit up. 'Oh, of course she won't mind. Thank you, Mrs Tanner,' she said and flushed with pleasure.

'Don't you be thanking me, love,' said Mavis. 'Madge goes a bit mad when she makes the butties, you'll be doing me a favour. And there's no shortage of cake here. We made too many for the WVS so you can take some home for Christmas.'

Gracie had never felt happier. Her mam loved cake.

Granny Ida and Granda Bertie would bring food round to the house on Christmas Eve so the family never went hungry at Christmas, but they always argued with their son and the Christmas atmosphere left as soon as they arrived.

Suddenly everyone stopped talking and looked towards the back door when they heard someone shouting and running down the path.

'It's Melly from the Seaman's Stop,' said Elsie. Not someone Mavis approved of due to the amount of time she spent down in the Silvestrian.

'What's that woman doing here?' said Doreen as she removed a row of pins from between her teeth. Doreen didn't care for her much, either.

She didn't have long to wait for her answer as the back door burst open, and Melly, holding onto her side with her hands, tried to catch her breath.

'Oh, God in heaven,' she spluttered as she bent over. Mavis was already at her side, as was Elsie. They were all silent, fearful, something was very wrong. Mavis had lived through the war, as had Elsie, they had known the worst, heard the worst and lived through hell. Nothing could truly faze them and it had left them able to recognise danger before it fully revealed itself.

'What is it, Melly?' asked Mavis as she held onto her arm and Elsie guided her towards the table.

'Here, sit in the chair,' Elsie said as she pulled a chair out. 'Pammy, get some water. Tell us what it is, Melly!'

'It's the baby, the one who belongs to the Sister Biddy works for.'

'Sister Horton?' said Elsie.

'Louis?' said Mavis.

Melly took a gulp of the water. 'That's right, that's the one. He's been kidnapped. Disappeared into thin air, he has, with that Polish girl who's cleaning at the hospital.'

The room fell quiet. Gracie stopped cutting the fabric and placed the scissors on the table.

'Why would she do a thing like that? Where would she take him?' asked Mavis. Panic was rising but she needed more information.

'I have no idea,' said Melly. 'She doesn't know anyone. She lives at Malcolm's place so she has nowhere to take him. Biddy left him outside in the pram for a sleep and from the upstairs window I saw Eva take him. I thought nothing of it, thought Biddy must have known, but Biddy, she's told the police she thinks the Polish woman is his real mum come back to get him.'

The air left the room as everyone gasped. Each one knew the circumstances of his life and the fear Emily and Dessie had lived with, falling in love with the child, counting the days to his adoption.

'The police have searched her room and there's money in her bag and even a passport because she came here from America.'

A heavy silence fell, broken by Mavis. 'Does Emily know?'

'No, she doesn't. Biddy is with the police and I have to go back because I saw her take him. Biddy said to tell you, Mavis, to get to Emily before the police do. The police have more cars coming and they are driving around the streets like maniacs, looking for her.'

A small voice piped up, 'I think I might know where she is.'

Mavis turned to the youngest person in the room. 'You, Gracie? How, love? What has it got to do with you?'

'I know the Polish lady is working on nights with my nan and I know my nan did a very bad thing – she wrote a letter to the children's services complaining about how Louis was being raised. Grandad told me because he wasn't happy about it.'

There was another sharp intake of breath around the room.

'That doesn't surprise me in the least,' said Elsie. 'I'm afraid she was always a bitter one, your nan, Gracie.'

Madge placed her arm around Gracie's shoulders. 'Don't worry, it's not you,' she said.

'Well, come on then, Melly, come with me. We need to take Gracie to the police to give them this information,' Mavis said and grabbed her coat off the back of the kitchen door. 'Elsie, you come with me to Emily's. This is going to be bad and it will take both of us.'

A piercing scream filled the room that made everyone jump.

'Oh, Holy Mother of God,' said Mavis, 'Victoria, you're in labour.'

'No, I'm not,' Victoria gasped. 'It's just the Braxton Hicks, I'm practising. The pain, it's just a bit of wind.'

'Pass me her coat, would you, Mam?' said Pammy.

Mavis began lifting coats down from the nail on the door.

'Don't no one tell Mrs Duffy anything,' said Mavis, 'she'll go out of her mind.'

'She'll have to go some to catch up with Biddy,' said Melly.

'I bet,' said Pammy. 'You go to the police, Dana and I will get this one to the hospital.'

'No, no, really, it's just wind,' said Victoria.

Mavis shook her head. 'Victoria, love. You'll be feeding that wind a bottle in a few hours. I don't think you've got very long by the looks of you and you are best up at the hospital because we all have to go now – and anyway, Emily is always banging on that the first should be in the hospital.'

'Come on, Doreen, you come with me. Let's go and man the switch,' said Madge. Everyone was heading out of the door when she asked, 'Does anyone know where Mrs Gaskell is? She was supposed to be coming this morning.'

'I have no idea,' said Elsie as she turned out of the gate, linking arms with Mavis and heading down to the Dock Road, while Gracie and Melly made their way back to

Malcolm's and Pammy and Dana hooked onto Victoria, one on each side, and Madge and Doreen made their way up to the hospital.

'She's probably had enough of us lot already and gone back to being the hermit,' said Madge. 'Can't say I blame her – look at the state of us, kidnapped babies, satin gowns all over the show, a baby about to be delivered miles from home and, to cap it all, it's snowing. Hardly the bridge set, are we?'

Chapter 21

As if by a miracle, they had just stepped over the entrance to the receiving ward when the noise Victoria made ensured they were noticed as Sister Pokey and Teddy came running over.

'Oh goodness me, what is going on here?' said Sister Pokey. 'No, forget that, a very stupid question. Lovely to see you back with us, Nurse Davenport, it's a contraction, just breathe through it, it will soon be over.'

Victoria wasn't listening to a word she said. She was already lost in a world of pain and preoccupation.

'Porter,' shouted Teddy to Jake, who was walking through the door that led to the wards, pushing an empty wheelchair. 'We need to transfer a patient to the new maternity block, straight to labour ward, please, Jake.'

Dana completely ignored Teddy, her gaze fully fixed on Victoria, as was Pammy's.

'Come on, Victoria, you will be fine,' said Pammy who had helped the midwife deliver five babies at home, in a minor, peripheral way, but as a result, childbirth held no fear for her. It was a different story altogether for Victoria, who was an only child from a family where such things as childbirth and pain were never spoken of.

Teddy's eyes never left Dana's face. 'Actually, doctor,' said Sister Pokey, 'I don't think there is any time for that! Nurses, I know you aren't in uniform, but could you stay, please? Half the staff are on a Christmas shopping day because we expected this to be a quiet one – it usually is, at this time.'

'Oops,' said Dana, as Victoria's waters went, 'it looks like we're off.'

Within minutes, Victoria wasn't just panting, she was pushing too.

'Trolley,' roared Teddy as he leapt into action and, kicking one of the brakes off, he pulled a trolley across.

'Isn't Roland with you?' asked Pammy.

'Roland, no, he's gone to the match with Oliver. I had to cover here.'

'Oh, no!' Victoria did not hold back and screamed her dismay. 'Can someone get him, pleeeease.'

Pammy turned to Teddy so that Victoria could not see her face. 'Can he be found?' she mouthed to Teddy, who mouthed back, 'No. Unless you want to head over to Anfield and search the kop?'

In seconds he was at Victoria's side with his arm around her. 'Sister-in-law, please don't panic, but I'm afraid that you and my niece or nephew in there are going to have to make do with me for the moment – and frankly, I think we both know how useless my brother would be. I'd just like to say that for your first baby, this is all going swimmingly well.'

Victoria grabbed at the air with her free hand. 'Dana, Dana,' she gasped, 'it's another one, it's coming!'

Dana was on the opposite side to Teddy and they were both helping Victoria to sit on the trolley Jake was holding in place.

'Off you go,' said Sister Pokey, to Teddy and Dana, 'take the bay. It's out of the way and Jake, fetch the Entinox, fast, and get back here as soon as you can. Oh, the blue light is flashing over the desk – something is coming in. It looks like we are going to be busy. Nurse Tanner, I know you are off duty, but may I borrow you for the afternoon?'

Teddy and Dana pushed the trolley towards the bay just as Beth marched through the doors of casualty. 'Sister Antrobus sent me down; apparently there's a blue light coming in. But what are you doing here?'

A scream filled the unit and Beth turned her head. 'Do I know who that is?' she asked.

'You do. It's Victoria and it looks as though she is well on the way to delivering her baby.'

'Oh my God!' Beth felt an overwhelming surge of emotion. 'Are you sure?'

'I am and the lucky little one is going to be delivered by Teddy and Dana by the look of it because there's no time to get her to the maternity unit.'

'Dana and Teddy?' said Beth. 'Did I just hear you right?'

'Yes, you really did,' said Pammy. 'Have I got time to find a uniform before this blue light comes in?'

As if on cue, the sound of a siren filled the air.

'I would say, no,' said Beth. 'And have you looked out there?'

Pammy turned around, the snow had changed from a light flutter to a heavy fall. Sister Pokey appeared at their side.

'That is in for Christmas, if you ask me,' she said. 'Look at the sky, it's so heavy.'

Behind the ambulance parking up outside, they could see nuns making their way up from the convent.

'They start the ward carols, tonight,' said Sister Pokey.

'I don't know why,' said Pammy, 'but they always make me cry.'

Sister Pokey laid her hand on her arm. 'That's because you feel the music in your heart, Nurse Tanner.'

Dr William's car pulled up outside Miss Devonshire's house and Dr Gaskell turned around in the passenger seat to face his wife in the back. 'Are you sure you want to do this?' he asked her.

'I most certainly do,' she replied. 'Let me have fifteen minutes and if I can't persuade her to change her mind,

I'll come out for the reinforcements. If she insists on continuing along this path there is nothing for it. We will have to lock her in the pantry whilst I think of another plan. Is that all right with you, Dr William?'

Dr William looked surprised. 'That's fine by me,' he said and grinned as he winked at his patient in his rear-view mirror. 'Let's face it, no one can make the situation any worse. She is deadly serious. I telephoned Strawberry Fields from the surgery and they have been told to prepare a cot and to contact suitable parents on their list for adoption. They waste no time in that place. A potential family can receive a call at nine in the morning and the baby will be with them before lunch. Miss Devonshire means business.' He turned on the windscreen wipers to clear away the snow and wiped the misted window on the inside with his leather glove.

Just as Doris was about to step out of the car, her husband spoke and she sat back in. 'All my professional life has been spent trying to make things better for people, to heal not just the patients, but their families and society as a whole. God alone knows, it's not easy working in such poverty, but we try to make people's lives better. When I meet someone like this, who is immune to reason, who takes a position because it makes them feel good, important – or whatever it is they do it for, it makes me wonder, is it all worth it? There will always be a Miss Devonshire, out to make mischief and misery.'

Doris placed her hand on her husband's shoulder. 'Of course it is. You are only upset because you feel powerless and that's not something you are used to. Trust me on this, I think I can really help. Leave it to me.'

Dr Gaskell patted his wife on the hand. This new woman wasn't only answering him back, she had decided that she could solve the biggest problem to face St Angelus for some considerable time. 'I will happily leave this one to you, my dear.' Dr Gaskell got out and opened the car door for his wife. The brim of his trilby hat immediately began to collect the snow and she smiled up at her husband.

'Fifteen minutes,' she said and, pulling her scarf up over her hair and the collar of her coat up to protect her neck, walked down the drive to the front door. She held her head high, felt no nervousness whatsoever. She reached out her hand and lifted the door knocker with confidence. She was in control. She had information – and information was power.

Chapter 22

Pammy had found a clean apron in the utility room that she slipped over her neck and fastened around the back. Beth and Sister Pokey would receive the patient and she would hover in the background in case they needed her. As soon as the ambulance men barged in through the doors, sister was at the head of the trolley.

'Can you get the houseman please, Nurse Tanner?' she said to Pammy, but Pammy didn't need to, Teddy was already on his way.

'How is she?' Pammy asked him. 'Shall I go in?'

'She's very calm and loving the Entinox. She's too far advanced for any Pethidine. We don't want to deliver a flat baby and I was worried about that, but she doesn't seem to need it. The labour suite is free in the unit so Jake is going to take her down there next as long as she doesn't have any dramas on the way.'

'Teddy, Victoria is a lady, she will be very in control, you should know that. She would rather die than be seen to be out of control. You are from similar breeding.'

347

'That doesn't make her immune from complications, Pammy, but you are right. She didn't threaten to hit me over the head once, or strangle Dana. Remarkable for a first baby, but everything is just fine.'

'Have you heard, Teddy – someone has taken Emily and Dessie's baby? I'm not panicking because Gracie knew where he would be. It looks like his mother has come back for him.'

Teddy looked incredulous. 'What? Are you serious?'

Pammy felt a blast of cold air and looked towards the doors as in walked Malcolm with her mother, Mavis.

'Oh, good Lord, what is going on?' Pammy exclaimed as she saw Biddy, looking distraught and carrying Louis in her arms behind them, with Gracie shivering at her side. A policeman walked in next to Ida, the night cleaner.

'Doesn't look as though he's been kidnapped to me,' said Teddy, who sprang over to Sister Pokey's side as a trolley with a figure lying on it was then pushed in. 'Right, what have we here?' he asked and looked down into the face of a young woman who was barely alive.

'Hello, Dukie,' said Mrs Gaskell as the door opened.

Miss Devonshire blinked and looking past Mrs Gaskell, took in the snow and said, 'Hello, Doris, I am not sure to what I owe the pleasure, unless of course it's your husband who has sent you.'

Doris felt a flutter of anger. The old Doris would have

been sent – this Doris chose to come herself. 'Actually, I decided to come and I think you know why.'

Miss Devonshire took a deep breath and let out a low sigh. Doris could see that, somewhere in her mind, she was searching for a justification to send her away, but there was none. They both knew that.

'Look at that snow. You had better come in before you freeze to death.' Miss Devonshire stood back to let Doris into the immaculate and perfect home that had once belonged to her parents. Watercolours from Cornwall, placed ridiculously high up on the wall, marked out the path to the sitting room. 'Can I offer you a drink, tea?'

Doris had brought her handbag in with her and she slipped it down her arm. 'No thank you, Dukie, I have something important to talk to you about and the sooner we get this over with, the better.' Doris smiled. She felt totally in control. Walking over to the window she looked out to the car where her husband and Dr William sat waiting patiently. The snow had reduced her visibility, but nonetheless, she could see her husband's face, looking anxiously towards the house.

'It's always been a nice part of Queens Drive here, hasn't it? It's a long time since I was last here, but I recognised the house, immediately. If I remember, last time, I wasn't offered tea.'

Miss Devonshire didn't comment. 'Do sit down,' she said and waited for Doris to sit. The fire was laid, waiting to be lit in the evening, and in the corner of the room was what looked like a brand-new television.

'Oh, you have a television, how nice.'

'Yes, don't you?'

'Not yet, no. We thought of it, for the coronation, but then we were away and so, well, the moment passed. We are getting one now though, I have just decided – Oliver may visit more often if we have one.' She laughed and then felt immediately guilty at the mention of her son's name. She was trying her best to lighten the mood, would try to talk Dukie down a little, lower her defences. She would only play her trump card if she had to.

'You know why I'm here, don't you?'

Miss Devonshire picked up the scatter cushion next to her, plumped it up and then placed it on her knees, her suddenly trembling hands folded on top. In an instant, she had lost the mettle that made her the tyrant she was known to be.

'I do, and I have to tell you, there is nothing you can do because I have evidence which is irrefutable.' She sprang to her feet and left the room, to return only seconds later and place the first and second letters of complaint, along with the weigh sheet, into Doris's outstretched hands. 'Even your husband would have to take note of that,' she said, finding a new confidence as she sat down.

Doris read both letters slowly and carefully. 'I understand how you have had to take this into account,' she said as she folded the letters, but it is obvious by the handwriting that they have been written by the same person, someone who has an axe to grind. Dukie, I have held that little boy, I have fed him his bottle and he is as healthy now as my own son was at that age – which is a miracle, given how poorly Louis was when he was admitted. He has been very well looked after. You have to change your mind. You cannot take this child away from the people he thinks of as his parents just before Christmas, breaking all their hearts, not to mention those of the entire staff of the hospital and everyone who knows them and place him in Strawberry Fields. It is frankly absurd.

'You know that once the Fields accept him the legal status is that he is theirs and they could have him with a new family within hours. No one knows that better than you.' Her voice became as tense as a finely tuned violin wire as she spoke. As she said it out loud, she could barely believe what her old friend was doing and what she was having to subject her to. It was hurting them both, something she hadn't anticipated.

Miss Devonshire looked as though she was about to break until Doris saw the resolve slip into her spine and she sat upright. 'I do appreciate what you say; however, I'm afraid that, on the basis of those letters, I have to do my job – indeed, my duty. She has also lied and someone who is fit to be a parent cannot lie. What on earth would she lie about next?'

Doris smiled, weakly. 'What about you, Dukie?'

'What do you mean, what about me?'

Doris sat forward and folded her hands on her knee. She didn't need a cushion to protect her, she had the force of the truth behind her. 'Haven't you built your own life on the back of a lie? What makes Emily Horton's lie any worse than the one you have been living with for all of these years?

Chapter 23

Beth had undressed Eva and placed her in a hospital gown. 'She looks jaundiced,' she said, 'is stick-thin, oedematous ankles and probable abdominal ascites. Her pulse is rapid, probably due to the pain and her temperature is 104.'

'Thank you, Doctor,' Teddy said and Beth blushed. She was always being ribbed for trying to guess a diagnosis ahead of the doctors. 'Let's speak to everyone who has brought her in and see what information we can gather. It's hard dealing with a patient with zero information.'

'I only know she had the baby on the bathroom floor,' said Ida.

'I know nothing,' said Melly. 'I only clean her rooms, but she asked where she could wash her clothes and I could smell something very funny in the scullery when she was in there.'

Malcolm now stood at the side of the trolley, holding

Eva's hand. His eyes were moist and, instinctively, Teddy was gentle with his questions.

'She's collapsed a number of times,' said Malcolm, 'but she was always all right after and I thought it was because she was so thin. The Disprin worked a treat.'

With a start, Teddy recognised his patient. 'I remember her,' he blurted out, 'I saw her outside the main entrance. She asked me where the admin block was and you are right, Malcolm, she looked faint and then quickly recovered.'

'We only know what we read in the letters at Malcolm's,' said Biddy. 'She's Louis' real mother and she has been as far as America and back and it wasn't her fault that Louis was left.'

'She called him Elijah,' said Ida.

The doors opened and no one spoke as a stricken Dessie and Emily walked in and Biddy walked towards them. Emily took her son and for a moment, there was a gulf between them as Biddy stood back. She was paralysed by guilt, thought she had let everyone down. Dessie spoke – Emily was incapable as conflicting emotion coursed through her veins.

'It was no one's, fault, Biddy. He's left outside to sleep in his pram every day. She could have taken him from anywhere, so please, please don't blame yourself.' He opened his arms wide and encircled them around his wife, Biddy and the boy who was his son, aware that he might not be so for much longer.

'I'm going to have to ask you all to leave the area, please, I have to draw the curtains now,' said Sister Pokey. 'Everyone to the waiting room please.'

Teddy put a hand on Malcolm's shoulder. 'I'm sorry, but she is very poorly and we need to find out what is wrong.'

As soon as the curtains were closed, Teddy began to palpate Eva's abdomen and said to Beth, 'A Cusco's speculum, please, and Sister Pokey, can you grab the gynaecologist on call and alert the theatre, please?'

'Right away, Dr Davenport,' said sister as the curtain fell back into place.

'Are her obs still the same?' he asked Beth.

'Yes, her pulse is 120, her temperature is 104 and her blood pressure is 110 over 90. Exactly what it was when she came in through the door. I'll fetch an instrument trolley.'

As Beth left, Teddy noticed his patient open her eyes and took advantage of the few moments he had with her while she had rallied round to consciousness.

'Hello, Eva, you don't feel very well, do you?'

Eva shook her head.

'How long have you had this pain, can you remember?'

He could barely hear her reply and placed his ear close to her mouth. 'Since I had Elijah,' she whispered.

Teddy shook his head, it couldn't be possible. Beth reappeared with an enamel trolley and glanced at Eva, who had slipped back into unconsciousness.

'Sister has called the gynaecologist on call, he's on his way,' she said.

'Good. It may not even be related to the birth, but I can't find anything else to go on at the moment. Her chest is clear. It could be a urinary tract infection, I suppose, but the retained abdominal fluid tells me otherwise. The night cleaner says she had her baby spontaneously on a bathroom floor and I'm wondering if there are any retained products? If there were, she would have bled to death by now, unless it was something small, causing a chronic problem rather than acute.'

'Wouldn't she have collapsed before now?' asked Beth.

'Yes,' said Teddy. 'I suppose she could have had a low-grade infection and fought it off with her own immune system for a time, but this long? I doubt it. Can you hold her knees for me?'

Beth eased Eva's knees up and let them fall partially to the side and then held them in place. Teddy stared at the curtain, his eyes almost closed, concentrating hard on what he could feel. He removed the speculum, threw it into the bucket and it clattered against the side with some force. The only response from Eva was a fluttering of her eyelashes as he tore off his rubber gloves. Beth retook Eva's blood pressure.

'What is it now?' he asked.

Beth peered at him over the top of her glasses and he instantly detected the warning set of her jaw. '100 over 80,' she said. 'It's dropping.'

Teddy looked alarmed. 'She definitely has retained products. Her uterus is as hard as a cricket ball. Call theatre now and I'll run her up there myself and assist, tell the gynae to meet me there.' He kicked off the brake, swung the trolley around as Beth lifted the curtains. 'Here, help me!' he shouted and Jake took the other end. 'Up to theatre now.'

'I haven't lived a lie,' said Miss Devonshire, 'my past is no one's business.'

Doris felt desperately sorry for her, she always had. The reason their friendship had faltered was because of Oliver. Once he was born, Doris couldn't bear to see the pain in her friend's eyes and her friend couldn't bear to see the pleasure in her own. It might have been easier if Oliver had been a girl, but she doubted it. Doris reached out and placed her hand over that of her old friend.

'Dukie, you had a baby. Your parents wouldn't let you keep it so you gave him up for adoption. He was a little boy. I saw him, I held him, remember?' Miss Devonshire nodded her head and a tear plopped onto the back of Doris's hand. 'I haven't ever forgotten him, so I am sure you haven't. He looked very much like Louis, didn't he? Dark brown hair and dark eyes?'

There was no response.

'Look, what I am saying is, I don't really think you can make objective decisions with regard to adoption, do you? I don't think you should be doing this job. You are so professional and so good, but your past, the past you cannot change, clouds your judgement and you cannot be blamed for that, or help it. It isn't your fault, Dukie...'

Another tear plopped and she lifted her hand and wiped her eyes with the back of her hand. 'It was all so long ago,' she said.

'It was, but if I haven't forgotten Robert, you can't have done either. You were his mother. Please listen to me; I was always your good friend. I cried too when you had to give him up, you know I did. You don't know this, but I fought and argued with your parents here, in this room, when you were locked up in that awful mother and baby home. Your father wouldn't budge an inch. He was more interested in what the neighbours would think than how his daughter felt. You had spent six weeks feeding Robert and caring for him, loving him. It was too cruel, barbaric – and you had a double blow, your Francis killed in the war only weeks later. You had the worst grief to bear, Dukie, and now, you are letting it get in the way of another child's happiness, another family. Of a couple like the one who adopted your Robert. You can't deny them that, for all the wrong reasons, can you? Louis isn't Robert, the circumstances aren't the same.'

They both jumped as the door knocked. Doris felt irritated, thinking it was her husband, trying to hurry her along. As she opened the door, leaving Miss Devonshire to dry the tears that had fallen unhindered, she was shocked to see Gracie shivering on the doorstep.

'Goodness me,' said Doris, 'what are you doing here? Why aren't you at the nurses' home with Mrs Duffy?'

'My nan sent me, she's at the hospital with the others, She told me I had to come and say that she wrote the letters – she pushed the one through the door this morning. She asked me to tell the lady that she's very sorry. The baby's real mam is back now, but she's very sick.'

'Who is at the hospital, Gracie, and why? Come on in, you're frozen. Come and explain and then maybe we should go to the hospital too.'

Doris looked out of the door and down the path. The drive was white, covered in a layer of snow. She worried if they would be able to get to St Angelus in the car, if they waited much longer. She lifted her hand to her husband and Dr William who waved back. Both men looked frozen as they banged their hands together to keep them warm. 'Yes, we can all go to the hospital now.'

Sister Pokey sent everyone home – and Miss Devonshire sent Louis home with Dessie and Emily.

'If she is his real mother and it wasn't her fault, then I am afraid she will be able to have her son back. It will be a matter for the police, not me, but that is the truth of it. I am sorry,' she said to them. Emily looked up into her face. She didn't know what had happened, but a kinder Miss Devonshire stood in front of her today.

Emily could barely see for the tears pouring down her cheeks. Dessie held onto her and rocked her from side to side.

'I fully understand if you don't want to take him back home with you now,' Miss Devonshire added, 'all things considered.'

'No!' Emily shouted the word and hugged Louis close to her. 'We are taking him, he is coming back with us, he has been ours, *is* ours. I understand, but while she…' Emily couldn't bring herself to say the word 'mother', 'Eva is here, he will come back to his bedroom, his cot, his home. It's his *home*.' She sobbed the last words.

'Shush, Emily, let's not frighten Louis. Come on, we will take him,' said Dessie, he and Emily realising that it might be the last time he ever said those words.

Pammy checked on Victoria, who was not progressing as quickly as quickly as she had at first. She looked in through the portal window and waved to her and Dana, who was laying a cold cloth on her friend's brow.

Teddy was already scrubbed and in theatre, relieved that the anaesthetist was already there from the previous operation. He rescrubbed and they were ready to start in record time.

'I have no idea when she last ate,' said Teddy, 'but it

could have been three hours ago when she finished her cleaning night shift here.'

The anaesthetist was in the process of intubating his patient. 'That's helpful,' he said with an eyebrow raised and a sigh.

'Sorry,' said Teddy.

'Well, we have no information and therefore no choices,' the surgeon interjected. 'It looks to me as though we are fighting the clock here anyway. If we weigh risk against caution, risk wins hand down.'

Minutes later they were reeling at what they found. The gynaecologist looked at Teddy and the anaesthetist over the top of his mask, his tools of surgery balanced in his hand.

'Hysterectomy is the only chance we have of saving her life here on the table,' he said. 'And there is only a very slim chance of survival here. I am sure this is the primary growth we have stumbled upon, given her history, possibly a minute retained product and chronic infection behind it. I'm guessing it's turned malignant over time.'

'She's so young,' said Teddy.

'Yes, that will have worked against her; the cells will have reproduced rapidly and I don't yet know what is on the inside. I think she may have the beginnings of septicaemia too, and who knows what else we will find...' The atmosphere in the theatre was charged. 'Are you with me, gentlemen? Sister?' he asked as he looked at Teddy, the anaesthetist and the theatre sister.

'We are,' they replied in unison. The gynaecologist nodded his response and worked quickly and skilfully to bring the procedure to a close in the fastest time possible.

As they cleaned up after the operation three long hours later, the men were silent as sister cleared away the instruments.

'Sister,' said the gynaecologist, 'can you make sure no other operations are performed in this theatre until the walls have been thoroughly washed down and swabbed? This theatre is now classed as dirty until it is sterilised.'

The theatre was silent as was often the way after an operation when all the parties involved knew the best had been done, but it wasn't enough. The blood-filled buckets were removed, the aprons and greens stripped off, hands scrubbed – and still no one spoke.

They were on their way back down to the receiving ward before Teddy asked the gynaecologist the question everyone downstairs would.

'Is there a chance she will she make it?'

The gynaecologist was unequivocal in his answer. 'No. I was surprised we didn't lose her on the table. You rarely see anyone that advanced, but when you do, it's always a shocker. More common before the days of the NHS when women bore everything in silence. It was almost always too late then. I'm more surprised she has recovered from the anaesthetic. The blood transfusion may help, but it won't last for long. I've given her penicillin and a hundred milligrams of Pethidine and written her up for more. At least she will be relatively pain-free now. We will keep the drip up, obviously; she is a young woman but she's lost a huge amount of blood. In my best opinion, she was too poorly for surgery. I would give her four to six hours. She is a very, very sick young lady in the most advanced stages. She could have dropped dead at any moment over the last weeks. Frankly, quite incredible that she hasn't. She must have had a very strong reason to keep battling on.'

Back at home, Dessie and Emily had barely spoken. There was nothing to say that could change anything or make the situation any better, so Emily sat with the baby who had stolen her heart and forced herself not to cry. To laugh and play with his fingers, to kiss him and feed him, to will him not to sleep because she wanted to commit every waking moment to memory. She didn't even notice when Jake entered the house. Barely lifted her head to the sound of murmuring voices and only responded when Dessie tried to take Louis out of her arms.

'What are you doing?' she demanded to know. 'Where are you taking him? You can't, not yet, he's ours for tonight.'

'Emily, love, Eva, his – his mother, she's dying and she's asking for him. Jake is here, Matron has sent him.

He says that Dr Davenport asked him to tell us she only has a few hours at the most. Matron says she's not forcing us to take Louis, that it's entirely our choice, but I think we should, while there is still time, and let her hold him. What do you think?'

Emily shook her head and pulled her son into her chest.

'Emily...' Dessie stood in front of her and, reaching down, lifted Louis from her arms. He knew that if he didn't make this happen, she would regret it. 'Come on,' he said. 'Let's go back to the hospital. The poor woman has no one but Louis – and us. I don't know about you but I feel I owe her a thank you at the very least.'

Emily didn't speak, but she stood up from the chair and took the coat Jake was holding out to her.

'I've got the van,' he said. 'It's already getting dark and the roads are bad. Doreen and Madge have gone to fetch Malcolm from the Seaman's Rest, because that's where the girl, Eva, has been staying.'

Teddy wasn't surprised to discover that his brother was pacing up and down like a caged lion.

'Where have you been?' Roland demanded to know.

'Roland, I don't know where to begin,' said Teddy. 'Who is in with her?'

'Dana and a midwife. Dana was, rather, she went to fetch a hot drink for me about five minutes ago.'

Teddy smiled. 'Let me go and chase that for you,' he said and disappeared as quickly as he had arrived.

Dana was in the maternity unit kitchen with her back to him when he stepped in. She was laying up a tray and, thinking it was one of the midwives, didn't turn around.

'I hope you don't mind,' she said. 'I've taken a few biscuits; our mother needs some energy. We thought she was going to be quick for a primigravida, but she's run true to form and is going to take forever!'

Dana turned around with a smile on her face which slipped as soon as she saw it was Teddy. 'Oh, it's you,' she said.

He moved to the other side of the table. 'Yes, it's me. Did you get my letter?'

Dana avoided his eyes and stared at the tray. She absentmindedly picked up a teaspoon. 'I did, but I'm afraid it doesn't make any difference to my position. Things are still as they are.'

He reached out and grabbed her hand and the teaspoon fell and clattered on the saucer. 'Dana, please don't make it forever. Please, it's Christmas, will you at least talk to me? Just talk, hear me out. If you want to walk away and never speak to me again, I will understand, but at least let me have one night. Tomorrow, can we meet, just to talk? I may have a niece or nephew by then and you may have a godchild. It's a new beginning, isn't it?'

Dana smiled and his heart leapt. 'Tomorrow? At the rate she's going, I doubt it.'

A midwife called through the kitchen door, 'Oi, you two, you're missing all the action. Delivery under way in room three!'

'What?' exclaimed Dana and almost ran out of the kitchen.

Pammy had offered to special-nurse Eva and stay with her until the end, or when the night staff came on, whichever came first.

'Do you know, there isn't a day when my nurses don't fill me with pride?' said Matron to Dr Gaskell, Dr William, Doris and Miss Devonshire as Elsie made teas and coffees in her rooms.

'So much for a quiet Saturday, Elsie,' Matron had said when the others left to return to Mavis's house and save the pan of scouse that was still sitting on a flame on the stove.

'Oh, indeed, we have the best working here, Matron.'

Elsie slopped back into the kitchen to Biddy who was sitting on the stool, red-eyed and fretful.

'I feel so bad, Elsie,' she said.

'Well don't,' said Elsie. 'Save your tears. From what I've heard, that poor girl isn't going to make it. I'm done here. I think you and I should go and see your friend Malcolm. I saw the look on his face. I think we all need a drink tonight, don't you?'

'I'll fetch Madge and Doreen too – they are in the

switchboard room. Let's go and drown our sorrows, eh? This is one night the Sylvestrian isn't out of bounds. And Doreen's been asking me a lot about Malcolm these past few days,' said Elsie.

Eva was in a side room on ward two. Dusk had fallen and the snow had continued to fall and now covered soot, fog and smoke-stained Liverpool in a blanket of sparkling white. Emily and Dessie sat on each side of Eva's bed and Louis, fast asleep, lay next to her in the crook of her arm. He was exhausted by his day's activities, which was just as well as Eva continued to drift in and out of consciousness. Emily, always the nurse, kept one eye on the drip and the other on her pulse and breathing.

It was Dessie who began to speak first; Emily watched as he picked up Eva's hand.

'I don't know if you can hear me, love,' he said, 'but your little lad, he is the bonniest in all of Liverpool. He's going to be a clever boy too, always alert he is, takes everything in. I just wanted to say thank you, because the past months while we've been looking after him, they have been the best of my life.'

Dessie was only whispering, but his voice broke and Emily could see that her husband was struggling with the emotion of it all. She slipped her warm hand into Eva's cold one and squeezed it.

'Thank you,' she whispered, 'I promise you that if you need me to look after your Elijah, he will be the most loved and most cared for child to have lived. He will want for nothing.' She felt an imperceptible squeeze on her hand and once again, struggled with the tears in her eyes.

Pammy came into the room and picked up Eva's chart, checked the observations, and settled down into a chair next to the window. Emily laid Eva's hand on Louis' back, Dessie stroked the top of her other hand that lay in his own.

As Pammy looked out of the window she saw a procession of capes and candlelit lanterns meandering across the car park as the nuns appeared at the ward doors and filed in. Pammy turned and looked out of the cubicle glass and saw that with the nuns were Matron, Dr Gaskell, Doris his wife and the head of children's services, Miss Devonshire.

'Oh they are going to sing carols,' said Pammy. 'This always makes me cry.' She turned in her chair to watch the choir and felt her heart swell as it always did as they began on the strains of 'Silent Night'.

I am such a lucky girl, thought Pammy. She thought of her mam, Mavis, taking everyone home to feed them and making a detour to collect Mrs Duffy and take her home to explain everything that had happened to them. She thought about Anthony, who she was seeing that evening, and as she turned to Emily and Dessie and Eva, she thought how lucky she was to know such selfless and kind people. The strains of 'Silent Night' filled the room as Malcolm walked in with Doreen and Madge. Dessie rose to offer him his chair.

'No, you sit,' said Malcolm who had tears in his eyes.

Pammy watched as Doreen slipped her handkerchief into Malcolm's hand and, placing her hand on his back, comforted him. *Aye, aye*, thought Pammy, who became more like her mother, Mavis, every day. Pammy guessed she had just witnessed the start of something special at the end of something they were all still grappling with.

Eva opened her eyes. She didn't speak, but she did look down at her son, and bent her head, resting her lips on his hair as he soundly slept. They all lifted their heads to watch the choir so none of them noticed Eva's tears fall onto Louis' scalp or her lip pucker onto his skin or heard the words as they left her mouth, 'Kocham Cię, I love you.'

Matron held up the lantern that she always carried around the wards each Christmas and caught Pammy's eye and saw her tears. That girl always cries at the carols, she thought. She must have a very good heart.

As the carol singers finished and moved away, Emily turned back to Eva and she could tell straight away, by the beautiful and peaceful smile on Eva's face that belied her anguish, it was over. She took her hand, lifted it, felt for her pulse and whispered, 'Dessie, she has gone.'

★

Dana left the labour room in search of Roland, who she found with Teddy, smoking cigars in the day room.

'Well,' she said, feeling almost giddy. 'Do you two want to know the news?'

Roland didn't answer, he couldn't. Beth came running around the corner. 'Sorry, I only had to clean the theatre down – I mean as in wash all the flamin' walls and it took forever,' she said. 'Any news?'

'There is indeed,' said Dana. 'Victoria has had a baby girl.'

There was an eruption of shouts as Roland headed straight to the labour room, leaving Beth with Dana and Teddy. Beth immediately took her leave. 'I'm half-starved,' she said. 'I'm off to find out what's going on down on ward two. What a night!'

'A girl,' said Teddy. 'Did she manage without the forceps, is everything…?'

'Yes, all good. She's had the great contraction, third stage is complete and the midwife is just checking the placenta. Everything is there.'

'Good, you know about the girl, Louis' mother?'

'Yes, I heard upstairs,' said Dana. 'That is very sad.'

Silence fell and Teddy, scared she was about to walk away, spoke again. 'Did she say what she wanted to call her?'

Dana walked over to the window and looked out at the snow. 'No, she did say one thing, though, this is my snow angel.'

Teddy laughed. 'She is too.' He slipped his hand into hers. 'Dana, will you forgive me? Let me try and prove to you that I am not that man?'

Dana had forgotten what his skin felt like, the familiar firmness of his hand. He was so close, she could smell him. It was all still there, the frisson, the excitement, the love.

'Teddy…'

'I know. I know I have so much to prove, I could take forever, but please, if you feel half as much as I do, you will want to try and find a way. Do you?'

She turned to face him, forced too to face the truth.

'I do want to.' It was almost a whisper and he was so overcome with emotion he couldn't answer and, instead, as he felt her move towards him, placed his lips on hers.

Doris deposited Miss Devonshire at her front door as her husband kept the engine running.

'What are you doing for Christmas, Dukie?' she asked.

'Oh, I will go to mass, and then have a quiet day in front of the TV.'

'Nonsense, I won't hear of it. You will come to us. Don't think you are the only one, Matron is coming too.'

And a few minutes later, as she sat back in the car, she turned to her husband and smiled as he lifted the handbrake. 'Home, James,' she said. 'Will this old car make it?'

'It will,' he replied. 'Unlike that poor girl. Did you just invite Dukie for Christmas?'

'I did.'

'And Matron, too.' Her husband shook his head in amazement. 'I don't know what has happened to you, my dear, but I fully approve.'

'Good, because I've invited Dr William and his family too.'

Dr Gaskell threw his head back, roaring with laughter, and she felt a warmth flow through her at the sound of him. It had been years since he had laughed with her like that.

'I'm going to get the sherry out when we get home,' he said. 'No cooking for you. Let's have one of those cheese and toast type suppers we used to have years go.'

Doris turned and looked out of the window. I just have one little thing to do first, she thought to herself, and imagined the pleasure she would feel when she lifted the lid and threw her little blue pills to the bottom of the bin.

About the author

Nadine Dorries grew up in a working-class family in Liverpool. She spent part of her childhood living on a farm with her grandmother, and attended school in a small remote village in the west of Ireland. She trained as a nurse, then followed with a successful career in which she established and then sold her own business. She is an MP, presently serving as Parliamentary Under Secretary of State in the Department of Health and Social Care, and has three daughters.